IN THE NAME OF GOD

In the Name of God

Stephen J. Gordon

Apprentice House
Loyola University Maryland
www.ApprenticeHouse.com

© 2011, Stephen J. Gordon

978-1-934074-62-6 Paperback
978-1-934074-63-3 Hardcover

Printed in the United States of America

First Edition

Book Design by Andrew Zaleski

Published by Apprentice House
The Future of Publishing... Today!

Apprentice House
Communication Department
Loyola University Maryland
4501 N. Charles Street
Baltimore, MD 21210

410.617.5265
www.ApprenticeHouse.com
info@ApprenticeHouse.com

To my wife Becky, and to AJ and Esty,

Michal and Avrohom, Jeff, Alana, and Sophie —

you keep my world in balance and give me much to smile about.

1

I stood in the bathroom of the synagogue and stared at the tears silently running down my face. The weeping had come on suddenly. I had just washed my hands, looked in the mirror, and started to cry. Uncontrollably. There was no warning. There never was.

On the other side of the door and down the hall was a banquet, and I had a date waiting for me at our table. She was absolutely great: intelligent, attractive, fun.

I wasn't ready. But this wasn't the first time Alli and I had gone out, and I thought these paroxysms were all but gone. Sometimes, though, sometimes I could be driving down the street, I could be sitting in a restaurant, I could be thinking of a moment a thousand miles away and I would be overwhelmed by tears.

Applause filtered up the hallway and through the door. I washed and dried my face before anyone could come in, paused for a final look in the mirror, then headed out. The paneled hallway led to the main hall, where I found my seat at Alli's table, which was blessedly along the right-hand wall. I sat down as invisibly as I could and looked around.

What was I doing here? As peaceful darkness covered the city of Baltimore, I was attending, of all places, the annual banquet of Beit Shalom Synagogue. The fact that I was in a synagogue — albeit the social hall — was laughable, because I was, to put it mildly, pissed off at God. But I didn't want to go there; it took too much out of me. So the fact that I was at this banquet had more to do with Alli and the guest speaker, Eitan Lev, than anything else. Alli had heard of the banquet through a friend and thought the guest would interest me. She was right.

Eitan Lev was the latest candidate for Prime Minister of Israel. He was a former general, a war hero in Israel — a war criminal in the Arab countries — and the most popular Israeli politician in recent memory. He was an unstoppable general who placed the lives of his countrymen above all else. He was eloquent, plus had a political savvy that impressed Washington and London.

I looked at Alli on my left. She was bright as well as stunning, with beautiful shoulder-length dark-blonde hair and cerulean eyes. She was a graduate student at University of Maryland in physical therapy. Allison was fit and athletic; originally she had wanted to go into phys. ed., but her parents thought she'd be wasting her intellect. Physical Therapy, then, was a natural alternative, she had explained. It was okay with me. If it's physical, it must be therapy.

"Look at all the security," Alli said, looking around the room, interrupting my thoughts of her.

Indeed. The social hall was a modest-sized rectangle of a room with a mirrored wall behind the head table and elegant flowered green wallpaper on either side. The lighting from the chandeliers was subdued, yet I had spotted the security people the moment I had walked in. There were two small, but solid-looking men standing to either side of the head table, plus one standing below the raised dais. Then another man — this one taller and thinner — stood at the double doors to the kitchen, and a fifth, an older fellow, near the main entrance. They were all *Shin Bet*, Israeli security. I knew the type. These guys were not local law enforcement — there was a distinctive hard, youthful Middle-Eastern look about them. This last fellow, the older man at the main door, seemed more out of place. He was probably in his late thirties/early forties, while the others were in their early twenties. The younger men all had full heads of hair; his was thinning and his eyes had more than a few wrinkles at the corners. Additionally, he wore stylish small black wire-rimmed glasses, so he no longer had the perfect vision of younger agents. It also wasn't lost on me that from where he stood he could see everything — and I bet he had seen plenty in his day. He was the boss.

"I'm glad I left my knife at home," I muttered to myself.

"What?" Alli looked at me, eyes wide.

"Just kidding."

Actually, I wasn't. I always carried a folding knife. My current one was a three and a half inch Benchmade ATS 34, combo blade — half straight edge, half serrated. I knew there'd be security here with a metal detector as part of it, so bringing a knife would have been a bad move, to say the least.

I scanned the room again. In addition to the *Shin Bet,* there were also some Baltimore cops, but I knew they just didn't have the same experience as the Israelis. Fact of life.

We had just finished our main course — stuffed capon in a decent orange sauce, some kind of funky potatoes and broccoli — when Mr. Lev began speaking. He had received a standing ovation as he approached the podium, and then, when the audience quieted down, he stood at the mic and thanked his hosts. The room was packed. In addition to the capacity crowd sitting at tables, there was a contingent of press with their omnipresent video cams, plus local, state, and national dignitaries.

Mr. Lev began talking about the situation in the Middle East...how fragile life is for everyone, the security needs, the monetary needs, and the importance of American moral support. The former general spoke eloquently. His English was quite good. Impressive actually.

My mind began to wander and I continued to look around the room. Except for Alli and one or two others — adult students of mine — I didn't know anyone. I enjoyed the anonymity. For a moment or two, I watched the security guys watch the audience. Then I scanned the group myself. Nothing unusual struck me. I shifted my gaze to the waiters and waitresses. When Mr. Lev had started his address, the caterer's crew mostly headed into the kitchen. A small group stayed out in the social hall, leaning against a back wall, to listen to his remarks. There were three men and two women. All were dressed in matching black dinner jackets and pants. They were mixed in age, from a woman in her forties with red hair to a young man in his late teens. The teenager had close-cut black hair and was watching the guest speaker with interest. Actually, they all were watching Mr. Lev with interest.

"Will you stop playing with your food," the woman next to Alli said to her husband, breaking into my thoughts.

"Give me a break, Eileen, I'm not playing with my food. I'm rearranging it on my plate."

Eileen was a petite woman in her early forties with long, straight brown hair. She had small oval glasses that John Lennon may have once considered, and was wearing a black dress that shimmered with gold thread across the shoulders. Her husband, who was a few years older, had salt and pepper hair and an intense stare.

"What, are you nervous or something?" the woman pressed.

"How would you like me to start a food fight right here? I've got the broccoli ready to go." He stabbed a stalk of broccoli and held it up.

"Oh that's great, Howard. Security will take us away. We'll make all the papers."

"Your *obit* will make the paper, Eileen, if you don't leave me alone."

I listened to the good natured marital sparring and had to

smile. Almost immediately my happy feeling was replaced by a familiar ache in the center of my abdomen. I began to feel a slight tremor radiating out from my mid-section. If I didn't get a handle on it, it would wash over me, turning me into a wreck faster than you could say "dishrag."

I set up a breathing pattern to force relaxation.

The speaker was still going on...something about the importance of the territories to Israel's defense. I barely heard what he was saying.

Howard and Eileen, the couple next to Alli, were holding hands now.

My throat began to tighten.

I wiped my forehead with my napkin. Alli smiled at me. I weakly smiled back. Did she see what was happening to me? I could walk out now; no one would mind, right? Would the Israeli guard at the main door stop me? I mean I had just come in. Hell, *I'd* stop me if I were in his place.

The guard had other things on his mind. His eyes were on a table on the other side of the room. I looked at the other security guys and then at the waiters leaning near the kitchen door.

This feeling, a weakness spreading throughout my body, would subside. I knew that. I just had to let it come and let it go.

After a moment I leaned over to Alli and asked her to pass the water.

She handed me a half-filled carafe that had condensation running down its side. I refilled my glass and took a few swallows. Another moment passed.

"...We will not leave any city undefended," Mr. Lev said, pounding the lectern with his right fist.

Suddenly there was applause and then the entire roomful of guests jumped up, enthusiastically.

The speech was over, and I rose with Alli, likewise applauding. The emcee, a short, slightly rotund tuxedoed man in his forties, came to the mic.

"Thank you, General. And now dessert will be served." I half smiled. A significant political speech was one thing, but dessert, now *that* was important.

I spied chocolate cake being hustled out of the kitchen by the waiters, and backed off the sarcasm. I never met a chocolate cake I didn't like, and the way I felt, I needed to get something sweet into my system to help me refocus.

In moments, the cake was in front of me, and in a few moments more, I was licking the fork clean. "Not bad," I commented to Alli. "Richer than I thought." Why did I sound like an idiot?

My stomach was settling back down and I could feel myself relax.

Howard, the man next to Alli, turned toward me. "So, do ya think they're gonna hit us up for money?"

I smiled. "I'll give them your name."

Howard laughed.

"Do you and Eileen argue here often?"

He laughed again. "Only on special occasions. Like if it's Monday or something."

I smiled.

As the evening wound down, and now that I was feeling better, I continued the audience-watching I had started earlier. It was a relatively young crowd. The attendees looked pretty mixed: some men dressed formally — doctors and lawyers I'd guess — but also some regular folk. I could only guess their professions, but frankly I didn't want to.

The group began to sing *Birkat Hamazon*, Grace After Meals, and while they were doing that I looked at the waiters again. They were scurrying about, clearing the tables. The young waiter, the teenager who had been leaning against the back wall watching the guest speaker, caught my attention again. He was clearing a table over to my right. He was definitely young...perhaps 16 or 17. To me, he also looked foreign...not Middle Eastern, not Hispanic. I wasn't sure. I couldn't place him.

I watched him move about, collecting plates and filling a large oval tray balancing on his left arm. There was something else.

He was sweating. I looked at the other waiters. They were hustling too, but while they looked busy, they all seemed not to have worked up the same perspiration. The powerful air conditioner was keeping the hall fairly cool. A number of women, in fact, were wrapped in their husband's suit jackets. This guy didn't seem to feel the A/C at all.

Mr. Lev began to leave. Grace After Meals was finished and he came down off the dais, shaking hands. He paused for a moment to whisper something in the emcee's ear, and then began to weave his way through the crowd. Lev's *Shin Bet* minders took their positions. While the head man maintained his overview, the two men who were on either side of the head table moved right in front of him, staying very close. The man from the kitchen and the agent who had been standing below the dais moved to either side of him. I was surprised they didn't have someone to the rear.

As Lev began to head in my direction — the exit was behind me to my left — I looked past him. The young waiter was probably twenty-five feet from the general and his attention was clearly not on his work. He looked from his tray of plates to Mr. Lev, then back to his plates. He'd let another moment pass and then he would watch the former general again.

And then I noticed it.

He was slowly moving toward him.

I looked at the *Shin Bet* guys. They weren't watching him. They didn't even see him. Two images filled my mind. Yitzchak Rabin moving through a crowd after a concert one Saturday night in Tel Aviv and a young man pumping three bullets into him. The other image was Bobby Kennedy lying on the floor of a hotel kitchen, a pool of blood beneath his head.

I found myself moving toward the young waiter. The almost debilitating feeling I had experienced earlier was gone. All I saw was the sweating young man. He came closer, slowly, fixed on the general. Lev was now, perhaps, ten feet from him. If the Israeli continued in the same direction, in a matter of seconds the two would intersect.

The waiter put down his tray.

The crowd was still applauding. Lev was shaking hands as he slowly moved toward the exit. The Israeli guards in front were trying to clear a path. Lev continued to smile and shake hands. "Thank you. *Toda rabba.* Thank you."

The waiter's left hand slowly moved inside his jacket. He was now five feet from the general. I could clearly make out the shine on his forehead and upper lip. His eyes didn't waver from the guest of honor.

The guards were looking the wrong way.

I moved a heavy-set man to the side as I stepped forward. From behind me I heard him say, "Well *excuse* me."

The Israeli was probably wearing Kevlar or something similar under his frilly shirt, but it wouldn't matter. The bulletproof vest wasn't covering his head.

The entourage passed right in front of the waiter, the bodyguards looking but not seeing. The boy's left hand came out of his jacket holding a large caliber automatic. It looked like a Beretta. For a brief moment he pointed the gun at the ground as if it were too heavy for him. I took the final step toward him. As his hand came up I grabbed it and twisted it sharply, up and back. Even as I heard the sharp crack of wrist bones, I swept his left foot out from under him.

As he collapsed to the floor, I stepped back and shouted, "Gun!"

2

For a very long moment the waiter didn't move. He just lay there on his back, the unfired automatic beside him. The shock of being thrown to the floor momentarily stunned him. His eyes had gone wide when I swept out his feet, but now they came back to life. I knew he was in pain, but I also knew he must've been pretty pumped up, either on drugs, pure adrenalin, or both.

In another second he began to get up, but in that second the *Shin Bet* agents were on him. The tall, thin agent who had been standing beside General Lev on the way out, kicked the waiter's left knee from behind, forcing him to collapse. His partner, the agent who had been near the dais, simultaneously shoved him over backward onto the floor, and pinned a knee into his gut. Before the waiter could let out a gasp, the agent pressed the barrel of his own automatic into the boy's forehead. The young waiter grimaced in pain.

"Don't move," the Israeli said with a slight accent.

I looked up to see what else was happening. When the first two *Shin Bet* agents knocked the waiter to the floor, three other agents surrounded the guest of honor and hustled him unceremoniously out of the room. He disappeared, enveloped by his guards, out the front double doors. I had no doubt there was a bulletproof car waiting for him.

In seconds, Baltimore police and Israeli security sealed the exits. They needed to find out what was going on and no one in the hall would leave until they had a handle on what had just happened.

Who was the waiter? Was he working alone? Was he a religious fanatic? Did someone put him up to this? He was so young. Was he a paid assassin?

Some questions, of course, would wait for a private interrogation, but the critical one for now — was he acting alone — had to be answered before the crowd dispersed. Neither the Americans nor the Israelis wanted to let the waiter's partner — if there was one — walk out with everyone else.

I looked around the room to see how the crowd was reacting. For the most part, there was silence as dapper men and elegant women just watched. A camera crew from Channel 13 — a cameraman and a well turned-out woman reporter — were recording the action. They were frantically hustling to get shots...some of the crowd and some of the police and security agents doing their work. Were they filming when I broke the waiter's wrist? Maybe they were framed on the general as he was leaving and I could be seen with the waiter in the background. That's not what I needed...to be immortalized on video... my visage played and replayed all over the world.

Maybe the Israelis and the Baltimore police wouldn't check the camera. Maybe there was nothing to worry about.

Yeah, right.

The news crew weaved their way through the guests toward the Israelis pinning the waiter to the ground. They were, at most, six feet from me and getting ready to set up a camera shot. The reporter, probably about thirty with big blonde hair set off against a black evening dress, stood facing the camera with the suspect on the floor in the background behind her. The cameraman raised his camera and looked through the eyepiece.

"Not now, Miss Turner." A silver-haired plain-clothed police officer came over, his badge hanging from the breast pocket of his sport coat. He began escorting her away from the trio on the floor and handed her over to a uniformed officer.

"Wait." The senior Israeli agent, the older man with stylish wire rimmed glasses, stepped in. He turned to the reporter. "Were you filming when the general was leaving?"

The cameraman, a tall, skinny man with sandy-colored straight hair, answered: "Not the whole thing. I got his speech and then a few seconds of him coming through the crowd."

"Play it back for him, Bobby," the woman reporter said.

The senior Israeli interrupted, "Do you have a monitor we could use?"

"I've got an 11 inch in the van," Bobby put in. "Be better than trying to see through the viewfinder."

The plain-clothed cop flicked a thumb toward the door. "Get it. And find a quiet place to look at it." He turned to a black officer standing beside him. "James, go with this guy."

The officer and the cameraman moved toward the doors.

I watched them exit. Well, they were going to check the tape, and I'd find out soon enough if I were on that video. If the police or the *Shin Bet* noticed me, I wouldn't be hard to find in this closed room.

When I turned back to the scene in front of me, the Israelis were pulling the waiter upright. Another officer stepped in, handcuffs open. The crowd around them watched in silence. While the first Israeli kept his automatic pressed into the waiter's forehead, the cop spoke to the boy, "Put your right hand behind your back." He did as he was told. The officer locked the handcuff into place around his right wrist. "Now your other hand." The boy complied.

As the officer began to wrap the other handcuff around the waiter's hand, the waiter screamed in pain. I smiled to myself in satisfaction. His wrist was broken for sure. They snapped on the handcuff despite his howls and escorted him away, not being particularly mindful of his injury. I hope they questioned him before some sensitive doctor gave him a pain killer. He'd be less likely to be forthcoming if he were feeling just fine.

In the minutes that followed, the audience began to relax. Some people sat conversing at tables, while others milled about the hall. The volume had definitely come up in the room.

I located a virgin piece of chocolate cake and headed back to my seat with Alli.

"Okay," Alli said as I sat in my seat, "what did you do?"

"I took another piece of cake."

"Not that. You know what I mean."

"What?" I asked, shoving a fork-full into my mouth.

"You're the one who shouted 'Gun!' What did you do?" she pointed to where I had taken down the waiter. "You were walking over there and the next thing he was on the ground before we knew what was going on."

I reached for a glass of water and smiled slightly. "Don't you think Baltimore has the best water in the country?"

"Gidon!"

Somewhere above us a helicopter was hovering over the building. If I could hear it in here, it must've been deafening outside.

"Are you going to tell them, the police?"

"If they ask."

"Why won't you say anything to them?"

I cut another small piece off my chocolate wedge. I looked at Alli. How old was she? Maybe eight years younger than I. I was beginning to feel the gap. But it wasn't only that. It's what happened to me between when I was her age and where I am now. On the other hand, that's why I continued to go out with her... because she still seemed innocent.

"Okay," I began, "you know I like to keep to myself sometimes. Low profile..." I trailed off.

"Gidon, in this community, when you do what you do, there's no such thing."

"It's sort of a conflict, I know." I let a moment go by as I played with the cake in front of me. "I need the publicity for work, yet..." I didn't finish the thought.

I looked at Alli. I loved her lips. They were great lips.

I had to tell her something. "With these guys — the Israelis — they'll file away everything you say. I don't want another file open on me."

"Another file?"

"You know what I mean." I knew she didn't and I wasn't going to let her ask.

She looked at me for a long moment.

The door to the room opened and in walked the older Israeli agent and the plain-clothed cop. Had they reviewed the newscaster's video tape? What did they see? My guess — or was it my prayer — was that they didn't see very much of the entire episode, my actions included.

I watched them from a distance as the silver-haired plain-clothed cop and the Israeli huddled. The more I thought about it, the more I began to get annoyed. The *Shin Bet* should've been more careful with their charge. You can't anticipate everything, but still, if I hadn't been there, Eitan Lev, front-runner for Prime Minister of Israel, would be lying in a pool of blood. The Israelis are still good, but times have changed even for them.

I let another moment go by as I watched the Baltimore de-

tective and the chief Israeli security man. Chances were someone would be able to identify me as the one who shouted "gun."
The question was, could I extricate myself without making
the Israelis more curious about me. I wasn't worried about the
Baltimore cops.

"I guess you're right," I turned to Alli. "I really should talk to
the police."

She nodded. "I'll save your cake."

"No nibbling."

Alli smiled and I headed over to the edge of the room where
the cop and the older Israeli were talking. As I approached, one
of the younger *Shin Bet* agents immediately appeared in front of
me. He wouldn't let me pass. He was my height with short black
hair. The man couldn't have been more than twenty-five. He was
not in good humor. "Yes? Can I help you?" he said this quickly,
almost challengingly. But that could simply have been because
English wasn't his native language.

The cop and the older Israeli looked over at me.

I locked eyes for a split second with the *Shin Bet* man in front
of me, then looked past him to his boss. "I'm the one who shouted 'Gun!'"

The older Israeli waved off the younger security man who
took a step to the side. The Israeli in charge gestured, "Come."
He held out a chair for me at a nearby round dinner table. The
younger Israeli remained close.

I took the seat the boss offered, and he took one just a few
feet away. I looked at the table. It was covered in a navy blue

tablecloth and had a half-emptied cup of coffee near me. The rest of the table looked equally abandoned — partially finished water glasses, discarded cloth napkins, centerpiece candles burned almost all the way down, silverware scattered.

I turned to my new Israeli host. He was watching me. The Baltimore cop stood to his right. He was watching me too.

The Baltimore cop spoke up, "You are..."

"Gidon Aronson."

"Gidon?" the Israeli repeated, somewhat surprised. He must have been expecting a more Anglicized name. "*Atta m'daber Ivrit?*" He was asking if I spoke Hebrew.

I didn't say anything. I shrugged as if I didn't understand.

"I'm sorry," he said. "You don't speak Hebrew?"

I wasn't sure whether that was a question or not. "No. But I get that a lot from Israelis. My parents named me after the Biblical character."

"I know that Gidon," the man said. "He used spies and psychology against his enemies." He held out his hand, "My name is David Amit. I am in charge of security. You saved Mr. Lev's life. Thank you." He paused. "So, what did you see? What happened?"

I took a breath. It seemed the thing to do...you know, like I had to think about this. "I saw the waiter stop what he was doing and watch Mr. Lev work his way toward the exit."

"And?" the Baltimore cop asked.

"The waiter put down his tray and moved very deliberately toward Mr. Lev. And he was sweating...a lot."

"Why didn't you say something then?" This again from the cop.

"Didn't think of it. Besides, nothing had happened yet. And then there wasn't enough time." I turned to the Israeli. "Your men were looking the wrong way."

The Israeli looked at me, ignoring what could have been an accusation. "So what did you do?"

I knew they would ask this, and I kept it simple. "I saw him pull out a gun, so I sort of tripped him...knocked him down."

"A very brave thing to do," the Israeli observed.

"No choice."

"Did you notice anyone else, anyone with him?"

"Not that I could see. He was focused on Mr. Lev."

"You're pretty observant," the Baltimore cop said.

I shrugged. "Sometimes."

"What do you do for a living, Mr. Aronson?" This, again, from the cop.

"I teach." Before anyone could ask something else, I said, "How do you think the waiter got the gun past your guys?"

The younger Israeli agent, the one who had blocked my path earlier, leaned over to Mr. Amit and whispered in his ear. The senior Israel nodded, then leaned back, looking at me.

Out of the corner of my eye I saw one of my adult self-defense students watching us from a nearby table. He was a medium-tall, slightly chubby balding man who was always asking me questions. *Don't come over here...don't speak to me*, was all I could think.

I looked at him, but then turned back to the men in front of me.

"So you don't think there was anyone else with the waiter?" Amit asked again.

"No, I didn't see him interacting with anyone other than to wait tables."

"Unless there was someone in the kitchen you couldn't see," this from the younger Israeli standing beside his boss.

"Maybe, but during Mr. Lev's speech, the waiter spent the entire time out here in the hall."

The cop seemed surprised. "You noticed that also?"

I smiled what I hoped was a good smile. "I was bored, so, I looked around."

The young Israeli agent leaned over to his boss and whispered again. The senior agent looked up at his man and said, *"Kain, ani yodey-ah."* Yes, I know.

I looked at them looking at me.

One of us needed to say something, so I did: "Why don't you check the TV crew's camera. Maybe they got something on tape." Of course I already knew they did that, so I tried to make it sound like an innocent, helpful suggestion. I'm not sure it came out that way.

"Yes, thank you for that idea," the cop said. His comment sounded equally lame.

Amit turned to me. "Gidon, you are an interesting man. I would love to speak with you some more." He smiled pleasantly.

"Where can we reach you if we need to get in touch?" the cop asked.

I gave him my home number and stood up. Amit held out his hand and I shook it. "Thank you for your help. As I said before, you saved Mr. Lev's life."

I shrugged again, trying to look embarrassed. I seemed to be shrugging a lot lately. "I'm glad I could. Good luck." I headed back to my table, not waiting to be dismissed.

I heard them start to talk behind me, but my hearing wasn't good enough to make out what they were saying. I wondered how long it would be before they paid me a visit at home.

"So, how'd it go?" Alli asked, as I approached her.

"Not as good as I would have liked. I always say too much."

"Too much? I don't understand."

"Neither do I," I smiled. I really had no idea why I wasn't more forthcoming. Was there a reason not to be? Old habit, I guess. I let out a silent breath. Man, I was too tired for all this. I looked at Alli, "So, did you save my cake?"

"I did."

I looked down at it, but it wasn't calling me anymore.

There was movement to my right, from the head table. The plain-clothed cop who interviewed me, had walked over to the head table and had picked up the microphone from the dais. He flicked the switch on the mic and the loud speaker popped to life.

"Ladies and gentlemen, I'm Lieutenant Kuper. Thank you for your patience. Everything is under control. Mr. Lev is safe. We have the man who we think is responsible in custody. If anyone has information that can help us, please see me. Otherwise, you are all free to go. Thank you, again, for your patience."

There was a murmur about the room. I watched for a moment as people began to file out past the police. I nodded to Alli and we joined the slow-moving exodus. We stepped out in the hallway, which was lined on either side with display cases of menorahs, shofars, and other Judaica, and then we eventually found ourselves outside the building.

The May Sunday night air was cool, and compared to the close confines in the social hall, it was liberating. We stood with the synagogue behind us, looking out onto Seven Mile Lane, a main suburban street, but of modest size. As invigorating as the air was, though, when we emerged from the synagogue, it felt as if we were stepping into a crime scene. Police cars with their blue lights flashing were parked almost bumper-to-bumper along the curb in front of us. A uniformed officer wearing an orange reflective vest was standing in the middle of the intersection, directing traffic. I was half expecting to hear the distinctive squawk of police radio, but the cops had lapel walkie-talkies.

Out on the sidewalk there was already quite a crowd. Not only had all the dinner guests emptied into the public area in front of the synagogue, but there were several groups of local residents there as well. Even the opposite street corners were filled. Ahead of us on each corner was a mixture of old and young gawkers, neighbors probably, brought out by the light and sound show that accompanied the police. There were elderly couples in bathrobes, men and women in warm-up suits, and kids on bicycles. I looked up into the night sky. The helicopter was nowhere to be seen; no reason to hang around once the dignitary and his would-be assassin were gone.

Alli tugged on my arm, wanting to head to my car. She began to lead the way to the right, through the crush of people. I found myself looking across the street to the bystanders. On the far corner, behind a young couple holding up an infant, was a group of kids...teenagers, I'd guess. They were standing close together, alternately looking at the crowd — us — and shifting their feet. A few had cigarettes dangling from their lips. One boy was on crutches. The crutches caught my attention; they were the aluminum type and glinted in the artificial white light of the synagogue flood lights.

As we continued to move to the parking lot, someone was approaching us from the right. It was the slightly chubby adult student I spotted earlier while I was talking to the *Shin Bet* agent. I had prayed that he wouldn't come over to me in front of the Israeli and he hadn't.

"Yo, Sensei!" the student called. God, he was loud.

"Hi, Lenny." Alli and I stopped walking.

"So, what d'you think? Exciting, huh. What were you doing?...Helping out the Israelis, right?"

I looked at Alli and shared a smile with her. "That's it, Lenny, you know me."

"Good. They need help these days. They *should* go to you." He paused. "Well, that's all I wanted to say. Gotta go. See you Wednesday night."

"So long."

As I watched him move toward the adjacent parking lot on the right, another figure caught my attention. David Amit was standing at the edge of the crowd, near the curb in front of us, surrounded by his men. They were still scanning the group. All were looking about; all but Amit. He wasn't interested in the mass of people. He was looking at me.

A black sedan pulled to the curb. The Israelis, without exchanging any words, got in, and quickly pulled away. After the car turned a corner, I let my gaze drift back to the kids across the street. While some of the bystanders were beginning to head off, they hadn't moved. They were still huddled on the opposite street corner, taking in all the action.

Alli tugged on my sleeve once again and we made our way to my dark red Jeep. Thanks to the fact I had previously backed into my space, we were able to pull right out. I cut off a middle-aged tuxedoed man in a black Lexus and then headed out. We drove toward downtown.

Alli lived down in Federal Hill, a historic area of town just beyond the Inner Harbor. To get there we headed south on I-83.

The drive went quickly — at this time late Sunday night there wasn't much traffic on the highway — and for a long stretch, we rode in silence. Then as the lights of downtown bloomed ahead of us, Alli spoke up. "So, what's the plan for tomorrow?"

"Well, while you're mending bodies and manipulating joints and muscles, I'll be battling a class of middle schoolers."

She looked at me, confused.

"I'm subbing. 7th Grade American History."

"And you *enjoy* that?" she asked smiling, slightly sarcastic.

"Don't you know I'm bent."

"Uh huh, that's what I like about you."

"Not the average, young professional medical-type that you're used to."

"Definitely not." She reached over and put her left hand on my thigh.

I looked at her for a moment. What was I doing? Did she have any idea that what I did to the waiter tonight was because I had to and partly because I enjoyed causing him pain?

Maybe I needed some therapy. Well, she *was* a physical therapist.

Alli lived on Montgomery Street, a sleepy, tree-lined cobblestoned road one block from Federal Hill Park. Years ago the city had bought many of the Federal-style row houses because they had fallen into disrepair, and then provided incentives for new owners to fix them. The results were impressive. The buildings had been renovated, keeping within the original styles of the masonry, moldings, shutters, and more. The houses had regained their aura of an earlier — much earlier — time.

I found a parking-for-residents-only spot across from her house and pulled in. I hung a guest parking pass from my rearview mirror and then stepped out. Alli met me at the curb. She took my hand and we walked over to her doorstep.

"So, you're a hero." She turned and suddenly seemed very close.

I looked into her sky blue eyes. They were clear and vibrant.

Mine were probably bloodshot from fatigue.

A young couple walked past us, arm-in-arm. I could hear them talking about the Afghani restaurant they must've just visited.

Alli was still looking at me.

I smiled, thinking about what happened tonight. "We all do what we can."

"It *was* very brave of you." She was getting even closer.

"You're pretty brave yourself, going out with me."

"Mmm."

I kissed her. Softly at first, slowly...enjoying her lips on mine.

Okay, I wasn't *that* tired. Still, how smart was this? Two months ago, there'd have been no qualms. I probably would have pinned her to the door.

I needed to go home. That was the smart thing to do.

But her lips were great. I moved over to the side of her neck.

She smelled amazing. Alli wore just a hint of perfume, but her own scent wouldn't let me go.

Her arms went around me and I placed mine around her. My right arm — and I didn't ask it to — slowly glided down to the small of her back.

Another moment went by. She was too young for me. I knew that. Energetic, exciting, but too young. She was in school — graduate school — but still school, and I was on the other side of life.

"Come inside," she breathed into my ear.

"I would love to, but...I can't."

I pulled away from the embrace, ever-so-slightly. I kissed her again, very softly.

She looked at me.

"I really would love to," I repeated, "but I'm old and I have things to do for tomorrow."

She laughed at my mention of being old. "Are you sure?"

"Am I sure I'm old?"

"No, I know you're old," she smiled again. "Are you sure you have to go back?" She kissed me once more.

"No, I'm not sure."

She kissed me again.

"I'm really not sure."

If I stayed and we ended up where I knew we would, it might give her the wrong impression. Was that a problem?

I pulled away a little more, probably an entire millimeter. My right hand stayed on the curve of her lower back. "I'll call you tomorrow."

"It *is* tomorrow." It must've been after midnight.

"Even better. I'll call you later. Dinner?"

"If you insist."

"I do."

I kissed her again and then waited for her to retrieve her keys from her small handbag. She unlocked her front door, then stepped inside. "Goodnight."

"Goodnight," I smiled. She closed the door softly.

I turned and scanned the street. All was quiet. I let out a breath and went over to my Jeep. I was excited to be with Alli, no doubt about it, but the relationship left me exhausted if I dwelled on it too much. Alli was fun and eager, and I was just...I don't know what. I got into my Jeep and headed back uptown.

My modest house was tucked away behind Charles Street, just north of the Johns Hopkins Homewood campus. I made it in ten minutes due to nearly empty streets. The Homewood area was almost park-like and, thanks to the University, had an energy unique to college life: vibrant foot traffic, student activities, eateries, sporting events, and more. As it was after midnight, that energy was dormant for now, but would awaken with the day in six hours.

Once inside my house, I headed to the first floor office, pulling off my tie and opening my collar. I went over to my desk and flicked on the desk light. It cast the room in a shadowed aura that partially hid its periphery. The desk was a mess as usual with papers scattered all over. After digging out the phone and its base from a mound of magazines and catalogs, I flicked on the message system. As it cycled, I looked around the partially darkened study. An M.C. Escher print hung on one wall, a bookcase against another, an oversized chair — a chair and a half the saleswoman had called it — against a third. My scan came to rest on a long, scroll-length parchment hanging on the wall next to my desk. On the parchment was a hand-drawn Chinese poem that had been given to me more than a few years ago. In the flowing brush style of classical Chinese calligraphy with its thick and thin black characters, the poem told of dragons' wings and the creation of heaven and earth.

The answering system clicked to the first message: "Sifu, this is Jon. The ten gis you ordered came today. Mr. Kenshi brought them himself. He sends his regards. He said the broadswords are on back-order, but he'll make some calls."

I smiled, envisioning the middle-aged Japanese importer who ran a small martial arts supply business out of his clothing store not far away. He didn't need to come by, but he often did. I was honored he felt that way. Mr. Kenshi loved to sit in my office, share a story or two or three, and laugh his deep abdominal laugh.

"Oh," Jon went on, "I think we may have a new student. She's tall, has long blonde hair and an amazing smile...a junior at Hopkins. And let's just say that if you need help teaching her, I'll be there for you. No problem. She saw our demonstration at the student union. About teaching her, really, I can give the intermediate students to someone else, and I can help her get started. She'll probably be by tomorrow." There was a pause, then, "That's it. I'll see you tomorrow."

"Did you get her phone number?" I asked the machine.

"Oh," Jon's voice came back on, "her name is Evy, and I got her number. Bye."

Click.

The second and final message was from the 7th grade teacher whose class I was covering. She just wanted to remind me about class and where she was leaving her lesson plans.

I turned off the machine, then gathered my material for tomorrow's class. I had some notes, a copy of the 7th Grade text —

a two-inch thick hardcover volume called *The American Nation* — and a game of *Monopoly.* I knew the teacher; she wouldn't mind if I digressed from her plans, as long as I covered her material. I was glad she was flexible that way.

Finally, after I procrastinated enough, I took a final look around the room, turned off the light, and headed upstairs.

3

The lone sentry, dressed in army fatigues and a checkered *kaffiyah*, walked along the edge of the roof, easily drifting into the crosshairs of my nightscope. The early morning hour was black, moonless...perfect for what we had to do.

I shifted slightly. I was lying on my belly amidst the rubble of a demolished building, waiting for the little signal that would go from my brain to my right index finger, now lightly caressing the trigger guard. I thought about it, but didn't think about it. Not yet. Not yet. The moment wasn't right.

The sentry, I could see through the telescopic sight, was clean-shaven and had a strong jawline. Though I couldn't discern his eyes, I imagined they were hard with a fair amount of anger and hate in them. He stood atop a three story building, one of two structures still intact in a neighborhood filled with mounds of broken concrete and protruding rods of reinforcing iron. Between where we had taken cover and the sentry's stronghold lay 100 yards of flat, open street, illuminated by the stark white glow of halogen floodlights.

I had expected more guards, considering what was inside. There'd be plenty, I knew, just on the other side of the ground-level door facing us. My *Sayeret Matkal* team would deal with those men soon enough.

The night air was completely still and totally silent. A cool Mediterranean breeze would have been welcome, but that was fine. I didn't want even the hint of a breeze altering a millimeter of my shot's trajectory.

As I watched, the sentry up on the roof reached the end of his walk, turned around and moved back the way he had come. The crosshairs in my sight stayed on his head every second. He stopped about halfway to the other side and scanned the deserted street below him, looking first to his right, then taking a long look to his left. After he was satisfied nothing was amiss, he continued his circuit.

He had taken just one step when it happened — the entire neighborhood went dark. One moment there was light and then... nothing. There were no streetlights, no lights inside buildings, no floodlights. Just blackness. The building itself seemed to vanish into a void.

But not the guard in my sights.

I took a breath, let it out slightly, then squeezed the trigger. There was a muffled puff, but there was no sound as the guard was knocked off his feet. He wouldn't be getting up. As I emerged from between two broken cinderblock walls, three men stood up to either side of me. *Kadima*, I thought. Forward.

We began to run toward the building.

Our footfalls barely made a sound on the old paved road. As we ran, I quickly looked right and left beyond my men. No enemy soldiers, no pedestrians, no one was there. In five seconds we were halfway to the building, crossing the center of a street that had been ablaze with white light just moments ago. The block-like structure ahead grew larger.

A figure appeared at the door in front of us. To my left there was a muffled burst of weapons fire, and the figure at the entranceway was thrown backwards, a cluster of dark spots blooming over his chest.

Another figure appeared at the door and then, before anyone could react, the entire area exploded with light.

The building's lights had come back on, and with them every floodlight in creation suddenly turned the street scene to daylight. We were totally exposed — seven figures in black in the center of a barren, white no-man's land. They weren't supposed to have generators.

Oh God.

Automatic weapons opened up from every window in the building. The explosive torrent overwhelmed me.

The men to my left were hit — two in the chest, one in the head. I didn't see what happened to the others, though peripherally I saw they were all down. I ran, zig-zagging toward a pile of rubble beyond the downed men on my left. Glass and pebbles crunched beneath my boots.

The pile of debris ahead of me wasn't a pile; it was a mountain. It didn't matter. I needed cover. I scrambled up the front, while chunks of stone were blown apart inches from my head.

The peak was too far away. I clawed at the rocks and pushed with my legs. Any moment a torrent of 7.62 mm rounds would tear through my torso and skull. The shots could be on their way right now.

The top got closer. A rock next to my head shattered at a bullet's impact. My face suddenly tingled and I knew I had been hit by shards of stone.

I pulled myself over the crest and let myself roll to the other side.

The rubble gave way under me, creating an avalanche. I began to roll and tumble. Somehow I lost my weapon.

As I fell, cascading dust and powder masked everything around me. It was a long way to the bottom, much longer than it logically should have been. With every tumble, I felt sharp stones cutting and jabbing my arms and legs.

Finally, thankfully, I stopped rolling.

At the bottom of the stony heap, I didn't move for a full five breaths. With my eyes closed, I mentally checked my joints and appendages, then flexed my fingers and moved my legs. My left arm hurt at the elbow, but I could still move it. After waiting another moment, I stood up, looked at the mound that was now sheltering me, and listened.

The night was quiet again. No weapons fire, no voices, no footsteps.

I turned to find my way around the debris and came face-to-face with a man holding an AK-47. Stars flickered over his head. He was dressed in army fatigues and a *kaffiyah*. He was clean shaven and had a strong jawline. He was the man I had shot on the roof. I knew I had shot him just behind his temple, but there wasn't a mark on him. I looked past his assault rifle to his eyes. I had been right: they *were* filled with anger and hatred.

He smiled coldly and raised the weapon, pointing it at my face. My mouth went dry.

As he pulled the trigger, the muzzle flashed brilliantly, blinding me with white-yellow light.

I sat upright in my bed and let my bedroom come into focus. The presence of the room slowly faded in from the edges. I knew my eyes were open, but that muzzle flash, the night battle, the soldier I couldn't kill, that reality remained in front of me.

Sweat rolled down my cheeks and I could feel my heart hammering in my chest.

After another moment, I consciously began regulating my breath to slow my heart. In a minute, it was almost down to a healthy race. I looked around. Everything was right where it should be...the dresser across from the foot of my bed, the mirror on the wall, the upholstered easy chair in the corner. The violence and the images that had just enveloped me hadn't changed any of that.

I slowly swung off the bed and stood up — but didn't move for a long time. Feeling a little uncertain in the darkness, I sat down on the edge of the mattress and let my hands rest on my thighs. My palms were cold.

Too slowly, the images in my head began to dissipate and the events of the evening crept in. That was too much reality for the middle of the night. I climbed over to my pillow and rolled onto my back. The ceiling hovered over me. Finally, I closed my eyes and attempted to go back to sleep.

4

The Sanford Stein Day School was located just outside the Beltway in the northwest part of town. In fact, you could see the school from the highway. It was a sprawling, yet modest campus with lower school and middle school wings, a gym, and well-maintained ball fields.

I parked my Jeep next to the basketball court, grabbed my *Monopoly* box and a navy blue backpack, and headed toward an overhang-protected main entrance. As I approached the curved sidewalk near the entry doors, I thought about the school's descriptive name. It was a "Day School," a private Jewish school that taught a traditional general studies curriculum, complemented by a Jewish Studies program that included Jewish History, Hebrew Language, Bible, and other classic texts. I was never quite sure what the "Day" in "Day School" meant. I did know that this school was culturally in the middle of the Jewish spectrum, a Conservative tract that kept many of the traditions and was dedicated to community service.

I walked up to the main doors, two pairs of steel-framed glass and checked my watch: 8:15. My second period class would begin at 8:50. I shifted the *Monopoly* box from my left hand to my right and tried the closest door. The handle wouldn't budge. Thanks to terrorism and concerns for general safety, entry doors, it seemed, were always locked. To the side was an intercom and I pressed the call button.

Looking through the glass door into the lobby, I could see the main office diagonal from me, about twenty feet to my left. The receptionist sat at her desk behind a sliding glass window. From where I stood, she appeared to be in her early fifties with an older Mary Tyler Moore look about her. She reached below her desk and the lock buzzed open. I crossed a well-polished tile floor, past a huge mural depicting smiling boys and girls, and over to the receptionist who had slid open the glass partition.

"I'm Gidon Aronson. I'm subbing in the Middle School this morning."

"Yes, Mr. Aronson, it's good to see you again."

"Thanks." I paused a moment. "It's Janice, right?"

"That's pretty good. I'm impressed," she said smiling.

"I *always* remember the important people."

She laughed. "Do you remember how to get upstairs?"

"I do. It's where I put my keys that I can't remember."

"They're probably with mine somewhere."

I waved and headed down a blue and yellow corridor and around a corner to a staircase. In moments, I was on the second floor and rounding another corner. As I walked past a door on my right marked "Teacher's Lounge," I noticed that my heart rate seemed to have picked up. Twenty 7th graders whose regular teacher was away. What was there to be nervous about, right? Give me an assassin in a crowded banquet hall any time. *Oh, relax.* I knew what I wanted to do; I just needed to get into class and start rolling. I continued past wall mounted displays of student art — multi-colored cubist paintings that looked Picasso-esque — and down to the Middle School office. The door stood open.

The reception area was relatively small. To the left was the secretary's desk partially hidden behind a chest-high partition and shelf. About ten feet behind the work station was a closed door with the nameplate "Dr. Saltzman, Headmaster" on it. To my right were two copying machines, and against another wall was a grid-like hive of teachers' mailboxes. A number of them were overstuffed with papers, while others looked sadly empty, as if those teachers were unloved.

I turned back to the secretary's desk. Empty. In fact, no one was in the room at all. Perhaps there was a meeting behind the headmaster's closed door. A nearby analog wall clock clicked to 8:20. Class would start in thirty minutes and I wanted to arrive early so I could establish dominance over the 13 and 14 year olds. I knew where to go; I had subbed for Mrs. Cayhan before. I just needed her lesson plans. I stepped over to the collection of mailboxes and began looking at the names printed above each one.

"Can I help you?"

I turned to see a very striking, petite woman who was probably in her early thirties. She was slender with shoulder-length blonde hair framing her sparkling eyes. A tapered white sleeveless dress flattered her figure and revealed toned, tanned arms.

"I'm Gidon Aronson. I'm subbing for Mrs. Cayhan."

"Right. I knew you'd be coming in. Carol told me."

"You are...?"

"I'm sorry. I'm Katie Harris. I direct student services here." She put out her hand, which I shook. Her grasp was firm. "You're taking her 7th Grade American History class, aren't you?"

"I am."

"You know, you can save me a trip, if you don't mind." She pulled a pink slip of paper from a nearby mailbox and then leaned over the shelf to fill it in. I noticed she wrote with her left hand — always a good sign in my book — and I also noticed she wasn't wearing a wedding ring. The fact there was no tan line where a ring would have been hadn't escaped me either.

As she continued to write, I tried to watch her without staring. As she leaned over, her hair had fallen slightly away from the back of her neck to reveal a thin gold necklace. It went perfectly with her tanned skin and the color of her dress. So no one would think I might be leering, I stepped back and turned to peruse the walls. There were class photos, a bright yellow flyer announcing the arrival of the yearbooks, a calendar, and two State commendations. After another moment, I looked down at my tie — for some reason I suddenly hoped it was one of my more stylish ones — only to see that it had flipped around so that seam and label were now forward. I ever-so-nonchalantly flipped it back. I looked up to see Miss Harris watching me. She was smiling at my deft maneuver.

"It's my natural energy," I said. "It just spirals right off me. All my ties flip."

"Uh huh," she smiled back.

"Really." I smiled back. After a moment I pointed to the slip of paper in her hand. "What do you want me to do?"

"Just give this to David," she named the student on the note. "It's a pass to let him come to my office."

I took the note which had the words "The Harris Get Out of Class Pass" printed across the top.

"Cute."

She smiled, not as impressed as I would have liked. "He's not due to see me until 9:00, so that should give him more than enough time to copy down his homework."

"No problem." I put the paper in my shirt pocket. "So, what does a director of Student Services do?"

"Oh, I teach, I coordinate the efforts of tutors, our school psychologist, other teachers and administration. Basically, I'm the official advocate for the students."

I was thinking about asking her where her office was — in case *I* needed help — when the headmaster's door opened. Out came an attractive middle-aged woman with short tapered dark hair that made her look both attractive and business-like. I recognized her as Diane, the Middle School secretary. As she emerged from the headmaster's office, she was talking over her shoulder: "I'll call her office and see if she can come in." Diane sat down at her desk and picked up the phone. Before she began dialing, she looked up at me: "Mr. Aronson, hi. How are you?"

"Pretty well, thanks."

"Give me a second and I'll be right with you." She began dialing.

"Gidon, it's nice to see you." I looked up to see the headmaster coming out of his office. He was a tall man in his mid fifties, a little husky as if he could've been a football player in earlier years, balding and clean shaven. The knot on his Jerry Garcia tie hung an inch or two below an unbuttoned collar. He exuded warmth.

"Thank you, Dr. Saltzman," I said, shaking his hand.

"So I hear you had a little excitement last night."

Oh God. What did he know and how?

The headmaster turned to the two ladies in the room. "Do you know that Mr. Aronson stopped an assassination at the Beit Shalom banquet last night?"

The women looked at me. I just looked back at headmaster.

"It's a small community, Gidon," he laughed. "I have several friends who saw you."

I just shrugged. "I'm just glad Mr. Lev is okay."

"What did you do?" the secretary asked.

Dr. Saltzman didn't give me a chance to respond. He put his hand on my shoulder. "He flipped a waiter who was about to shoot Eitan Lev."

"I didn't flip him," I said, shifting my weight, unconsciously. "I just tripped him before he could do any damage." I felt the three pair of eyes on me, waiting for more explanation. I shifted my weight again. "Really, it wasn't a big deal."

I needed to leave. I didn't want to talk about this.

Katie Harris stepped closer. "Excuse me, but you're subbing for Carol, right, in about fifteen minutes? Do you know where her lesson plans are?"

Was I that obvious in my discomfort, or was she extremely intuitive? It didn't matter. I took her lead. "She said they'd be in her mailbox."

Ms. Harris stepped over to the grid of mailboxes, located one along the top row, and pulled some papers from it. "7th Grade American History. Here they are, with your name on them."

"Thanks." I took them from her. "If you will excuse me, I need to look at these and set up before class starts." I turned to the Headmaster and his secretary. "It was good seeing you."

As I headed down the hallway, I could feel my shoulders slowly relax. When I paused to get my bearings, I heard footsteps behind me. I smiled as Katie Harris approached. "Bless you, bless you, bless you for getting me out of there," I said.

"You're welcome, you're welcome, you're welcome." There was that luminous smile again. We walked together. A moment went by then she said, "You've taught this class before, haven't you?"

"A few times."

"They're good kids."

"All nice and rested and full of energy, right?"

"Yup," she smiled again. "Just for you."

We rounded a corner and headed down another corridor. This one was carpeted and had bulletin boards to either side. Room 235, Mrs. Cayhan's room, was the second classroom on the right. We stopped in front of it.

"You know, your reputation precedes you."

"My reputation?" I wasn't sure what she meant. I broke a guy's wrist last night and threw him to the ground. Did she mean that?

"As a teacher. I've heard the kids love it when you substitute."

I laughed. "Is that a good thing? Maybe it's because their regular teacher isn't here."

"No, they enjoy your class. Really."

"I'm glad." I let a moment go by. "Have you been the special services person here a long time?"

"I started this past September."

"And you like it here?"

"Very much. I love the kids."

As we talked, I noticed that she hadn't asked about last night. I wasn't sure what that meant. Maybe she just didn't want to pry. That was refreshing and appreciated. I was sorry I hadn't run into her before.

"Well," she said after a moment, "if you ever need help with any of the kids, or ideas for getting across a lesson, let me know."

"I will. Thanks, again, for the save," I said.

"My pleasure."

With that, Ms. Harris headed down the corridor and I opened the door to my home for the next forty-five minutes. I looked around. The room was the traditional rectangle, with the teacher's desk in front, facing rows of students' desks. On the far side of the teacher's desk — opposite me as I walked into the room — was a wall of windows, some covered by Venetian blinds. Behind the teacher's desk and facing the room was a whiteboard, with a matching one on the back wall of the room. This rear whiteboard was flanked by two bulletin boards. The one to the left had a display on the Presidents of the United States, while the other highlighted different geographic terms such as *peninsula, isthmus,* and *basin* — with matching illustrations. I took this all in and also noticed that the air conditioner was on, putting a slight chill in the room. In a matter of minutes the room would be filled with young hyperactive bodies that would add some heat.

I put my notes, the packet from the teacher, and my *Monopoly* game down on the desk and took a deep breath. The teacher's notes spelled out Mrs. Cayhan's plan for the day, plus the students' homework. I picked up a black marker from the ledge below the whiteboard and posted the overnight assignment. No sooner had I finished the last line than the bell rang, signaling the end of the current period. Actually, it was more like an electronic buzz, but it was warning enough. I gathered my notes, sat on the edge of the desk, and waited.

In a minute, two girls — one tall, dressed all in black with spiky hair, and one short and thin with blonde hair tied up in a sort-of bun — came in talking. They took two steps then froze in mid-stride.

"Mr. Aronson, are you subbing today?" the smaller of the two semi-shrieked.

"I sure am," I said smiling.

The petite girl immediately headed back out to the hallway and announced my arrival, using a decibel level disproportionate to her size. Within minutes the entire room was filled. There were probably eighteen or twenty kids and there was only one desk to spare. The new period bell rang, and we were off.

"Okay," I announced, "your homework is on the board and I will be passing out your drill, so please settle down."

The buzz in the room quieted as I passed out Mrs. Cayhan's drill for the day: an analysis of a political cartoon about big business in the late 1800's. It showed a giant Cornelius Vanderbilt, the railroad baron, straddling a group of railroad tracks. He was holding a leash in each hand that was attached to different railroads. The students' task was to answer a number of questions about the cartoon.

I looked out at the students in the room. There were tall and small kids, round and thin; some were in shorts and T-shirts, others in jeans and more fashionable tops. As I watched the boys and girls get down to work, the young, petite girl who had announced my arrival raised her hand. She was sitting in the front row, dead center.

"Mr. Aronson, are you subbing all week?"

"No, Arielle, just today. Mrs. Cayhan will be back tomorrow."

She raised her hand again.

"Yes, Arielle," I smiled.

"How'd you remember my name? I mean you're not here that often."

A boy diagonally behind her with close cropped blonde-hair and a cherubic face burst out with: "It's because you ask so many questions, Arielle. God!"

"Thank you, Zach," I said. "Actually, I try to make my mind very impressionable, like a field with undisturbed snow on it. Then when I need to remember something, it makes an impression and I remember it." I paused. "That, and the fact that you ask a lot of questions, Arielle."

"If you say so, Mr. Aronson," Arielle said.

I smiled again. "Back to work."

Just as the class had settled down, the door opened and in walked a dark-haired boy, dressed in jeans and a black and orange Orioles T-shirt. He began heading for the lone desk in the back left corner of the room.

Our eyes met. "Stop," I said.

Everyone in the room looked up.

"You're Josh, right?" I loved being able to call them by their names. It made it personal, essentially saying I may be a sub, but I know who you are.

"Uh huh." Josh answered, frozen in place near the door.

"Do you know what time it is?"

The boy wasn't even flustered. "I know I'm late. I'm sorry." He wasn't. You could see it in his expression and in his body language. He was smiling and looking at his friends.

"Do you have a late note?"

The entire class was watching the two of us. Except for our exchange and the low rumble of the air conditioner, the room was still.

The boy in the Orioles T-shirt looked at me. "No."

I didn't say anything; just looked at him

"Mrs. Cohen let us out late."

I addressed the class: "How many of you are in Mrs. Cohen's class?"

About fifteen students raised their hands. I thought that might be the case.

"Class started eight minutes ago, Josh. It's not fair to all of us, and besides, you missed my explanation on the secret to re-membering Arielle's name."

A moment went by. We needed to get past this.

"Don't take advantage of me, Josh. I don't appreciate it."

He sat down without further comment.

"Okay, ladies and gents," I began, "we have miles to go before we sleep, so let's take one more minute and then we'll review the drill." They all got back to work.

A hand from a girl seated in the center of the room went up. She had her knees pulled up close to her chest, her feet resting on the chair.

"Yes?"

"Could you turn down the air conditioner. It's *freezing* in here."

I looked at her. She was wearing shorts and a sleeveless flowered top. She was rubbing her own arms, trying to get warm.

"We *can't* turn down the air conditioning, Sammi," Zach, the boy who had earlier needled Arielle, spoke up again. "The knob is broken."

I walked over to the window-side of the room and took a look at the wall unit. It was a system similar to the units found in many motel rooms that controls both heat and air conditioning. There were only two knobs: one to select the function and one to control the temperature. The knob for the temperature was missing, leaving only the metal post.

"You can't turn it," Arielle spoke up from the front. "It's stuck. You need a pliers or something."

I looked at it for a moment then grabbed the small post between thumb and forefinger and rotated it to the left. It was a little resistant, but it turned. Immediately, the tone of the unit deepened and the air blowing out became warmer.

"Oh my God, how did you do that?" someone in the back asked.

I just smiled. On the way back to my desk I caught a glimpse of the wall clock. It was almost 9:00. I pulled Katie Harris' note from my shirt pocket. I asked for David Leder to come see me, and a short, disheveled-looking boy with wire rim glasses came over. I handed him the "Harris Get Out of Class Pass" and off he went.

The remainder of class went smoothly. After reviewing the drill and then working on vocabulary relating to their chapter, I pulled out my *Monopoly* board. Since the lesson was on the rise of industry in America, I thought it would be interesting if they could redesign the *Monopoly* board to reflect that era. They could rename the railroads and utilities to something more era-appropriate, and then could also replace the street names with other monopolies of the time, such as the Standard Oil Trust. I divided the class into four groups and gave them time to come up with suitable names. Ten minutes before class was over, we reconvened to share their ideas. They loved it, and I was pleased. Not all my ideas went over so well.

The bell rang shortly and the class filed out. Most of the kids said good-bye; some said thank you. I ushered two stragglers out — two boys who took an incredible amount of time gathering their books and binders — and then collected my own belongings.

I went back to the office. It was much busier this time, filled with teachers and a few kids. Teachers were moving from mailbox to door, from door to copier, from one office to another. Students were just hanging out.

I looked at Diane, the secretary who had welcomed me warmly. She was at her desk and had the phone cradled between her ear and shoulder — she must've been on hold — but was talking to a teacher beside her about report cards, jotting down notes on a Post-it pad, and directing traffic in the room — all at the same time. She saw me walk in and waved me over with her free hand. She handed me a blue sheet of paper emblazoned "Substitute Pay Form," then went back to her traffic direction.

I found a shelf to lean on and filled out the paper.

By the time I was finished, the room had emptied. I handed the form to Diane, thanked her, and headed out. As I walked down the corridor filled with the student cubist art, I hoped I would bump into Katie Harris before I left. I smiled picturing her smile. My thoughts shifted to Alli. I owed her a phone call to set up dinner tonight, but I'd deal with that later. My mind went back to Katie.

I headed down to my office on North Charles Street. This area of town was a few miles north of the city center and had a mixed commercial-residential feel to it. On the main street, stores lined either side, however, the road itself was not all that wide. In fact, it was one-way northbound, and where the shops were mostly at street level, apartments filled the upper two stories. I pulled into a tenant's only parking lot behind my building, then headed around front.

My modest place of business was located between the offices of a radio station and a natural food restaurant. Both had been there when I first rented my place. I had never set foot in the radio station — no need to — but I was familiar with the natural foods place. It was run by a Latino husband and wife who seemed to always be there.

I hustled up the five steps to my entrance: a single, nondescript glass door that had orange paper lining it on the inside so you couldn't see through. There were no signs, no markings of any kind as to what lay inside. I unlocked the door and walked in.

The entranceway soon gave way to a decent-sized hardwood-floored open room. There weren't many accouterments to give away what went on here. The walls — simply painted white — were pretty much bare; there was a punching bag hanging from supports in one corner, and there was a lone bookcase against the back wall that had a shelf-full of arm and leg pads and a collection of miscellaneous books. Two good-sized windows, both of which were open, let in plenty of light.

The one thing that gave away the purpose of the room was a young man in his mid-twenties, holding a pair of Chinese broadswords. He wore loose black pants and a red T-shirt with a black dragon emblazoned on the back. At the moment, he was moving vigorously about the room flashing the swords, constantly rising up on one leg, and then sinking low. I watched from the side.

After about thirty seconds he came to a stop. He turned to see me and came right over.

"Sifu, hi."

"Good morning, Jon."

Jon was about five-ten, lean, and curly-haired. Sweat was running down his cheek and the front of his T-shirt was patterned with wet spots like an ink-blot test.

"That last section looks good," I said. "Smoother than last week. Not bad for a young guy."

"Thanks. Some old guy showed me what to do."

I smiled. The "old guy" was me.

He smiled back, then asked: "Did you get my message last night?"

"About the uniforms and about the new student? Yes. I look forward to meeting her."

We walked through a door and into my office. Like the main room, the office had the essentials: a desk, some chairs, plus a tall filing cabinet. The only elements of luxury were an old sofa that I had rescued from a second-hand shop and a TV/DVD player. On top of the filing cabinet was a green towel. I tossed it to Jon.

"So how'd last night go?" Jon asked, mopping his face.

"You know, Oh Young Student, there aren't too many people I let pry into my private life."

"If I didn't pry, you'd end up telling the whole class anyway."

I smiled because it was true. I sat down in the desk chair and looked up at my student. "It was definitely an interesting night." I told him everything, from spotting the waiter to the discussion with the *Shin Bet* guy. The only thing I left out was my emotional state at the beginning of the evening.

"So what do you think about the Israeli dude?"

"He'll be by. He knew I wasn't giving him the entire story. And while that may not affect his investigation, these guys hate not knowing everything about everything."

"So he doesn't know your background?"

I shook my head. "I don't think so. Maybe by now. I don't know."

Jon began playing with one of the broadswords, moving it from side-to-side. "So, when do you think he'll show up?"

"This morning, I'm sure. I had to give him my home phone number. He'll trace me here."

"Anything you want me to do, Sifu?"

"You may want to offer me a can of soda when he comes in."

He smiled, knowing exactly my intent.

"After that, be invisible. Don't give him a reason to notice you."

"I'll be as clear as a fresh mountain stream."

"Uh huh."

With that, Jon went back to his work-out and I went about some paperwork. My attention span for that was about five minutes, so I left my desk and went about my own martial routine. It was very dull to look at: several sequences of stretching exercises and then a lot of standing around and staring off into space.

About an hour later the door buzzer sounded. Jon and I exchanged glances and he went to see who it was. In a minute he came back, as expected, with David Amit, the *Shin Bet* man from last night. Amit looked a little more worn than the evening before. He was wearing a sport coat with an open collar — Israelis detest ties — and his thinning hair was slightly disheveled. He came in alone, though I doubted he was by himself.

"*Boker tov,*" he said almost flatly. "Good morning."

"Good morning. What can I do for you?"

"Is there a place where we can talk privately?" He looked at Jon.

I led Amit into my office. I opened a folding chair for him and placed it opposite my desk. I grabbed the cushioned desk chair across from him.

He sat in his seat with his legs crossed, ankle on the opposite knee, and tried to look casual. "You didn't tell me everything last night." He looked around the dojo office. "Where did you train?"

"Here and there. It doesn't matter does it? What can I do for you, Mr. Amit. You know what I told you about the waiter was accurate."

He uncrossed his legs. "You said you didn't see the waiter talking to anyone, that you thought he was working alone."

"From what I could see."

"We don't think so. We don't think he was by himself."

"Okay, but as I told you, I didn't see anyone else."

There was a knock on the office door. It was Jon. "Sifu, excuse me. I thought you'd like something to drink." He looked at me and I could almost see a smile on the corners of his mouth. He handed me a can of Coke and a plastic cup.

"Thanks." I turned to the Israeli. "Mr. Amit, do you want anything to drink?"

"No thank you."

Jon left the room.

The Israeli went on: "We think he's part of a larger group."

"So?"

"So, we'd like your help."

"I helped last night. Did your job for you."

Amit didn't react; he just looked at me. After a moment, "What unit did you serve in?"

I poured the soda into the cup and then began to fiddle with the empty can. "Why do you ask questions you already know the answers to?" I paused. "How is Mr. Lev?"

"Mr. Lev is fine. We need your help," he repeated.

"I'm just a teacher. Go to the police."

"They can not help us."

"Why not?"

"The waiter is involved in a group that the police don't know very much about."

What he meant was he knew the group, but probably didn't have the time or the resources to infiltrate them. I looked down at the can of soda in my hand and put my right index finger against its side. About halfway down I began to make a slow drilling-type movement with my finger. Amit looked for a moment at what I was doing then turned back to me.

He sat forward in his chair. "You teach here. You can maybe get one of their group to join your class or use one of your students to get close to them. Maybe one of the girls... preferably someone in high school."

I was on my feet. "That's it, we're done. 'Use one of my students!?' You know your way out."

Amit stood up casually. "They were watching you last night when you came out of the synagogue."

I looked at the *Shin Bet* man. I looked at his black wire rim glasses and at the lines at the corner of his eyes.

I looked right into his black pupils. "Mr. Amit, it's time for you to go."

"Consider this your *meluim*, your reserve duty."

"We're not in Israel."

"You are involved."

"I am not involved. I helped you last night, that's all."

"I'm sorry you feel this– "

"Just tell your bosses in Ganei Yehoshua that you couldn't recruit me."

His right eyebrow went up as I mentioned the location of *Shin Bet* headquarters in Tel Aviv.

As I finished this last statement, I pushed my right index finger through the side of the aluminum Coke can. This time both Amit's eyebrows went up. I pulled my finger out and then tossed him the can.

"Like I said, I can't help you."

Amit looked down at the punctured can and then back at me. "You are a very interesting man, Gidon." He said the same thing last night after my interview. I didn't like it.

He turned to leave, but looked back. "You asked me last night how the waiter smuggled a gun past us. He hid it in a tray of silverware. He had help."

"We're done, Mr. Amit. *Atah meyvin*? Do you understand?"

"Yes, I understand."

"Good. Let me see you out."

I escorted him out of the office and into the main practice hall. Without looking around I could tell Jon was not in the room, though I knew he was nearby. I walked the Israeli agent to the entrance.

There was nothing else to say, so he just looked at me and then opened the glass door and went outside. I locked the door behind him.

"Shit," I said aloud. "Now he'll be back."

Jon appeared at my side. "I thought you were pretty chill."

I looked at my finger. It was bleeding from where I punctured the soda can. "Not chill enough."

5

I needed to get my meeting with Amit out of my system. Fortunately, I had a class to teach in a few hours and that would distract me. Unfortunately, my growing distaste for what just happened would come out somehow, either in my physical handling of my older students or in what I said. In any case, not good. I needed to mellow out. Jonathan took off to get some work done: his family was into commercial real estate and he had to check on some properties, so this left me alone.

I worked out for an hour and a half — not the meditative stuff I did before, but intricate, active physical movements — and then I showered and went next door for lunch. I ordered a roasted vegetable sandwich, and instead of any number of natural iced teas, I opted for plain water. As I sat at a table facing the room, I reviewed my actions of last night. I replayed how I handled the waiter and my conversation with the police and *Shin Bet*. The only thing I could have handled differently is what I said to the Israelis. I could've been more forthcoming, but I wasn't sure what that would have accomplished, except for revealing personal information I wanted to keep to myself. I shrugged and bit into the sandwich.

After finishing my sandwich and draining my glass of water, I headed back to the studio to call Alli. Since I had a late afternoon class, she volunteered to come by after work so we could go out to dinner from there. I still wasn't sure what was going on with us, but we might as well continue seeing each other until our feelings became more clear — one way or the other. Lord knows what she was expecting. Lord knows what I was expecting.

By the time my five o'clock class came around, I was feeling better... more upbeat, more centered. Something continued to nag at me, though. Amit said that last night someone was watching me when we came outside. I wasn't convinced he was telling the truth, but if he was, I should've noticed.

With all this bouncing around my head, I let Jonathan start the new beginner's class. There were about fifteen new faces for this session, and they were all crowded in front of him. Half of the group were ten and eleven year old boys and girls, while the rest were older kids and adults. The three older students were in their late teens/early twenties — college age — and two were co-eds. The ladies were slender, while the lone young man was more filled out. They joked with each other, obviously good friends.

For the most part, the newbies were dressed in T-shirts and shorts. A few of the after-school kids had white *gis* from a previous martial arts experience. Since this was the first class, of a new session I didn't make uniforms a requirement. That would come in time.

Jon divided the entire group into three rows of five and had the class spread out across the room. He kept younger kids up front, the older, taller students toward the back.

After the traditional bow, Jon led the workout, beginning with head rotations to loosen their neck muscles. In the minutes that followed, he took them through more stretching routines from top to bottom — head, arms, trunk, and legs. He worked on balance exercises for kicks: they stood on one leg, with the supporting knee slightly bent, and then they extended the other leg. Most of the students were able to keep their balance for the allotted time. Some, though, teetered on their supporting leg and kept falling over. The college women seemed to do well, as did a few of the younger students.

At one point Jon and I made eye contact, and with a slight nod he called me over. "That's her in back," he whispered, "the one I left you a message about last night."

I looked at the college kids in the back row. He had described the new love of his life as being tall with long blonde hair and an amazing smile; a junior at Hopkins. Both college girls were on the tall side and both had long hair, so I couldn't tell which one he meant.

"All right, everyone on the floor, on your backs," Jon got back to work. "Leg lifts."

He had them supine, with hands tucked under the small

of their backs for support. Jon ordered them to raise their feet about a foot off the floor. He modeled everything from up front.

"Now, hold it." Everyone, including Jon, froze with legs off the ground.

As he worked them — and probably harder than he had to — I wandered up and down the lines to see if I could make anyone nervous. For the most part, they all seemed pretty focused. But then they hadn't seen me hit Jon yet.

The after-school kids in front began to moan. The class was still in the leg-raised position. One student dropped his feet to the floor. Then another kid did the same.

"Keep those legs up there." The students struggled to lift their legs. "Okay, now on your bellies. Push ups on the knuckles, except for you kids in front. You guys just use open palms."

Jon clenched his fists, put them on the floor, knuckles down, and began counting as he pushed up. The class began to follow. I watched the coeds. They were in the middle of their line, and the one on the left, seemed particularly driven. She was dressed in shorts and a white T-shirt and had long blonde hair that was held together by a silver barrette. She was keeping up with Jon's vigorous count.

"Okay, relax."

Everyone moved into a sitting position and the few students who attempted the knuckle push-ups gingerly opened their hands. The blonde college girl with the barrette was one of them. Now that she was sitting up I got a better look at her. She was, indeed, a looker. Young, slender but curvy, she had beautiful clear skin, high cheekbones and dark eyes. Her face was red with exertion and beads of sweat had formed on her upper lip. I could also now make out her T-shirt. It had a beautiful depiction of Chinese zodiac symbols, from dragon to tiger to snake, and all signs in between.

I moved behind her so she couldn't see me. I caught Jon's attention. Out of her line of sight I pointed to her and he discretely nodded. I smiled.

Jon continued with crunches and more leg stretches. Finally, he turned to me and said, "Okay, Sifu, they're all yours."

The class turned to me and I headed to the front of the room. "Good afternoon, everyone." I was dressed in a pair of black military-issue BDU pants and a turquoise T-shirt depicting an Oriental mountain scene. Very untraditional for a martial arts class. "Anyone ever hear the expression, 'Your money or your life'?" I looked the group over.

There were a few murmuring acknowledgments.

"Well, it's not true...not anymore. I know of a young man who was on the "A" train in New York a number of years ago with his girlfriend. They were headed to a movie when two guys came up and demanded his money. He gave it to them. Guess what happened next. They wanted his watch...then his ring...then his girlfriend."

I paused for effect.

"And today," I scanned the faces as I spoke, "even if you give them everything, they might just shoot you for the hell of it... just because."

I turned to Jon and waved him over. He hustled and stopped right in front of me.

"Reach for me, please," I said to him.

Jon took a step forward, reaching for me with an open right hand. I parried his arm, side-stepping his grasp. I simultaneously swiveled his far shoulder backwards toward me and swept his right foot. He collapsed to the ground. Jon lay there for a moment, and then sprang to his feet.

"A fight's over in less than three seconds, one way or the other. If you want to be the one standing, you better be good. Let's get started."

I began with basic fist and horse stance. With Jon's assistance, we circulated through the ranks to make sure everyone was on the right track. I noticed he often returned to the blonde college girl to adjust her arm and hip positions.

In what seemed a matter of moments, the sixty minute class was over. I gave them my homework expectations and then wished them all a good evening. For the most part, the students both young and old left the room, buzzing about what they had just learned.

As the last of the students filed out, Alli walked in. She was wearing white slacks and a green polo shirt that had a white "Northwest Physical Therapy" logo above the left breast. "Hi there," she smiled.

"Hi there." I leaned in and kissed her.

"Good class?"

"Yeah, pretty good. Jon has his eye on a *very* attractive new student, a college junior he says." I looked around for my senior student but didn't see him.

"I saw him outside, talking to this awesome-looking blonde."

"That's her."

"No policy about dating students?" she asked smiling. I didn't know if she were serious or not.

"For me, yes. Him, no."

"Sounds fair. So, where do you want to go to dinner?"

"How 'bout Little Italy? Haven't been there in a while."

"Okay, nothing too fancy, though. I'm not dressed for it."

"Fine with me."

"And why don't we ask Jon to come along. He's never joined us."

"Sure, but the boy is *busy*. He may already have plans."

No sooner had I said it, then Jon came back into the room with a huge smile on his face.

"Don't tell me," I said. "You have a date."

"Tomorrow night," he beamed.

"Jon, Jon, Jon," I said. "You must be losing your touch."

"What?"

"Not tonight?"

"I guess she needs the time to dump whoever she's currently with."

"Uh huh."

"So since you're free," Alli said, "you can join us for dinner."

"Definitely," he looked at me, "If it's okay with Sifu."

"Oh, I suppose." I smiled, then turned to Alli. "Let me just change my shirt and I'll be ready to go."

"Me too," Jon said.

With that, I headed to my office to change while Jon went to the men's room to quickly wash up. Once in my inner sanctum I pulled off my T-shirt and changed into a blue polo that I kept around. My black cargo-BDU pants would be fine for a casual evening. Besides, I didn't have another pair of pants. When I returned to the main hall, Alli was checking her cell phone. Jon soon joined us — he had changed into Dockers and a sport shirt — and we were off.

Alli and I rode in my Jeep and Jon followed us in his Mitsubishi Eclipse. We headed down I-83 — the same road I took last night to Alli's — but instead of heading to Federal Hill, I turned left onto Eastern Avenue.

Little Italy, just east of the highway, is just a few square blocks of narrow streets, row houses, eateries, and minimal parking. Curb-side spaces are all but impossible to come by, particularly at dinner time. We circled the block a few times until we came upon a middle-aged couple just getting into their late-model Audi. I waited patiently and then pulled into their spot. Jon, in his Eclipse, drove past, continuing his search. He turned a corner and disappeared.

Alli and I got out and walked toward where Jon had disappeared. Before we made it to the end of the block, Jon came sauntering around the corner. "There're three spaces just up the street."

"Naturally," I said.

As we crossed onto High Street, I scanned the area we had just left. A number of pedestrians were walking in our direction. Several were dressed up: sport coats or semi-dressy skirts and nice blouses.

I stopped for a moment, letting Alli and Jon continue on ahead. I looked back toward where we had parked, and I saw a group of four boys, hanging out at the line of cars. The kids were probably about sixteen or seventeen, and for the most part were dressed in jeans and T-shirts. They looked out of place among the young marrieds and professionals. I could see that one of the boys had a cigarette dangling from his mouth and he was on crutches...not the wood version, but the aluminum type. Every few seconds the quartet looked over at me. I watched them watch me.

Jon and Alli came back for me, thinking I was just taking in the scenery, and the three of us returned to the task of picking out a restaurant. We settled on a new place called Testa's, and stepped inside. By now it was 6:30 and the restaurant was moderately full. I was glad to see that they were busy so early in the week. A tall, balding *maitre d'* dressed in a black dinner jacket met us, and inquired as to the number in our party. As he checked a seating chart, we looked around. The place was relatively small, but filled with booths along the perimeter and tables in the middle of the room. The decor was continental, with dark woodwork, and Rubenesque paintings on the walls.

In a matter of minutes, we were seated at a table near the back and had menus in hand. A young, perky waitress came over a few minutes later, carrying a bottle of olive oil and a basket of warm bread. She filled the small saucer in the middle of our table, and I wasted no time in tearing off a piece of the warm bread, dipping it into the olive oil, and popping it into my mouth. As we knew what we wanted, we ordered: Alli had settled on Veal Parmesan, Jon went for spinach ravioli, and I was having linguine with mushrooms and sun-dried tomatoes.

While we waited for our food, Alli turned to Jon. "So, I understand you have a life besides karate."

"There is no life besides karate," he said smiling. "Okay, there is something else I do between workouts. My family has some commercial properties in the city and I help manage them."

"Like businesses or offices?

"Mainly offices and apartment buildings. My dad got started when he was relatively young — probably in his early twenties. I guess I'm the heir apparent, though I don't know if it's what I want to do the rest of my life."

"Jon's father wants him to try the business for a while before making up his mind," I said.

"Sounds practical," Alli commented. "He's a sharp man, I bet."

"And very generous," I added.

"Sifu helped my father out a few years ago and he wanted to repay the kindness."

"The place I have, the dojo, is a present from him."

"Wow."

"Yeah, wow. And he won't hear of me paying rent or anything. Incredibly magnanimous."

Alli didn't ask what I did for him, and Jon didn't volunteer any information. I was glad for that. Instead, Jon just tore a piece of bread from the basket in front of us and dipped it into the olive oil.

"So," Alli said after a moment went by, "did Gidon tell you about last night?"

"A little bit."

Bless him. He had more of an inside track as to what happened than Alli, even though she was there, but he didn't say anything. Jon also knew about the *Shin Bet* man coming to see me. That news I hadn't shared with Alli.

"So, what d'you think," she looked at Jon. "Why would anyone want to assassinate the man running for Prime Minister of Israel?"

"Someone doesn't like his politics. Or could be a religious thing — you can never tell when it's the Middle East. Or maybe he was just paid."

"I vote for that," I said quietly.

"That he was just hired to kill him?" Alli asked. "Why?"

"I'm tired of young fanatics killing in the name of God."

"What do you mean?"

As I looked at Alli I could see Jon looking at me, too. I just shrugged, trying to blow it off, not wanting to pursue this.

"So, it was an exciting evening," Jon jumped in. "Not your typical banquet."

Alli came back to it: "Do you think he was working alone? I mean what are the chances of that?"

My eyes drifted to the front window, and in my mind I could picture four boys near my car across the street...the four of them...and one was on crutches. Last night when we came out of the synagogue, there was a group of boys watching the excitement. One of them was on aluminum crutches. The metal had glinted in the police lights.

"So, how 'bout them O's," I heard Jon say.

I looked back at Jon and Alli. "What?"

"The Orioles, boss," Jon repeated. "Do you think they'll do better this year?" He turned to Alli. "I have a friend who has a skybox. Anytime you want to go to the game..."

"Thanks," Alli responded. "Save it for your new girlfriend."

Our meals arrived shortly and the conversation turned from the Orioles to the Ravens, to Jon's background, to Alli's work. When we finished the main course, our waitress returned and presented us with the idea of dessert. We looked at each other and we all shook our heads.

"Another time," I said to the waitress.

She brought the check, I paid it, and we headed outside.

Instead of starting to walk, we just paused in front of the

entrance to stretch — or at least to let our stomachs expand. By now the sun had set and the ambient light was beginning to recede. Street lights had come on and store signs had started glowing.

"Thanks for the treat," Jon said as we started walking up to the left.

"Don't worry, I'll just raise your dues."

"He's kidding, right?" Alli asked Jon.

"I'm never sure."

We continued heading up the street. As we did so, I nonchalantly looked around for the group of kids I had seen before. God, I hoped they wouldn't get in my face. As I scanned the area, there was no sign of them. The three of us ambled up the block, checking out other shop windows. The store fronts soon changed to private row houses. In front of several doorways residents were sitting on their marble steps, just taking in the neighborhood.

As we strolled I listened to Jon and Alli talk. I looked at them, smiled from time to time as they turned to me, but basically kept to myself. I was beginning to feel tired. The early evening air was quiet, and there was an orange glow to the sky as the city's high pressure sodium lights tinted the heavens. I watched as more than one couple walked past, arm-in-arm.

I started thinking about Alli again. I thought about the age difference...about the life difference. I just didn't know what to feel, or was supposed to feel, about her. Everything would be fine and then, as I spent more time with her, I'd become drained.

Like now. We started upbeat back in the dojo, then the discussion about last night, put me off. I just wished she hadn't asked me any questions. But that shouldn't be a problem, really, if everything were all right.

"So, Sifu," Jon said interrupting my introspection, "it'd be good to know a physical therapist in our line of work, don't you think? Now we just need an orthopedist. We could have them on retainers."

I brought myself back. "Not a great thing to advertise, though. 'Come to Gidon's karate class. We have a physical therapist and orthopedist on premises!' "

"I see what you mean."

We rounded a corner and headed up toward Jon's car.

"I got it," Jon said to Alli, "forget the retainer. You'll just have to join us."

"I think I'll just come after class, if I'm invited," she looked at me.

I turned to her to say Lord knows what, but then I saw Jon's car. Or rather I saw a kid, perhaps seventeen, sitting on the hood of Jon's car. He had a pair of aluminum crutches leaning against the front right fender.

As we approached, three other kids, who were leaning on an adjacent car, joined him. The boy on Jon's hood slid down and walked toward us. I guess the crutches were just an accessory, like sunglasses. He stood tall, probably five eleven, and was a little on the skinny side. He had curly black hair and cold, black eyes. Too cold for someone his age.

To either side of him were two boys, also around seventeen. The one on the right wore a backwards Yankees cap — I could tell because "Yankees" was written above the adjustable strap. In this town, wearing a Yankees cap was a definite statement of defiance. The third boy — the one to crutch boy's left — had a young Rasputin look about him with long, stringy dark hair parted in the middle. He was wiry and kept both hands wide open, fingers spread apart. Behind them was a fourth boy. This one looked younger and very uncomfortable. He was fidgeting and licked his lips nervously.

The three of us stopped in front of them, Jon and Alli were to my left.

I was not in the mood for this. Even as my heartbeat came up slightly, I let out a breath and relaxed. If the leader lifted his hand, or if it disappeared into a pocket, I'd hit him just like I'd punch a stone to break it.

My only thought was why didn't they just leave me alone. I wasn't looking for them. I was going out of my way *not* to look for them. The Israelis wanted these kids, I didn't.

The evening air around us was motionless.

I hadn't been in a street fight for a while. Didn't matter. First I'd take the leader, then the other three. I had my techniques picked out.

I looked into the leader's eyes and felt the blood move to my hands.

"Oh man, I don't believe this," Jon broke in. He stepped away from us and to the side. "I can't believe this is happening."

"What are you doing?" the leader spoke with a slight accent. I couldn't place it. Eastern Europe? Russia?

"Well, I don't want to get blood all over my clothes. That really sucks." Jon moved animatedly over toward the leader. "You guys are in for a treat. Well, I am anyway. You guys ought to be honored."

Alli looked at me nervously. She wasn't sure what was going on. The group of boys just watched Jon.

"Gotta tell you," he continued, "I never thought I'd see this. I've heard stories about this man," he pointed to me, "but I never thought I'd see him in action. I know he doesn't look like much, but, man, this is going to be over in *five* seconds. I wish I had video. Wait, I've got my phone." He pulled out his cell. "You guys don't know who this is, do you?"

They just looked at him blankly. The boy in back was really jumpy now. He looked like he was going to empty his bladder.

"This is Master Gidon Aronson. You can call him 'Sifu.' There's been a lot of shit in his life and he's going to hit you with all of it. Right now. I figure at least one of you will be dead before you hit the ground. The rest of you I figure, what Sifu," he turned to me again, "internal injuries, bleeding, ruptured things? Alli, you may want to stand over here with me. Once he gets cooking, you don't want to be in the way." He reached over and pulled her closer to him.

Jon was on a roll. He leaned over to Alli. "You are about to see a master craftsman in action." He turned back to the leader. "And if you think you're faster than him, forget it.

I never see it coming when he hits me and I work with him all the time."

Jon turned to Alli, who didn't look too steady herself. All the blood had drained from her face. "This is going to be really good," he said to no one in particular. Then to the leader: "So, go ahead, reach for something, or move a hand toward him. Go ahead."

No one moved. The only sound came from an air conditioner somewhere above us.

I could see the pulse in the leader's neck. It was moving fairly rapidly. I looked at the leader and...smiled.

A full two seconds went by when the nervous boy in back spoke up, "C'mon. Let's go."

"Shut up, Pavel," the leader spat out.

The leader continued to look at me. His cold eyes now had hatred in them. He didn't know how to get out of the mess he had put his group in. I knew that he knew I would kill him, and he didn't know how to extricate himself.

I looked into his eyes and said very softly, "Go away."

Another moment went by.

The boy to his right, the one with the backwards Yankees cap, tugged at his arm. "Let's go."

The group began to back up. Finally, they headed back across the street to an Altima Coupe and climbed in. With the engine roaring, they defiantly tore out of the space.

We watched as they disappeared around the corner. I looked over at Jon then at Alli. She ran over to me and wrapped her arms around my chest. Her entire body was shaking. I looked over her shoulder to Jon. "I 'don't look like much'?"

"Sorry."

"I'll let it go this time."

We stayed just like that for another minute with Alli's arms around me, then we slowly started walking again. We passed Jon's car and continued up the block. By the time we had gotten to the corner, Alli had unpried herself from me.

Finally, Jon asked, "What do you suppose that was all about?"

"I don't know. Revenge?...If they're connected to the guy from last night. Or maybe they just want me out of the way. Maybe they think I can identify them."

"Well, you can now," Jon said.

We turned and headed back.

"Are you going to tell the police?" Alli asked.

"I guess. I'll call them after I take you home."

We walked to Jon's Eclipse. He opened the door, but turned to Alli, "Are you okay?"

She nodded.

Jon got in, turned on the engine, and rolled down the window. "Dinner and an almost mugging. Not bad."

"Last night it was dinner and an almost assassination. I don't want to think about tomorrow night."

Jon half-laughed, "See you tomorrow," and pulled away from the curb.

I turned to Alli. "Time for me to take you home."

"Sounds good."

She leaned on me again and we went back to my car. The ride to Alli's place took ten minutes, and the entire time she held my hand. I didn't press for conversation. Talking about what just happened would be counterproductive and I didn't feel like filling the silence.

I found a parking spot on Battery Avenue on Federal Hill around the corner from her door, and didn't hesitate to pull in; there wasn't going to be anything closer. We got out of the car and I put my hand back in hers. As we strolled to her house, the night seemed refreshingly serene. The brick sidewalk looked particularly clean beneath the street lights and there was even a little more air movement here. The neighborhood was calm. Peaceful.

We approached her door and I let go of her hand. "Do you want to come in?" she looked into my eyes. "You probably could use a drink."

Alli still looked a little shaken and I didn't want to leave her alone just yet. Besides, I *could* use a drink. "Sounds good. I'd love t–"

I felt more than heard the movement behind me. I spun around, with my right hand already moving up for a block. I didn't know what was behind me, but I wasn't about to take a chance. A stainless steel hatchet flashed in the orange lamppost light.

The weapon came down — that's all I saw, that's all I was focused on — but I caught the arm that held it just above his elbow and redirected it, mostly with its own momentum, to the side, across the attacker's body. My movement was fluid. The man was now sideways to me and I punched him with my left fist just below the corner of his right eye. I heard his cheekbones crack. I hit him twice more. Blood spurted out of his ear. As he fell, I caught a glimpse of his face. It was the kid leader from the aborted mugging not more than thirty minutes ago.

He was using a hatchet. That's all that went through my mind.

I looked up to see his three buddies now standing over him. The one with the backwards Yankees cap was closest. Next to him was the straight-haired wiry kid and then the one who had seemed really nervous. He was already backing up. The kid with the Yankees cap began to reach for something in his back pocket. Before he could bring his hand out, I kicked him just under his belt buckle where the front of his pelvis was located. He collapsed straight downward, writhing in pain. I moved toward the other two. They turned and ran.

I went back to the leader, the kid who didn't need crutches, the kid whose eyes were among the coldest I had ever seen. He was motionless on the ground, the side of his face already turning a purplish red. His right eye was beginning to swell shut. I knew I had broken his cheekbones and probably part of his upper jaw. The hatchet he planned to cleave my skull with had fallen to the ground next to his side. I walked over to his right hand, the one that had held the weapon, and stamped down on it. There were several distinctive cracks.

I looked back up at Alli. She had gone pale again. She started trembling and then threw up. Several times. I put my arm around her shoulders and led her to her steps so she could sit down. As I sat holding her, I looked from the motionless figure on the ground to his partner doubled over in pain.

Shit. They just couldn't leave it alone.

With one hand still around Alli, I reached for my cell phone. In my contact list I found a number I hadn't used in more than half a year. I let my thoughts settle, looked back at the bodies, and then pressed "call."

6

While I waited for the ambulance and the cops, I left Alli's side and walked over to the leader, who was all but lifeless on the ground near me. His breath was faint and his face was swollen and discolored, particularly around his right eye and cheek. Up on the steps, Alli stared at me, unfocused. I'd tend to her in a minute, but first I had to find out as much as I could about this kid before the police blocked off the scene.

The boy's side pants pockets were pretty much empty... some change, a pack of matches, keys on a key chain. To get to his back pocket I had to roll him over slightly. As I did so, he moaned. Out of his back pocket I pulled a wad of bills. It looked like about $200 in tens and twenties, and they were wrapped around some sort of identification card. I held it up to the streetlight. The card was blue and white and emblazoned across the top with the words "Guardians of Heaven." Below that heading was a picture of the boy, scowling, and his name: Joe Gilkis.

That's all there was. "Guardians of Heaven," the boy's photo, and his name.

I turned the card over. The reverse side was all in Hebrew. Across the top it said *Shomrei Shamayim* — the Hebrew equivalent of "Guardians of Heaven." Below the heading the card went on to espouse how the member was a special person and charged with upholding the laws of the organization. In small print across the bottom of the card were two addresses. One was in Baltimore and one in Jerusalem. I made a mental note of both.

I turned the card over again. A membership card with no leader's name, no president or any authority figure.

"Ohh, help me. Please." I looked over at the other boy who tried to attack me. He was still on the ground, clutching his groin. Chances are when I kicked him, I broke his pubic symphysis and may even have ruptured his bladder. He'd be urinating blood for a while unless he got some serious help within the next hour or so. I expected that he would pass out any minute.

Returning to the boy at my feet, I replaced his money and membership card and headed back to Alli.

"Hey," I said softly, "how are you feeling?"

She didn't say anything. I put my arm around her again. I wanted to get her some water, but I also didn't want to leave her alone. In a matter of minutes that wasn't an issue. First, a trio of residents out on a stroll came toward us: a young man flanked by two women. They looked to be in their late twenties. The ladies wore a multi-colored tube top and a halter respectively, while the young man sported a collarless button-down white shirt. All had on jeans.

I watched as they came closer. At first they were oblivious to the bodies on the sidewalk, and then when they were about twenty feet away, they stopped and stared. Hands went to mouths, features paled, and they gave us a wide berth. I didn't say anything. I just watched their reactions to the figures on the ground.

A minute later other pedestrians came by. Most stopped.

By the time sirens drifted through the night toward us, a crowd had gathered. A young woman with close-cropped blonde hair and a backpack cut through the gawkers. She said she was Alli's neighbor, Didi.

"Are you okay? What happened?" She sat next to Alli, but on the other side.

"Attempted mugging,"

Didi turned to the two boys on the ground.

"Didn't go well for them," I said calmly.

Didi looked back into Alli's eyes. "Alli, let's go inside."

Alli nodded weakly. Didi put her hand on Alli's arm and they both stood up. After a moment they went into Didi's townhouse next door.

By the time the two of them had disappeared into the townhouse, the first police officer had arrived. He wasn't driving your typical police car. It was an old, dark green Jeep not unlike mine. The Jeep pulled to the curb in front of me and I could see the flashing blue light sitting atop the dashboard.

The cop opened the door and stepped out.

He was about fifty, wore a maroon polo shirt with a dark blazer over it. Physically, the man was about my height and balding. The hair that he had was salt and pepper and neatly trimmed.

I stood up and met him as he came toward me.

"Nate," I said. "Thanks for coming."

"Gidon," he said and we gave each other a quick hug. "Are you okay?"

"I'm fine."

He looked at the bodies at our feet. "What happened.?"

I gestured to the leader I recently learned was Joe Gilkis. "He tried to open my head with a hatchet." I pointed to the weapon on the ground near its unconscious owner.

"Foolish man."

"He's probably seventeen."

"Foolish boy."

"And that one," I indicated his now unconscious partner, "was reaching for something I didn't care to see."

"Old acquaintances?"

"New acquaintances. They're part of a group, I think, that tried to assassinate an Israeli dignitary last night. I stopped them."

"That was you? I heard about it on the news last night. Tell me about it in a second. I want to see what we've got before the paramedics get in the way." Nate stooped over the Gilkis kid and began to go through his pockets. He soon came up with the same items that I had — the keys, the matches, the wad of cash, the membership card. He dropped them all into a large plastic bag that he had pulled from a jacket pocket.

"Do you always walk around with an evidence bag?"

"Do you still carry that 3 ½ inch folding knife?"

I tapped my right side pants pocket and smiled. I let a second pass. "Glad you're here, Nate. I know it's been more than–"

"It doesn't matter how long it's been. I told you that. Anytime, anyplace."

I smiled in appreciation.

"Tell me what's going on."

Before I had a chance to respond, an ambulance arrived with its crew of paramedics. Nate directed them when they approached us. The two-man team set up intravenous lines on both boys. A second ambulance and two more cop cars arrived shortly. Nate took charge again. With badge in hand, he found the lead officer and ran interference for me...basically vouching for my character and promised he would find out what happened.

As the scene got increasingly crowded — the paramedics hovering over the boys, and the cops working both crowd control and the crime scene — Nate and I walked to Alli's stoop and sat on the steps. "Okay, start with last night."

I looked at my old friend and told him everything. I described the banquet, the Israelis, the waiter, and everything that ensued to this point, including the confrontation in Little Italy.

When I finished, he said, "They're not going to leave you alone."

"The Israelis or these kids?"

"Both. The Israelis because — well, you know how they are — and the kids because someone is pulling their strings and you're a witness. Worse. You're the one who fucked up their plans and they don't know what you'll do. Especially after tonight."

"I'm sorry about these kids," I nodded to the two boys on the ground in front of us.

"Why? They didn't give you much choice." We looked at the hatchet that was now being held in a plastic bag by a uniformed cop. Nate continued: "Someone corrupted these kids or at least took advantage of them and pointed them in your direction."

"They were pointed at Eitan Lev last night."

"And you got in the way."

"And I got in the way."

"It'll be interesting to see what happens next."

I let out a sigh. "I want to be left alone."

"I know, but this one's in your face."

"Yeah."

"I could be wrong," Nate said, "Maybe this will go away now." Neither of us believed that. He looked at me. "Shit."

I watched as the paramedics loaded the two boys into separate ambulances.

"I ought to see how Alli is doing." I stood up.

"Not used to the real you, huh." He stood up also.

"I'm an acquired taste," I smiled.

"I'm sorry."

"Me, too."

"I'll do what I can to keep the department from pestering you. But, I'll need a statement. Talk about deadly force."

"Mine or theirs?"

"We'll figure it out tomorrow."

I nodded.

"And if you decide to get into this, let me know."

"I will. Say 'hi' to Rachel for me. And to Laurie when you speak to her."

"Of course." He took a step away, then turned back. "Laurie's staying in Israel, you know."

"I know."

"Rachel's very upset."

"I know."

Smiling half to himself, Captain Nate D'Allesandro turned and sauntered toward the uniformed cop holding the bagged hatchet. As they began talking, I headed over to Didi's place. I climbed the three steps and rang the bell.

In a few seconds, Didi opened the door.

"Hi," I said. "How's Alli?"

"She's in the kitchen having some coffee. She's okay. Shaken up, but okay."

Alli's friend just looked at me, not making any move to open the door any further or to invite me in.

"I think she wants to be left alone right now."

I smiled. I guess I *was* an acquired taste. "Please tell her I wanted to check on her."

"I will." She closed the door.

I turned around, gave the scene of cop cars and police officers one last look then headed up the block and around the corner to my Jeep. Once behind the wheel, I put the key in the ignition, but then sat back, just staring in front of me. In my mind I could see the hatchet coming down.

Nate was right. The kid didn't give me much of a choice. I saw my three punches pounding him below his eye.

I then reran the image of Didi at her door. "*I think she wants to be left alone right now.*" And the door closing on me.

I closed my eyes for a long moment, then turned the key in the ignition and pulled away from the curb.

The drive up to my house went smoothly, with one exception. I didn't seem to be going home. My body and subconscious mind were taking me up the road to my dojo. Looks like I was going to work out.

At this time of night all the parking spots on both sides of North Charles Street were taken, so I pulled into my trusty Tenant's Only spot around the corner and walked to my studio. I passed the natural food restaurant and approached the cement steps leading up to my glass door. No one was on the street at this hour. The air was still. To the left of the staircase at ground level was a deep shadow cast by the streetlights. I stopped before proceeding and gazed into the darkness.

Someone was there.

I let a moment go by.

"Why don't you come out." My voice was calm. Calm and probably a little tired. If whoever was in there had a gun, it didn't matter if I invited him, or her, into the light. I could be shot just as easily either way. But, if the person *didn't* have a gun, then having him, or her, in the open was to my advantage — though at the moment I felt pretty depleted and didn't know how efficient I'd be.

"Come on out," I tried again.

After a long five seconds, a boy, probably fifteen or sixteen, emerged. He was a little smaller than me, skinny, and seemed hesitant to make eye contact. I recognized him.

"Pavel, isn't it?" I asked. It's what the head punk had called him.

Pavel was the fourth kid from the group that had accosted me in Little Italy. He was the one who nervously stood in back, urging his leader to leave me alone. During the attack at Alli's he had remained in the background.

"I'm sorry," he said stepping closer to me.

"It wasn't your fault."

"Are they okay?" Pavel seemed even smaller than before.

"I don't know." Neither of the kids who had attacked me would be okay.

"I didn't want to be there."

"I know."

A long moment went by.

"If it makes you feel any better," I said quietly, "I didn't want to be there either."

He smiled just a bit.

"I'm going inside for a cold drink. Do you want to come in?"

Pavel shrugged.

I took out my keys and headed for the steps. He watched me go up the stairs but didn't move. I unlocked the door, and turned back to him. "Come inside, sit down...we'll talk about the meaning of life or something." I opened the door, but he didn't move. "It's okay."

He looked up at me from the ground level, then came up the stairs. Once even with me, he turned back, looking up and down the street.

"They're not there," I said. I let a moment go by then headed inside.

Pavel followed me to the main work-out room. As he looked around the large hall I went into my office and grabbed a soda can from a small fridge tucked away in a corner. I popped the lid. "Want anything?" He was still looking around the bare room, not really paying attention to what I asked.

"I used to take karate," he said. "Our place had weapons on the walls, some mirrors, mats, paintings."

"Must've been nice. I'm poor."

He looked at me.

"Really," I said. "It's true. I'm living off the good grace of a student's father.

He looked at me, not understanding.

"I had a student who was a mess. Attitude, tough guy...got into trouble at school. Would pick on other kids. He'd follow them home, and a block from their house beat the shit out of them. One night, his father dragged him out of a party that was filled with drugs and crap, and brought him here."

"What did you do?"

"Beat the shit out of him." I laughed. "It was only fair."

Pavel just looked at me.

"Just kidding. I ignored him for a while then worked his ass off. Old Chinese way. I let him work off his aggression, taught him, fought with him, worked him some more. Took a while... long while."

"What happened to him?"

"He's a helluva martial artist now. Parents were so thrilled with what I had accomplished, they gave me this space. Not bad, huh?"

"Not bad," he repeated.

"Even without mirrors?"

"Yes," he smiled. "Even without mirrors."

I wanted to ask him some questions about himself, about what the hell was going on with his buddies, and about his own family, but now wasn't the time. "I've got some paperwork to do in my office, so if you just want to hang out, that's fine. Do you remember any of the karate you used to take?"

He shook his head.

"That's okay."

I walked into my office and sat down behind my desk. There really wasn't any paperwork, so I started opening drawers to see what was inside. In the bottom drawer beneath a folded tai ch'i poster was a martial arts supply catalog. I took it out and began leafing through it. Pavel wandered in. Without looking up, I finished the page, and then turned to him. "I'm going to work out for a few minutes in the other room. Make yourself at home."

Pavel didn't respond and I headed into the main hall. I pulled my shirttail out, so I'd have more freedom of movement and went about a basic series of fluid spinning motions within the internal Chinese pa kua system. The routine was more warm-up exercise than anything else, but it covered many of the rudimentary techniques of the art. I knew Pavel was watching from the side, and the warm-up exercise was as advanced as I wanted him to observe.

In a matter of minutes I had worked up a sweat, and any earlier fatigue was replaced with reawakened energy. The exercise moved me in a circle around a center point, and when I finished I stepped into the center of the circle and let myself settle down. My pulse was pounding and I could feel that my hands were warm and tingling. Before I knew it, twenty minutes had passed in the static posture. I turned to see Pavel sitting on the floor nearby. He was still watching me.

"How long have you been doing all this?" he asked.

"More than twenty years."

"A long time."

"To some, but it's what I do." I let a moment go by then headed to the bathroom on the other side of the room. I grabbed a towel, wiped my face, and then reentered the dojo. "I've got a shower in here. You've got to be tired and feeling pretty grungy. It's been a long night — for both of us." I wiped the sweat from my forehead and upper lip again. "Go ahead, the shower's yours. No one will disturb you. You'll feel better. Afterward, I've got some food in the fridge, if you want. Deli and pasta salad, I think."

He began to meander over to the bathroom.

"There's a little changing area inside before you get to the shower. Towels are in the cabinet below the sink."

I ambled back to my office, and by the time I sat at my desk, Pavel had gone into the bathroom. I waited two minutes then half ran to the closed bathroom door and leaned in. The shower was running. After another 30 seconds I tried the handle. Locked. The knob on the other side had a button lock in it — the kind you push in. I knew this because I had installed it myself. The outer knob had a small hole in it for emergency access. Insert a thin, rigid wire into the hole, push, and the lock will pop open. Additionally, I knew that if you turned the knob to the right and continued to exert pressure, the lock would also spring. The wire that came with the lockset was long since lost, so I turned the knob and continued the torque pressure. A moment later I felt — and heard — the mechanism click open. Hopefully, the shower muffled the soft sound. I slowly opened the door.

Pavel's clothes were dumped on a shelf to the right below a metal clothes hook. The shower room was just beyond another door. I carefully went through all his clothes. He had about ten bucks on him. That was it. Ten dollars and a blue and white membership card almost identical to the one I had pulled from his buddy earlier. "Guardians of Heaven." English on the front with the boy's name and photo and Hebrew on the back.

I looked up at the door in front of me. The shower was still going strong. I hoped Pavel was enjoying it. I silently exited the way I had come, the membership card in my right hand. I hustled back to my office, flicked on the little copier I had near my desk and copied the card — first the front and then the back. I checked the copies then ran back to the changing room. Just as I entered, I heard the valve on the shower turn and then the water cut off. I stuck the membership card back where I had found it, relocked the knob before I left, then pulled the door closed behind me.

When Pavel came out a few minutes later, I was back to the martial arts supply catalog. He came over, dressed in the same clothes he had before, but with wet hair and his face flushed from the hot water.

"Feel any better?"

"Yeah." He let a moment go by. "You said there was food?"

I looked at him. With his wet hair and old clothes, Pavel looked like a little kid. A little kid who had friends who liked guns and hatchets. I pointed to the small fridge. "Raid away."

"*Raid*?"

"Clean it out...Eat me out of house and home. And while you're doing that, I'll run to the corner market and buy some real food." I stood up. "Probably be back in ten or fifteen min-

utes, unless the 24 hour corner market isn't open 24 hours today. Make yourself comfortable. Eat, watch TV, read. Just don't
use the phone to call anyone...not your friends, not your family.
Okay?"

He looked at me. "Okay."

"Okay. And don't open the door for anyone. No one knows
you're here, right?"

"Right."

Pavel seemed uncomfortable with some of the colloquial-
isms I was throwing around, but I was sure he understood me.

"I'll be back soon."

"You already said that."

"I know." I headed to the front door, leaving Pavel standing
in my office.

Outside on the landing, I took a few deep breaths of the cool
night air then turned back to lock the door. I looked up and
down the street. All was quiet. Cars were parked on either side
of the road, shops were dark, and a slight breeze meandered
through the trees. I walked down to the sidewalk and turned
right toward downtown, knowing full well that the all-night
market was in the other direction.

As I walked I put Pavel and his friends out of my mind. There
was just the night air, the breeze, and the stillness of the street.
I walked slowly, leisurely, enjoying every step. When I got to the
corner, I turned left, crossed the street and headed back the
way I had come. The buildings on this side of the street were
almost identical to those on my side: storefronts at sidewalk

level, apartments upstairs. The streetlights here were similarly spaced: far enough apart so their amber glow lit the area yet cast shadows deep enough to hide some of the doorways. I kept to the curb side of the sidewalk, away from the building fronts.

I passed opposite my dojo and looked across to it. Except for the light just inside the front door, you couldn't tell if anyone were home. I kept walking for another half-minute and then paused in front of a used book store. Its entranceway was also in shadows. I let a few quiet moments go by then continued my leisurely pace. The casual stroll hopefully didn't reveal my new concern. Someone was hiding in the shadows of the bookstore I had just passed

Everything has a presence. If you're calm enough, and trained properly, you can feel where buildings, trees, and people are. I thought of the games we used to play to develop this. We would start with a partner moving slowly out of your field of vision. It would end, after much practice, in a darkened room with pre-positioned "attackers." I used to get whacked from all directions. Hopefully, that wouldn't happen now. Someone was definitely back there, and it was impossible to tell who it might be. A friend of Pavel's, a cop...anyone. All I could tell was that he or she was standing very still, trying not to breathe too loudly.

I moved on, crossing an empty intersection to the 24 hour market. Outside the entrance, was a small fruit and flower display. The place reminded me of the ubiquitous corner stores in upper Manhattan that were busy no matter the hour.

The door was open and I stepped inside. Two huge pedestal fans moved the air around and tossed my hair as I walked into the air stream. The place was congested with floor-to-ceiling shelves along the perimeter walls and chest-high shelves throughout the center area — all filled with boxes and cans of anything you might need...pasta, vegetables, cereals, breads, cookies. I grabbed a hand basket and wound my way through the aisles, picking up some cookies made by elves, cereal boxes, frozen pizza, and one percent milk. If Pavel were going to ingest pizza and cookies, he should have low-fat milk to wash it down. I paid with cash, smiled at the middle-aged Korean grocer, and headed out.

The walk back was more direct and I didn't pause to test my senses. There may have been someone else tucked away in the shadows, but I didn't care.

Back in the dojo, Pavel was still in my office, but now watching an old DVD of Steven Seagal wreaking havoc aboard a battleship. As I looked at the screen I saw Seagal shooting down a long interior corridor, a gun in each hand.

"Good movie," I said as I unpacked and stored the groceries.

"I've seen this a *beelion* times. Wait 'til you see him rip a guy's throat out." He moved an inch closer to the TV.

I just nodded. Without volunteering more commentary I went to a closet in the back corner and picked up a dark green zippered duffle bag. From inside the bag I pulled out a pair of binoculars. Over at my desk I then scooped up a bullet-shaped laser pointer from my middle desk drawer. Pavel remained hypnotized by the movie.

"I'll be right back."

He didn't even look up.

Without saying another word, I went to the small foyer just inside the front door. Where the dojo met the entryway there was a door to the side secured by a double cylinder lock...a deadbolt that needed a key on the inside as well as the outside. I unlocked the door with the key that had intentionally been left in the lock, and stepped into a common hallway. The passageway was dark except for ambient light coming in from a skylight and some small windows.

The hallway went to the left toward the back of the building. At the far end was an exterior exit plus the base of an emergency staircase. Silently, watching where I placed my feet, I climbed the stairs just one flight to stop in front of a small casement window. I wiped some of the accumulated grime from the pane and looked out onto Charles Street. Excellent. The view to the opposite side of the street was unobstructed to include a clear line of sight to the used bookstore. I peered through the binoculars. The ten power magnification was perfect. The doorway of the shop was almost tangible, but the shadow remained a sanctuary for whoever was there, if anyone. Night vision glasses might have helped, however, the point was moot as I didn't have a pair. If I had to guess, I'd bet that one of Pavel's buddies was hiding there, just out of sight. He had one friend left from his quartet. Maybe the buddy had followed Pavel, knowing he might want out. Maybe he was still looking for me. Either way it would not be good for anyone.

I took out the laser pointer with my right hand and smiled. It was one of the more powerful ones, and came with the standard warning label on the side about how it could cause damage to your eyes if not used properly. I looked at the doorway once again and pointed the bullet-shaped device across the street, pushing the spring button on the barrel. A red dot appeared on the driver's door of a white BMW parked in front of the book shop. I wasn't worried about the source of the dot being spotted. The angle had to be just right. It had to almost be shining in the person's eyes for him to spot it — and that wasn't going to happen. I moved the dot off the car and over to the store entranceway. With my left hand I held up the binoculars again and watched the blackness.

Slowly, I inched the red dot toward the doorway. I moved it along the entranceway wall and up the display window to the shadow's left. Whoever was in there — *if* the person were still there — had to see it. The red dot looked exactly like a laser gun sight, and hopefully the person would think someone was targeting him and react.

I steadied my hand on the window pane and moved the dot into the shadow at chest height. A second went by and I could make out some movement in the blackness. Suddenly a figured darted out. A man looked around frantically then began to run up the block to his right. I followed him with the binoculars. In the wide field of the prisms I could see that he was in his 20's, had dark, close-cut hair, and was dressed in jeans, T-shirt, and dark windbreaker. It wasn't Pavel's friend. It was an Israeli agent; one of the security men from the other night.

"Why Mr. Amit, you assigned a man to me." I waited another moment and then went back downstairs.

Pavel was still glued to the television. I put the binoculars and the laser pointer away and turned off the TV.

"Hey!" Pavel protested.

"So, what do you want to do?"

"Finish the movie."

I shook my head. "I'm going home. You'll come with me, okay?"

Pavel went silent. His eyes darkened and he looked down.

"C'mon. It's not often I invite potential students to my house."

He didn't catch the significance of the offer.

Still looking down he said in a low voice, "I should leave."

"No. You shouldn't."

He looked up at me. "Can I stay here?"

"By yourself?"

"Yeah."

"You just want to finish the movie, right? We can bring it with us."

"I'll be fine. You bought food. You've got movies." He paused. "I just want to be alone."

If he wanted to be alone, I thought, why did he come here in the first place? Ah, the contradictions of adolescents. But actually, it made sense: he wanted to be alone — safe and alone.

And he felt secure here. I understood that, because *I* felt secure here.

There was a lot to think about from the past 24 hours. The assassination attempt, the kids who were involved, the Israelis, my relationship with Alli — wherever the hell it was at this point. And regarding Alli, there was nothing to apologize for, right? This is who I am. I'm a nice guy; violent when necessary, occasionally, but otherwise, okay. This whole thing was a mess. I didn't want to think about it.

Pavel was looking at me as if I had just left the planet.

"Okay, I'm back now. You can stay here. But on one condition: no phone calls and don't open the door for anyone. I have a key and my student Jon has a key. He's a good guy. You can trust him."

"Okay."

I pointed to the cordless phone sitting on the desktop. "If I want to call you, I'll use this line. You'll see my name on the caller ID."

"Okay."

"Otherwise, don't answer the phone."

"I know."

"And if you need to call me, here's my home number." I began to write it on a pad near the phone.

"I thought you said I can't make any calls," he said smiling at me.

"Attitude. I take him in and he gives me attitude. You know what I mean."

"Yes, I've got it. Now, go home." He moved over to the television and turned it back on. The DVD had continued playing. Now Seagal was jumping over the edge of the battleship while tethered to a railing. Just as he cleared the deck, a helicopter blew up on the stern.

"Go," Pavel ordered. I was being dismissed. I went back to the closet and pulled out some new gi pants.

"If you want to get out of your clothes, you can sleep in these." I tossed them to him.

"Nothing in black?" Again the smile.

Pavel was definitely feeling better. Tomorrow I'd take him out and maybe we'd talk about his involvement with the gang. If any connection to the assassination came up, I'd just throw it to the Israelis.

"Okay, I'll see you in the morning."

"Okay."

Pavel went back to the movie and I left.

Once outside, I locked the door and walked directly to my car. All was quiet on the streets, so the ride home took only five minutes. My first stop on the way upstairs was my office to check the answering machine. There was one message. Maybe it was Alli. She had calmed down and wanted to see me.

It wasn't Alli. "Mr. Aronson, this is Carol Cayhan from the Stein School. You subbed for me today. Is it possible for you to take the class again tomorrow? I know it's late notice. The class is from 10:15 to 11:00. I left lesson plans on my desk.

Call and let me know...It doesn't matter the time. I'll be up watching the Home Shopping Network, or something. Thanks."

Two seconds of silence went by before I realized there were no additional messages. I reset the machine then looked up, staring across the room, but not really seeing anything.

The Israelis wanted me, some kids were trying to kill me, I had a runaway boy in my dojo, and my love life was about to become nonexistent. Did I want to teach a bunch of 13 year olds tomorrow? I picked up the phone and called Mrs. Cayhan. I told her I'd be happy to sub for her. She thanked me profusely, blessed my upbringing, said I was a real *mensch*, and then hung up.

As I thought about it, taking care of Pavel tonight was definitely a point on the side of goodness and mercy, but pounding that kid outside of Alli's, while it had to be done, was anything but *mensch*-like.

I sat down. No question the attack and my response would continue to bounce around my head for a while. I could compartmentalize it, but the intensity of my reaction, and its result, wouldn't fade so quickly. That hatchet coming down was a clear image. I could still see the orange streetlight reflecting off the stainless steel...and I could clearly hear the crack of the kid's cheekbones when I punched him in the face multiple times.

Shit.

Shit.

I stared out into the room.

I needed to work out again or something, but this time I really was too tired. After a few moments, I turned to the computer. Nate needed a statement from me; might as well write it down while it was fresh. Maybe that would help get those intense few seconds out of my system.

For the next twenty minutes, I sat at the keyboard and typed up the details of the attack. Time, location, my name, Alli's name, the number of people who were in the group that attacked me. I vacillated about mentioning Pavel, but finally decided to include him. He truly was on the periphery, but he was still there, and if I ever needed police protection for him, he needed to exist.

By the time I finished writing, my heart was racing again. Adrenalin was back in my bloodstream, brought on by reliving the action. Yet, there was still fatigue. After printing out the statement, I signed and dated it then tossed it onto my desk.

"Now, go to sleep," I heard myself say out loud. I stood up.

I looked at the comfortable upholstered chair across from the desk and shuffled over to it. *Don't sit there. Don't sit there. You'll never get up.*

The chair was looking at me. I just needed a moment to clear my mind before heading to bed.

Don't sit down. Go upstairs...You can do it. You're a disciplined man.

The room was dark, except for the wash of the desk lamp.

I sat in the chair.

For probably thirty seconds I just stared straight ahead, not seeing anything. I couldn't think. I couldn't really move. I blinked a few times.

Finally, after probably another sixty seconds, I stood up, though not too steadily. I headed up to the bedroom, but I had no awareness of climbing steps. I just found myself on the second floor. As I entered the bedroom, I unbuttoned my shirt and let it drop wherever.

I fell onto the bed and buried my head face down in the pillow.

7

The lone sentry, dressed in army fatigues and a checkered kaffiyah, walked along the edge of the roof, easily drifting into the crosshairs of my nightscope. The early morning hour was black, moonless...perfect for what we had to do.

I shifted slightly on my belly, amidst the rubble of a demolished building, waiting for the little signal that would go from my brain to my right index finger, now lightly caressing the trigger guard.

As I watched, the man on the roof reached the end of his walk, turned around and headed back the way he had come. He had taken just one step when it happened — the entire neighborhood went dark. The building itself seemed to vanish. But not the guard in my sights.

I took a breath, let it out slightly then squeezed the trigger. There was a muffled puff and the sentry was knocked off his feet. He wouldn't be getting up. As I emerged from between two broken cinderblock walls, three men to either side of me stood up as well. We began running toward the building...

8

The phone rang at 6:00. I would love to have said it caught me in the middle of REM sleep and that it took an eternity to break into my mind, but it didn't. I caught it after the first ring.

It was Nate D'Allesandro.

"Well, Gidon, he died."

"Who died?" I sat up a little more.

"The kid who tried to cut you in half. Hatchet boy."

"Okay." This morning I didn't feel one way or the other about his death. Maybe I was still tired.

"We need to talk about this some more. Just want to go over it all again."

"Can we meet at the dojo about two? I'm subbing this morning."

"That'll work."

"How's the other kid?"

"The kid you kicked in the crotch?"

"Yeah."

"Gregory Segev. He's still in recovery at Sinai, in case you want to pay him a visit."

"He'd *love* that. Keep an eye on him, though."

"In progress. See you at 2:00."

We hung up. I contemplated my ceiling for a moment, then pulled myself out of bed. An hour later, I had completed my morning workout, showered, and had something to eat — a bowl of cereal and some toast. Halfway through my first piece of toast I called Alli, not sure what to expect.

"Hi. It's Gidon." I probably didn't have to announce myself, but I felt like I needed to.

Her voice was quiet. "Hi."

"I need to talk to you about last night. I want to see how you're doing. Can I come by?

"Gidon, I don't know what to say." Pause. "Sure. Come by. I need to see you, too."

"Be down in forty-five minutes." I checked my watch.

"I'll be here."

"Did you sleep?"

"Not really."

"I'm sorry. We'll talk."

I hung up and finished my toast, knowing what probably awaited me at Allison's — a screeching halt to the relationship.

My first stop of the day was not Allison's, but the dojo to see how Pavel was doing. He was, no doubt, up all night watching my collection of action films. I circled the block once, spotted a man dressed in blue jeans and a windbreaker standing on a nearby balcony, then went to park. If he was on the balcony then his partner was at ground level, not too far away. That's the way to do it: a spotter and an agent or two on foot. As I walked up Charles Street, I wondered if Pavel knew what the hell was happening here and the potential for his own danger. I just wanted to keep him safe. I took the cement steps two at a time and let myself in.

The hallway was quiet but the lights were on. Hopefully, that meant that Pavel was still here. I'm not sure I would have been. I rounded the corner to the main hall and saw the boy. He had a broom in his hand and was sweeping the floor. I stood there watching him work.

"Wow," was all I could think of.

He turned around and smiled. "Thought I'd, you know, straighten up."

"Wow," I repeated. "You know how to make a sensei happy. Very *Karate Kid*."

He just shrugged.

"Did you sleep?" I went over to him.

"On your couch. Fell asleep during..." he paused.... "I don't know what movie it was."

I smiled. "Did you have anything to eat?"

"Pizza."

"Could have predicted that."

A moment went by, then Pavel said:

"Can you show me what you did to Igar last night?"

"Igar? The kid with the hatchet? The name on his I.D. was 'Joe.'"

"His American name. Wanted to fit in. We called him Igar. He called himself 'Joe.'"

"Very Ellis Island."

"What?"

"Long story."

I looked at Pavel. He didn't seem afraid anymore. Maybe it was teenage bravado. Maybe he thought I'd protect him from Igar's pals forever. Igar, who was dead now. Igar, who deserved to be dead now. Yet, he and Pavel were members of the same club, Guardians of Heaven.

"How did you know he was behind you last night?" Pavel asked. "And how did you hit him so hard?"

"Also a long story. Just keep sweeping. We'll talk later." I headed for the door, now that I had verified that he was all right.

"Where are you going?"

"To see a friend and then to teach about the growth of the cities in the late 1800's "

"What? I thought you taught karate."

"I do, but I also know about the growth of the cities in the late 1800's "

Pavel just looked at me.

"Just keep sweeping. We'll talk later."

I left, trying not to look up at the man watching me from the balcony across the street.

*   *   *

Federal Hill was just waking up when I pulled into a space near Alli's apartment. The shady street looked freshly scrubbed, ready for the new day. As I walked toward Alli's townhouse, a young couple in jogging outfits came toward me, leading a sandy colored Shiba Inu. The dog couldn't have been more than a pup, and had its tail arched forward, curving toward its spine. I stepped aside, letting the couple and their dog pass. When I approached Alli's building, I noted there was no indication that this had been a crime scene last night...no yellow "Police Line Do Not Cross" tape, no chalk marks, nothing. I climbed the two cement steps where we had sat last night, and rang the bell.

A moment later she opened the door, and for a second just stood there. Alli looked pretty good, dressed in white slacks and a mauvy sleeveless top. But her eyes were sad. "Hi. Come in."

I went over to her and kissed her gently on the cheek. She didn't respond. We walked over to a couch and sat down.

"The police were here already," she said, looking straight ahead.

"Oh?"

"They wanted to go over what happened last night."

"I'm sorry they had to bother you. I wish they could've waited."

"No, it was all right." A moment went by. "They said the boy you hit died."

"I heard that this morning, too."

"He tried to kill you." She looked right into my eyes.

"Yeah."

"And you killed him."

I just nodded.

"How do you feel about that?"

"Not particularly good. But I didn't have much of a choice."

Alli just looked at me. I wasn't sure what she was thinking.

"I wish the kid hadn't put me in that position," I said.

No reaction.

"It's upsetting, I know. It bothers me, too." I tried to sound soothing.

Alli kept her hands in her lap. "He tried to kill you," she repeated, looking at me incredulously.

I nodded again. She hadn't absorbed what I said. It would take a while.

After a long pause, I spoke up: "I'm sorry you had to see that."

"I can't get it out of my mind."

"Give it time," I said softly. I reached for her hand, but she pulled it away.

I couldn't make her feelings, or the images, go away. I couldn't make the images in *my* head go away.

"Give it time," I said once again.

I stood up and looked at her. "I should go."

I gently kissed her on the cheek, and not knowing what else to do, left her sitting on the couch.

9

The teacher's lounge at the Stein Day School was blessedly empty. It was a large room, painted light blue, carpeted, and had long, dark laminate tables arranged in a "U." Various Judaic and Biblical themed lithographs hung on the walls. A soda machine and a water dispenser sat against one wall, and a couch against another. Perpendicular to the soda machine was a counter and a sink, plus an ever ready coffee-maker. I sat at one of the long tables, my back to the soda machine, with Mrs. Cayhan's lesson plans in front of me. I looked at them, but my mind was back on Alli. I truly didn't know what to do.

Last night wasn't my fault. I didn't go looking for trouble. I did what I had to do. If I hadn't, I'd be dead now and perhaps Alli would be as well.

"Crap." I muttered to myself.

Alli was such a good person. Good looking, vibrant, intelligent. I just wished she hadn't freaked out so much. My mind did a quick playback to when we met — at a graduation party.

We were both friends of the graduate, a young man who had once been my student. We hit it off immediately.

This wasn't my fault.

I looked at the lesson plans again. Ten minutes to class. Immigration in the late 1880's and the rise of the cities. Skyscrapers, trolleys, Macy's, Pulitzer and Hearst, baseball. Mrs. Cayhan had left me a video to show — an easy lesson for a substitute teacher. I'd show it, but first I wanted to have a discussion about city life today.

City life today, where someone tries to kill you on the streets of downtown. Where innocent people are traumatized. What was I going to do about Alli? What was I going to do about Pavel...and his friends? With Pavel under my protection, would his buddies leave me alone? Would they leave him alone? I checked my watch, grabbed my teaching materials and headed to the classroom.

As I had done the day before, I wrote the homework on the whiteboard, and then waited, mentally reviewing my plans until the bell rang. A minute later, two girls, one tall and one petite — the same two who had arrived first yesterday — came in talking. As yesterday, they took two steps then stopped in mid-stride.

"Mr. Aronson, are you subbing today?" the smaller of the two semi-shrieked, starting the routine.

"I sure am, Arielle, " I said, smiling at our routine.

The petite girl immediately headed back out to the hallway and announced my arrival, using a decibel level disproportion ate to her size. Within minutes the entire room filled up. As the kids were taking their seats I noticed a dark-haired young man coming in wearing cut-offs and a white Orioles T-shirt. This was the same boy who had walked in late yesterday. He was on time today.

"Josh," I said raising my voice slightly.

He froze in his tracks and looked at me.

I smiled. "Glad you're here."

He looked at me as if I were from one of the outer planets, and then sat down.

Once homework was copied, we began a discussion of life in cities today. This led to a comparison between present society and what was typical in the late 1800's/early 1900's. As with most comparisons, there were some commonalities and some differences. This moved nicely into the video that Mrs. Cayhan had prepared.

Forty three minutes later, the bell rang, and before its reverberation had stopped, most kids were gone. I was still gathering my papers when Katie Harris, the student services woman from yesterday, poked her head in the doorway. "Hi."

"Hi."

She came into the classroom. "I saw you walking down the hallway before, and I wanted to say hello." Ms. Harris was clad in jeans, white top and black blazer, and with her blonde hair, the combination was striking. "Carol out again?"

"She called me last night."

"How'd it go?"

"Fine." I ejected the DVD from the player. "Discussion and a video. What could go wrong?"

She smiled, "You'd be surprised."

I smiled back. "How's your day going?"

"I was busy earlier. Not right now."

"No appointments?"

"Not until later."

I looked at her for a moment. "The kids must really love you."

"Thank you...but why do you say that?"

"Because you help them succeed."

"We all do."

"No, but I'm sure you spend extra time with them, and the kids know it."

I looked into her eyes. She was really focused on me.

"You, too, I'm sure. You wouldn't be here, Mr. Aronson, if you didn't enjoy it."

"Well, I'm a masochist."

She laughed and a thought occurred to me. "Two things. First, it's Gidon. Second, how are you with kids who don't like to talk about themselves?"

"What do you mean?"

"In order to help the kids, you must know them pretty well, right? Strengths, weaknesses, what they like, extra curricular activities. Home life."

"Sometimes."

"So, how do you get them to open up if they don't want to?"

"I have a few tricks."

She sounded as vague as I did when Pavel asked me how I do what I do. "I know, years of school coupled with real life experience. Let me tell you why I ask. A boy who's involved in a gang showed up at my door last night."

She raised her eyebrows.

"A by-product of my other work. Anyway, my guess is he's afraid of what the gang's gotten into and wants out. I want to help him, but I need to know more about the gang. Any ideas?"

"Tell me more."

I thought for a second. Katie Harris was very attractive. She had a definite presence; I could feel her in the room, even though she was still several feet from me.

"Do you have some time now?" I heard my mouth ask.

"Well, lunch in school just started, and I don't have any appointments until 2:00."

"How 'bout something to eat, then? We can talk over the finest cuisine under fifteen dollars." I wasn't quite sure what just happened; just that I sounded inane.

She smiled. "Sure. But we can't be out too long."

"Pasta...pizza? I know a place that's fast."

"Sounds good."

With that, I shuffled together my papers, and we headed out.

The restaurant I had in mind, Middle Eastern Pizza, was five minutes away, and as we were still on the early side — 11:15 — the lunch crowd hadn't yet descended. The shop was a cross between a restaurant and a pizzeria. Posters of Israel lined the walls, from bikini clad swimmers in the blue waters of Eilat, to a waterfall in the Ein Gedi reserve, to a café scene in Tel Aviv.

We sat at a small square table against the left-hand wall. Immediately a waiter came over, put down some napkins and glasses of ice water, and presented the menus. We looked at the selections. The menu boasted of pizza with multiple topping combinations...olives, peppers, pineapples, vegetables, mushrooms, anything you could imagine except meat. I ordered a "Pizza Darom," pizza with a sweet sauce and a falafel topping, and Katie ordered a "Haifa Pizza," a pizza with three different cheeses, mushrooms, peppers, and corn. While we waited for the food to arrive, we talked.

"So, tell me about this boy," Katie began.

"Do you want the short and to the point version, or the down and dirty one?"

"Kids' problems are rarely superficial. I'll take down and dirty."

I couldn't help but smile. "Pavel is about sixteen and with a gang that most likely tried to kill an Israeli diplomat." I knew she knew I was involved in that, but I didn't elaborate. "I don't think he was part of the assassination attempt, but still, he was a member of the group. Anyway, last night Pavel was with his buddies when they tried to kill me."

She looked at me, and her face lost any smile she had. "What happened? Are you okay?"

"I'm fine. I was down at Federal Hill with a friend. The gang probably figured I suspected them. Interestingly, I hadn't, but they didn't know that." They truly weren't on my mind until Amit mentioned it later on.

"So they tried to kill you?"

"Yup." I took a drink of ice water.

"What happened?"

There was no reason for great detail. I kept it general: "Four of them confronted me. Pavel and a friend took off when things got serious, but the two others, uh-" I had a quick flashback to pounding the hatchet kid in the head and then kicking the other one. "...the two others, um, didn't get away from me."

She didn't ask what that meant. "So, Pavel ran away and later showed up on your doorstep."

"My dojo step actually. I also teach martial arts, but you probably already know that."

"Word did get around the teacher's lounge."

I nodded, understanding...sort of.

"What's your sense of him?" Katie asked.

"Well, Pavel probably didn't really want to be with his buddies, doing the things they were doing. He seems like a good kid."

"And he's still there."

"In my dojo?..Probably in the middle of another Steven Seagal movie."

"Has he said anything about what happened?"

"Just that he was sorry." I looked around the room. Two men and two women, all dressed in business attire, came into the restaurant and were ushered over to a booth.

"He's obviously drawn to you and feels safe with you. Any chance his friends will come back?"

"Not those friends," I paused. "Maybe others."

"So what are your initial thoughts about what to do?"

I shrugged. "I don't want to expose him to other gang members, so I was thinking of just letting him hang around for a while. He'll open up when he's ready. Then, once I know something and have a handle on it, I may go to the police."

"Maybe you should talk to them now."

"It's too soon." I looked at Katie. "Anything specific I can do to get him talking?"

"Well, you're already making him feel secure. My guess is when he feels comfortable enough, he may give you the opportunity to ask him about the gang. That's what I would suggest... keep doing what you're doing and pay attention to what he says."

She let a moment pass. "I'm glad you didn't get hurt last night."

I smiled. "Me, too."

"And I think you're doing a wonderful thing for Pavel."

"We all do what we can."

She looked at me and the corner of her mouth turned up. "You can't take a compliment, can you?"

"Yes I can."

"No, I don't think so."

"Give me another chance."

"Okay," she paused. "I think you're doing a wonderful thing for Pavel."

"Anyone would do it."

"See!"

"I'm just kidding. Thank you...really."

We both smiled.

Our food arrived, which was good because I didn't know what else to say on the subject. I took a bite of my pizza, wiped my mouth with a napkin then turned to Katie. "So, how did you come to teach at the Stein school?"

"I'm from a small town in Massachusetts — Sharon — and came down here to go to college."

"At Maryland?"

"Actually, University of Virginia." She took a sip of her Diet Coke. "My love life took me here, and I worked in the public school system for two years. Then, I saw an ad the Stein school had placed for a student services person. I liked the idea of a private school, so I applied."

I wondered about her love life comment. "And you lived happily ever after."

She laughed. "I don't know about that. What about you?"

"Oh, I'm from around."

She laughed again. It was a great laugh.

"Sorry. Too vague. An old habit. I'm a Baltimorean. Grew up here, moved to New York for college, and then moved to Israel right after graduation. Joined the army. Stayed until my tour was over then came back."

"The *CliffsNotes* version of your life."

"All the rest is commentary."

"Disarm an assassin, foil would be attackers-"

"Leap tall buildings in a single bound."

"There's more to you than what you're telling."

"I hope so. So, born in Massachusetts, college in Virginia, student services specialist here. There's more to you than what *you're* telling."

"I hope so," she smiled.

The waiter returned, taking away our empty plates. We passed on dessert, and I asked for the check. After the waiter scampered off, I turned back to Katie. "Would you like to meet him...Pavel? We can go by now...won't take five minutes to get there."

The question took her by surprise. She thought for a moment. "Yeah, I'd like to."

"Thanks. By the way, do you know it's hard being a tough guy all the time?"

"I won't tell anyone. Promise."

We stood up.

"Sensei..." I heard the voice from behind and turned to see a thin, balding man in his late twenties, approaching.

He was dressed in a blue polo shirt and khaki Dockers.

"Daniel," I extended my right hand. "How are you?"

"Thank God."

"Things are good then?"

"Definitely good."

I turned to Katie. "Katie Harris, Daniel Katz, the owner of this establishment. Daniel is the only person alive who can own a pizza shop and stay thin."

Daniel shook Katie's hand. "They're my poppa's genes, what can I say. Pleased to meet you, Katie." He turned back to me. "Heard about you the other night at the banquet. Way to go."

"Daniel also used to be a student of mine," I put in.

"I'm coming back to class, you know."

"Anytime."

A boy probably in his late teens came out from the kitchen, wearing a red-stained white apron. "Dan, need you in back."

"Be there in a second."

I looked at the teenager. He was dark-haired, had a short scruffy beard as if he hadn't shaved in a few days, and a small hoop earring in each ear.

He turned to me. "Hi."

"Hi," I said back.

Without another word, he turned and went back the way he had come. Daniel watched the boy leave, but spoke to us: "Not a talker, but great with tomato sauce." He turned to Katie, "So, how was lunch? What'd you have, the Haifa?"

"Yes," Katie answered. "It was great. Had a sweetness to it."

"You can come back...with or without him."

"Thanks."

"All right," Daniel said heading toward the back, "see you soon, I hope." And with that, he vanished through a double-hinged door in back.

"I come here for the ambiance," I said.

"And for the tomato sauce."

"And for the tomato sauce," I smiled.

After retrieving our check and paying for it — my treat — we walked out. The ride to the dojo took longer than expected, as lunch hour traffic conspired to slow us down. Neither of us was bothered by the congestion, since we had plenty of time and the day was sunny and serene. Springtime in Baltimore had such potential for beauty. Typically, we went very suddenly from cool days in April to the heat of the summer. This year we seemed to be blessed by a real spring, with clear skies and temperatures in the mid seventies.

I parked in my tenant's space just off Charles Street, and then Katie and I walked around to the dojo. We passed the radio station and the natural foods place. Today, there were two round tables outside the restaurant, around which customers sat on metal chairs, eating healthy-looking salads and sandwiches. I did spot alfalfa sprouts hanging out of a young man's multi-grained sandwich and something leafy on his female companion's plate.

"I've never been down here," Katie said. "It's charming."

"It's a great area. Hopkins is not too far away, the Baltimore

Museum of Art is around the corner..." As I spoke, I casually surveyed the street, checking store fronts and balconies for any out of place pedestrians or customers. All appeared normal. I half wondered what happened to the agent who was hiding in the shadows last night and his balcony friend from this morning.

"Here we are."

I led Katie up the stairs to the front door, while pulling a key from my pocket. I began to insert it into the lock, but then stopped.

"What's the matter?"

I withdrew the key — I had barely touched the lock — then pushed on the door. It opened.

"Would you wait down the steps and to the side, please."

Katie looked at me for a moment. "Be careful."

She went back down the cement steps and moved over to a tree near the curb. I silently stepped inside.

The hallway was lit by an overhead fluorescent that hummed slightly. Probably a deteriorating ballast that I'd have to attend to. I hadn't noticed it before. I breathed evenly. As I approached the corner of the main workout hall I realized the television wasn't on. No DVD playing. No sounds of Pavel sweeping the floor. Or practicing karate moves he may have remembered from his past or just now picked up from Steven Seagal. There was no sound of running water from the bathroom. There was no sound at all. I turned the corner and looked in my office.

Pavel was there. He was on the floor beside my desk on his back. His eyes were open, but fixed on the ceiling. His brown eyes no longer had a luster to them. Someone had shot him just above the bridge of his nose.

I bent down, trying not to picture the boy who had come to me last night for asylum. I tried not to hear his voice as he argued with me to spend the night. Here was the young man who had come to me for some peace.

There was very little blood on his forehead, but there was a powder burn — stippling — surrounding the bullet's point of entry. Pavel had been shot at close range. I looked around. Nothing, based on a quick glance, seemed disturbed. Whoever had come in came with a single purpose.

I picked up a gi top from a nearby shelf and draped it over Pavel's head and torso. Forensics would consider this a disruption of a crime scene. For the second time in as many days, I placed a call to a friend who was a cop.

10

Katie and I sat on the floor of the main hall against the far wall while detectives and forensic specialists went over the office. We sat close to each other, not saying much of anything. Katie had already called school to say she wouldn't be in the rest of the day. I was feeling pretty awful.

"It's not your fault," Katie said.

"Well, let's see. I could've called the police. They would've taken Pavel...and he'd still be alive. I could've found out where he lived, returned him...and he'd still be alive. I could've stayed with him here...and he'd still be alive."

"Or you both could be dead."

"Maybe."

"You had a good plan with Pavel's well-being in mind. You were trying to *help* him."

I didn't say anything.

Nate D'Allesandro came out of my office and strode over to us. We got up off the floor.

"Well?" I looked at him.

"He was shot at close range, with what looks like a 9mm. We dug the bullet out of the back wall of your office. We'll know for certain about the caliber later today. Other than that, there's not a whole lot here."

"He knew the killer."

"Yup. Let him in."

"My guess is that one of his buddies followed us here, or just figured out that Pavel would come to me."

"Maybe he confided in someone."

"The wrong someone."

"And your office isn't disturbed," Nate confirmed.

"Not that I could tell."

"So what does that mean?" Katie asked.

"It means that whoever came here," Nate answered, "had only one reason to pay Pavel a visit."

The three of us let a few moments pass.

Nate turned to me. "Did you call Weather from your office phone?"

"No. Jon could have. Doubt it, though. He's of the cell phone generation, and I haven't used that phone in a while. Why?"

"It was the last number dialed."

"Pavel could've called someone and the killer didn't want that number showing up on redial."

"Clever."

"Thorough," I added.

"Pavel could've called Weather, couldn't he?" Katie asked.

"Unlikely," I said. "It's possible, I suppose."

"It was the killer," Nate put in.

Two attendants from the medical examiner's department came out of my office wheeling a gurney with Pavel's body bag. They minded their way through the dojo then maneuvered the stretcher through the front door.

Nate turned back to me: "Does 'Guardians of Heaven' mean anything to you?"

"You found his membership card." Nate wasn't surprised I knew about it. "No. I've no idea."

"We'll check. I know you'll check, too."

"I will." After a moment, I said, "For whatever it's worth, I put together a statement about last night." I pulled out a folded page and handed it to him.

"Thanks. This'll help, but if you don't mind, go over everything again. I just want to hear it one more time."

"No problem."

"And I want my detective to listen, too." He turned to a well-dressed, thirty-something man who was looking over some notes nearby. "Matthew, got a moment?"

Matthew came over — he was my height and had clear blue eyes — and once we were introduced, I gave them both all the details...the assassination attempt, my actions, my interviews, the incident in Little Italy, what happened in front of Alli's, and Pavel showing up here. Katie listened without reaction to what I did to Igar the hatchet boy and his buddy.

Nate looked at his detective, "Well, ideas?"

"I'd start with the usual background stuff and then I'd check with racketeering task force. Maybe they've heard of the gang."

"You'll make the call."

Matthew the detective nodded.

"What about last night? Do you see any legal problems for Gidon?" He meant that because I punched the hell out of Igar and he died as a result.

He looked at me, shaking his head. "It was definite pre-meditation on the kid's part. The response was clearly self-defense under life threatening conditions."

"That's my opinion, too. Thank you, Matt."

The detective turned to me. "You're Nate's Israeli army guy."

I let a moment pass. "I am."

He nodded then moved off.

Nate explained, "Just wanted another detective's reaction on last night...for the State's Attorney, if it comes up. Meanwhile, Pavel..." his voice trailed off. "We'll also follow up with the *Shin Bet* about the Guardians of Heaven. See what they know."

"Not much. That's why the Israelis came to me."

"And you're thrilled with that, I know. Well, we still have the kid in the hospital and the fourth kid from last night, when we find him."

"You'll let me know."

"I will." He looked toward the doorway where the medical examiner's men had taken Pavel. "I'm sorry, again, about the kid."

"Yeah. Thanks." And with that Nate headed out.

Katie put her hand on my arm. I smiled weakly.

"Nate seems like a good person. How do you know him?"

"A few summers ago his daughter was traveling through Israel and got into a rough spot. I helped get her out of it."

Katie probably guessed it wasn't an innocuous money issue or anything similar, but didn't pry.

In a matter of minutes, the forensics crew finished up for now, said their goodbyes and left. The dojo was now empty except for the two of us. We wandered into the office. The room was just as I had left it earlier today, except for the dark stain on the carpet near the desk and the missing plaster in the back wall, where the crime scene folks had dug out the bullet.

I looked at my desk. It all seemed untouched, even the pad where I had left my phone number hadn't been moved. It was still near the phone. I looked down at my papers, charts, and cordless phone that were all on my desk. "Pavel," I said to myself, "who did you call and why did you open the door?"

Even as I finished muttering to myself, I heard footsteps approaching from the hallway. We went out to see who it was. David Amit, the head of the Israeli team, was walking toward us, with two of his men trailing. They must have been waiting for the police to leave. One of Amit's agents was blond and high cheek boned, maybe with some Slavic blood; the other had dark, close-cut hair. I recognized the dark-haired man as the agent who was in the shadows the night before.

I was suddenly angry. Amit had put us at risk. He tried to make a link between the gang and the assassination, and I didn't trust that he didn't turn them onto me just to see what would happen. I moved toward Amit, my fury growing with each step. Maybe my rage about Pavel was surfacing. I didn't care.

As he opened his mouth to say something, I grabbed him by his shirt, swept his feet out from under him, and threw him to the ground. I turned to see the blond man reaching for me. I grabbed his arm, twisted it back against the joint, and he went flying also. The third man, the dark-haired one, was reaching inside his coat. I kicked him in the gut twice rapidly, not penetrating, but just enough to double him over. I heard the wind rush out of him. I violently twisted his shoulders, pulling him off balance to the floor. I spun back to the blond. He was about to get up. I moved in on him.

"*Maspeek!* Enough!" David Amit shouted, rising to his feet.

I looked at the Israeli chief.

"We saw who killed the boy." He motioned to the dark-haired man I had kicked. "Yaron saw him."

I backed away and let both agents get up. Katie was watching from the side.

Yaron spoke up, partially bent over. He had trouble taking a breath. "It was a woman or maybe a girl." He paused to inhale. "I was across the street. She came to the door and the boy let her in. She came out less than five minutes later."

"Can you describe her?"

"*Kain.* Yes." He straightened up.

"Tell the police."

Yaron looked at his boss who nodded.

"I'll tell you who to speak to." I instructed.

Amit turned to me. "I know about Lebanon."

We looked at each other for a long moment, each weighing what he had said. "Good. That's all you need to know about me then."

He nodded.

"*Shomrei Shamayim,*" I said.

"What?"

"Guardians of Heaven. Ever hear of it?"

He shook his head.

"It's the gang these boys belong to...Pavel and Igar. Maybe you can find out about the group. There's an office here and one in Jerusalem."

"I'll call Israel."

"It looks like all the members, or a great majority of them, are young Russian immigrants." I let another moment pass. "You can stop having me watched now."

"You knew?" the blond, high cheek boned agent asked.

"I knew."

The blond and Yaron exchanged looks.

"So, you'll tell me when you find something?" Amit asked.

"I'll tell you." I didn't know if he believed me. I saw no need to ask if he'd share his findings.

"All right, I'll be in touch. Here's where you can reach me... my American cell number." Amit handed me a card with only a phone number written on it. He turned to his men, nodded, and the three of them left without another word.

I put the card in a pocket.

"Do you know them?" Katie asked.

"They're *Shin Bet*, Israel security service and Eitan Lev's protection detail."

"Do you trust them?."

"Yes and no. We'll see."

"By the way, before, with those guys...wow."

"Didn't scare you?"

"No. More like holy moley."

I smiled. What a contrast to Alli. "I ought to get you back to school. I'm sorry I brought you into this."

"No, don't be. Pavel sounded like a good kid."

"He was."

My mind went back to my last image of him in the dojo and my warning about being careful.

"What?" She saw me drift.

"Why would he open the door after I told him not to...and who did he call?"

"A friend? Someone in the gang?"

"He wanted out of the gang."

Katie didn't say anything.

I walked back into the office and looked around. Nothing had changed of course. I sat at my desk. "He wouldn't open the door unless he knew who was there and trusted him."

"Or her."

"Or her."

I looked at the cordless phone on my desk. It was where it

had been when the police arrived, next to a stack of papers. The base/charger was off to the side.

"Who did he call?" I repeated.

"Let me have the phone." Katie held out her hand and I gave her the handset. "If this were a cell phone you could look at the outgoing call list..." she trailed off as she started playing with the buttons. There were several beeps. A moment later, "Guess what?"

She showed me the phone and a number on the display. "It's the phone number before Weather. Your phone has a complete call log."

I looked at her. "You're brilliant." I copied down the number.

"Are you going to call it?"

"Not from this phone. They'll have Caller I.D."

"You can block the call."

"Still, I'd rather not. There's a pay phone up the block. Do you have any change?"

"Yeah."

We left the dojo and headed up the street to the corner pay phone. We stood side-by-side next to the mini booth. Katie handed me some change and I just looked at it. Who do I ask for?...Pavel?...Guardians of Heaven? Who do I say I am?

I took a breath then dialed the number. The line clicked through.

"*Da*?" It was a female voice.

I hung up.

"What?" Katie asked.

"A woman answered speaking Russian."

"A woman?"

We both were thinking the same thing: Yaron, the Israeli agent, said he saw Pavel let a woman into the dojo, a woman who probably killed him.

"Do you have more change?" I asked.

She held out her palm with miscellaneous coins.

"I want you to call this time. A woman calling won't be as suspicious as a man. When she answers, ask for Pavel. You could be his girlfriend for all this person knows. Your voice should make her curious, particularly after I just hung up without saying anything...like I panicked. Don't give her your real name, but see if you can get hers. Okay?"

"*Da,*" she mimicked.

I fed the coins into the slot and redialed the number. Katie held the receiver off her ear so I could hear the exchange. In a moment, the call went through.

"*Da,*" I could hear the female voice at the other end.

"Hi, this is Shelley." Katie put on an animated, energetic voice. "Is Pavel there?"

Long pause, then, "No, Pavel is not here right now." Her English was perfect.

"Well, do you know when he'll be back?"

"No. I don't know."

"That's okay. Who am I talking to?"

She hesitated. "This is Bella. And who are you again?"

"Shelley. I'll try back later. Thank you." Katie hung up.

We stepped away from the booth.

"So what does this mean?" Katie asked.

"It means Pavel called a woman named Bella and either Bella came here and killed him or she mentioned it to someone who came here and killed him."

"Or Bella could be his sister for all we know, and someone else came here independently...someone else he knows."

"Thank you for that," I said smiling. "Another possibility."

We headed down the block to the dojo.

"I should get you back to school. Hanging around me may become dangerous."

"You'll protect me."

I smiled again. "I'd do my best, but I still should take you back to school. I need to make a phone call first, though."

Once inside, I dialed my student Jonathan on his cell. Because he managed the family real estate business, it was impossible to tell where he was. He could be anywhere from the Eastern Shore to Western Maryland.

"Hello," Jon answered.

"Hi, it's Sifu."

"Hi."

"Need a favor...actually several."

"Okay."

"Need you to take my classes tonight, if I'm not there. Wait a sec." I turned to Katie. "Do you have internet access on your cell?"

She nodded.

Back to Jon: "Never mind on the other thing. Got it covered. So where did I catch you?"

"At Evy's."

"Evy's?...The college girl from the dojo?"

"Yup."

"I think you set a record even for yourself. Sorry to bother you."

"I'll call you later."

I was being dismissed. We both hung up.

I looked at Katie. "We have the number that Pavel called. Can you do a reverse look-up and get an address?"

"If it's listed." She took out her cell and went on-line. After another moment of touching and typing, "No. No luck. It's not listed."

"I'll have to figure something out. Thanks. Now, it's time to get you back."

She touched my arm. "Are you sure you're okay?"

"No."

"I can stay longer, if you want. I told the school I wouldn't be back today."

"Thanks. I'll be fine. This is the way it is right now. I appreciate it, though."

With that, I took Katie back to school where she had left her car, and I spent a good part of the trip thinking about a relationship that could easily get started here. Maybe it already had. There was still Alli and that limbo. Of course, Alli was eight years younger than me — and there was the fact that I totally freaked her out. Katie was more of a contemporary; she had more life experience and seemed very together.

I pulled into the school lot and followed Katie's directions to the front of school and to a sky blue Mustang convertible, parked in the center of the lot, next to a group of mini vans.

I escorted her to her car.

"Thanks for helping me out today," I said. We stopped next to the driver's side door.

"I'm sorry about Pavel."

"Yeah."

"You're gonna follow up on the phone number?"

"I'll do what I can." I paused. "I know I've probably said this before, but I'm sorry I brought you into this. I didn't mean for you to be so involved...between the police, the Israelis, and helping me."

"I'm glad I was with you."

"Me, too." We looked at each other for a moment. "This may be random, but I'd like to see you again. I just don't know what to do next, because this whole thing might get dangerous very quickly. I don't want you in harm's way. I also tend to drop off the face of the earth sometimes to...to get things done. If that happens, please don't take it personally."

"Okay." She looked confused.

I gave her a dojo business card that simply had my Chinese seal on it next to my name and phone number.

"If you need me, though, call me day or night."

She gave me *her* business card. "If you need me, call me day or night."

I smiled. I looked over at the card I had given her. "The cards were a present from some students."

"My cards are from the school." A moment went by as we looked at each other. "Oh, let me have that for a second." Katie took back her card. She pulled a pen from her purse, and wrote down two additional phone numbers. "My home and cell numbers."

"Terrific."

She beeped open her car and I held the door for her. When Katie passed me to get in, she paused for just a second. It was enough. I leaned in and kissed her softly on the lips.

Katie smiled and sat behind the wheel. I walked back to my Jeep, wondering if I were nuts.

11

I drove back to the dojo with my mind reviewing not only the events of the past ten minutes, but those of the past few days. Until I had more information on Pavel's inner circle, there was nowhere to go with my questions. So, as I was scheduled to teach a late afternoon class, there was no reason not to take it, though Jon would cover the session if I wished.

I parked in my usual spot and walked around the corner. As I approached my steps, I saw Nate D'Allesandro across the street, getting out of his worn Cherokee. He paused for a break in the traffic and then sprinted over.

"Well, it *was* a nine millimeter at close range. No matches on the bullet. That'll take more time." He looked at me. "Any more thoughts on the Guardians of Heaven?"

I leaned against the wall of the steps. "Just that it's a gang of mostly Russian immigrant kids."

"There is a large Russian Jewish community here."

I nodded. "I know."

Nate looked up the block. "Baltimore is one of the major cities where they've settled."

"What about the boy who tried to shoot Eitan Lev?"

"Russian émigré also. The question is who wanted the hit? The kids can't be behind this...what do they know about politics?"

"Another question for your suspect."

"Already asked. He's not saying a word. At least not yet."

"Maybe they're hired guns."

"Young Russian mafia? Still, someone had to contract it."

I shrugged.

"Could be that sort of group," Nate admitted. "The way they came after you. Pretty vicious."

"Either way, as you said, someone has to be behind it. And what's the issue with Lev? He must've really pissed off someone."

"Ask your Israeli friends."

"I will. They're also checking the Guardians piece. There's an office in Jerusalem. Maybe that will turn up something."

"The card mentioned a headquarters here. We need to find it."

"I'll find it." A moment passed. "Any lead on Pavel's family?"

"Just came from them. Older parents... Pavel was their only child. They were devastated."

"I'm sure." I thought of Katie's suggestion about a sister named Bella. So that wasn't the connection.

"Their last name is Demirovsky. Live in upper Park Heights about a mile from the county line." He gave me the address.

"Do they have any extended family, any support?"

"The father has a brother here who has a wife and kids. So there's that."

"What'd the parents say about Pavel?"

"All I got was they hadn't seen him in a few weeks. He went to a boarding school in town."

"I'll stop by the parents' apartment after my class. I was probably the last person to see him alive. And he was staying with me."

"I don't know if that will bring them comfort or not…or more questions."

"I don't know."

"So, that's what there is for now." Nate sounded depressed.

"Well, I have something for you…maybe."

His eyebrows came up.

"An unlisted phone number…Pavel's last call. Apparently, my cordless phone has a call log." I gave him the number.

"Looks like we missed that. I'll tell the boys. Thanks. Though if the phone's not a land line, there's not much we can do. We're not the NSA. And if there's no GPS chip…" he left the rest un-stated.

A long moment passed. "We need to do something social, Gidon. Bring Alli by…or whoever."

"I will, Nate."

"Good." He looked up at the sky. "Alright, I'm off." And with that, he went back across the street to his car.

Once Nate left, I headed inside to prepare for my class... which meant I just had to change into my gi. As I entered my office, though, I found myself looking at the blood stain on the floor near my desk. I went to a storage closet, got a bucket, filled it with cold water then located a sponge. Soon, after some scrubbing, I had changed the dark, relatively small blood stain into a more brownish, 12 inch diameter splotch. I took some clean towels, absorbed what I could, and then left the remains of the stain covered for now with the towels.

"Sifu?" Jon called from the hallway.

"In the office."

Jon came in with his new friend, Evy. She definitely was a looker: tall, long blonde hair, barretted again in back. She was wearing a maroon T-shirt with a white dragon logo on it. The shirt was tucked into navy shorts and "bloused" at the waist.

"Hi," I said to her. "Back for more?"

"Definitely," she smiled.

"Nice T-shirt."

"That means that Sifu would like one just like it," Jon said to Evy, but smiled at me.

"I get some of my best T-shirts that way," I said.

Jon turned to Evy, "Class will start in about ten minutes. Why don't you start stretching out."

"Okay."

Evy headed out to the main hall and sat herself on the floor and immediately went into a full split.

"I could watch her stretch all day," Jon said.

"No you couldn't. You'd watch her for about ten seconds and then you'd have to attack her or something."

He laughed.

I looked down at the covered stain.

"Anything I can do, Sifu?"

"No, thanks. I'll have to take care of this later."

There were some new voices in the hall as the students began to file in. In a matter of minutes the class was underway: I broke them into ranks...just like yesterday. Then, unlike yesterday, I led the workout, not Jon. We did everything he had done the day before in terms of stretching and exercises, but I pushed everyone longer and harder: we held stretches half a minute longer and I added repetitions to all the push-ups, crunches, and karate movements. I had them stand in various stances until I saw legs begin to twitch. Everyone, from the kids to the adults, tried their best. Sweat was pouring off of everyone in the room; faces were red, and hair was plastered to foreheads.

As the class went on, I taught them movement in front stance, and then later how to get out of simple grabs. At the end of the instruction, I gave everyone time to practice with different partners. As I watched Evy, I could see she was full of enthusiasm. At one point, she was grabbing a fellow coed's wrist with the idea that the friend had to break out of her grasp.

As I moved closer, I could tell that she was really squeezing the woman's arm.

"Evy, not so tight," I suggested. "This is just practice. Don't let your partner escape, but don't make it unreasonably difficult either."

"Okay," she smiled.

She loosened her grip and then the friend rotated her arm, pulling against the thumb side of Evy's grasp. She broke open Evy's hand-hold.

"That's it. Perfect. Now, Evy, let your partner grab you."

The friend grabbed Evy's hand and Evy worked on breaking out of the grip. She whipped her arm around with enthusiasm and easily broke the hold.

"Very good. Now work the other hand."

As they continued, I circulated through the room, keeping an eye on everyone. Then, in a matter of minutes, class was over, and everyone filed out. Jon immediately gravitated to Evy and they soon disappeared. My number one student didn't even say goodbye. Evy had truly captivated him.

"Sifu," I heard Jon's voice from around the corner. He trotted over to me, but stopped a few feet away. He made a fist with his right hand and covered it with his open left palm. He bowed from the waist. "Thank you for teaching me. I'll see you later."

"May the force be with you. Have a good evening."

And with that, I was left alone. I wandered through the dojo, picking up miscellaneous articles of clothing that always seemed to get left behind — warm-up jackets, sweat shirts, small towels — and tossed them into a large bin in the corner. My plan for the evening was to head to Pavel's parents' place, so I went home, showered and put on fresh khakis and a striped Oxford sport shirt. I then headed to the address Nate had given me.

The Demirovsky's apartment was in a garden apartment complex off Park Heights Avenue, one of the main drags in northwest Baltimore. I parked in front of their building, a red brick two story affair, surrounded by clusters of other two story brick buildings. After double checking the number beside the front door, I went inside.

Pavel's parents were on the second floor. There was no natural light in the stairwell, the only illumination coming from a pair of exposed incandescent bulbs in the hallway. The dim lighting made finding the proper apartment somewhat challenging, and I had to almost put my face up against each door to read nameplates. Fortunately, there were only four apartments on the second landing. The Demirovsky's place was the last on the right. The front door was metal and painted a medium blue. I took a breath and rang the bell.

A moment went by and a woman in her mid-twenties opened the door. She was my height and had styled, close cut white-blonde hair, was conservatively dressed in a pin-striped suit and pumps. Her jewelry was minimal: a pair of pearl studs and a thin cloisonné bracelet. A heavy weight seemed to have rounded her posture...or so I imagined. "Yes? Can I help you?" I noted she didn't have an accent.

"My name is Gidon Aronson. I'm sorry to bother you now,

but I just wanted to wish Mr. and Mrs. Demirovsky my condolences. I saw Pavel last night and this morning, and I wanted to stop by."

"Come in." She opened the door and I stepped into an apartment that could've been transplanted from a home in Moscow, or so I projected. The room was painted white, but the living room and dining rooms were filled with dark, period-style furniture. There was a long couch covered with a dark flowery slipcover, dark end tables, a beat-up old television, and miscellaneous small tables — all covered with stacks of papers and books. There was no overhead lighting, just the red tinted remains of daylight coming in from the windows and the light from several wide, ornate-bodied table lamps. The overall feeling was one of clutter, though the owners probably knew exactly where everything was. An older couple — probably in their early sixties — sat on the couch surrounded by more people. Mrs. Demirovsky was on the left and she was weeping and rocking herself. She had wavy grey hair and what looked like an almost wrinkleless face. Her husband sat with his arm around her. Mr. Demirovsky had a full head of grey hair and a square face, creased with lines. His eyes were glassy with tears, and he just held his wife without saying anything.

The young woman who had opened the door, led me over to them. "Uncle David, Aunt Alla, this man came to see you."

As I looked at the couple on the couch, my mouth went dry.

Pavel's mom turned to me and held out her arms in my direction. I walked over, bent over, and took both her hands. She held my hands tightly.

"So, you knew my Pavel?"

"Just a little. I met him only last night. I teach karate and he came to see me."

She just looked at me with blue eyes filled with tears.

I continued: "I didn't know him very well, but he seemed like a truly sweet young man."

The father nodded.

"I just wanted you to know that he seemed like a fine boy and I'm sorry."

"Thank you, thank you," the father said.

"So you knew my Pavel," the mom repeated.

"Just a little," I smiled weakly.

She let go of my hands and I stood up.

"I'm so sorry," I repeated.

I suddenly felt like an intruder and I turned to leave. As I moved slowly toward the door, I passed a small round table that had a number of framed photographs on it. I paused to look at them. One was of Pavel and his parents at the beach. Pavel was in the middle and had his arms around both parents. Another was a group shot, probably of family members, taken in this apartment. Pavel and his parents were sitting on the left side of the couch, to his right was the young woman who had opened the apartment door, and then next to her was a boy about Pavel's age. He was about the same size as Pavel, and had long, stringy black hair parted in the middle. I stared at the face, which to me looked a bit severe...like adolescent attitude. I had seen that face before.

"Excuse me," I said picking up the photograph and walking over to the young, conservatively dressed blonde woman who had let me in. "Is this a family shot? I see you and Pavel's family."

"We took that a few months ago when we were all together for my aunt's birthday."

"So you're Pavel's cousin."

"Yes."

"And who is this boy next to you?"

"My brother, Alex. He and Pavel were the same age. They were very close...did everything together."

"You're cousins, but you don't have an accent. You're not from the Soviet Union...the former Soviet Union."

"No, my family grew up here in Baltimore. Pavel and his family came about five years ago. It was like a family reunion."

"And your last name is..."

"Moskowitz."

"From the famous Moskowitzes of Baltimore," I teased.

She smiled.

"Can you tell me a little about Pavel?" I slowly moved off to the side near the foyer. "I really only met him last night and I'd like to know more about who he was."

"Well, Pavel was a great kid. Bright, sensitive, a little awkward, I would say. I think he had difficulty adjusting here. He may have also been a little embarrassed. My aunt and uncle only speak Russian at home, and so Pavel's English probably wasn't as good as he wanted it to be."

"Did it cause problems at school or with friends?"

"Well, as I said, he was a bright boy, but school was hard for him." She laughed to herself. "My brother on the other hand, speaks English fluently but had other issues with school."

"Fights?"

"How did you know?"

"Just a guess. From the picture he seems to have a little bit of an attitude."

"Yeah, Alex is a pain in the ass." She laughed. "Both he and Pavel ended up going to a special school, a sort of boarding school. Pavel went because he had some learning issues. Alex went because he just had issues."

"A boarding school?"

"It's right here in the neighborhood, but the kids eat and sleep there. Sometimes they come home for weekends."

"Is this school only for Russian kids?"

"No."

"Of course," I nodded. "Alex is from Baltimore."

"By the way, I'm Abby," she held out her hand.

"Gidon." I shook it.

She let a moment go by. "You came here just because you met Pavel last night? That's so nice."

"Well, there is more to it. Pavel showed up on my doorstep. I think he was a little lost." I didn't need to go into details, particularly since her brother may have been involved in some horrible stuff.

"I actually put him up for the night."

"He was shot at your place?"

"Yeah." I was definitely not proud of that.

Tears welled up in her eyes. "It's horrible. Who would do that? Why would they do that?"

"I don't know. I'm sure the police will find out."

"I mean he wasn't into drugs or anything. He was such a good kid."

I just looked at her with nothing to say.

"I'm sorry, I'm sorry." She wiped away the tears using the palms of her hands. I noticed she wasn't wearing any rings, marriage or otherwise.

Before I could say anything else, a weathered older woman came over. "Abby, can I get you something, honey?"

Abby wiped her face again, then turned to the woman. "No, I'm okay. Thanks."

The older woman patted her on the arm, then moved off.

"My aunt from Florida. She's terrific." Abby tried to smile, but tears came again. "I'm sorry. I can't seem to stop crying."

"Don't apologize. It's a tragedy."

She pulled out a tissue. I wish I had one to offer her.

After a moment, I looked around, as if I were searching for someone. "I don't see your brother. Is he here?"

"No, he's at school. He called. Said he'd be here later."

I nodded. It was time for me to leave. "Well, again, I'm sorry for your loss." I moved toward the door."

"Thank you for coming."

I looked back at the Demirovskys sitting on the couch, huddled together. "Take care of them."

"We will." She opened the door for me and I left the apartment.

Slowly, pensively, I headed down the dimly lit steps to the front door. Pavel's cousin seemed very nice. Her brother, on the other hand, I knew was very different. Alex, the young man with long hair and severe expression, was the fourth member of the gang that attacked me outside of Alli's house last night. He and Pavel had taken off when things got rough.

I stepped outside and walked to my car. Dusk had settled on the city and I knew that whatever daylight was left would dissipate very quickly. I climbed into my car. I had the urge to call Alli to see how she was doing. I also had the urge to call Katie to see how she was doing. I did neither.

So, Guardians of Heaven wasn't an exclusive group. Alex wasn't Russian, though he had family who was. Who organized them? Did they have political affiliations? What was it about the Israeli candidate, Eitan Lev, that made him a target?

I needed to talk to someone who was tapped into the young community, someone who knew about the school Alex and Pavel went to, and knew the Guardians group.

Fifteen minutes later, I pulled into a parking spot in front of Middle Eastern Pizza. Dinner was in full swing and almost every table in the small restaurant was taken. I stood at the door and scanned for Daniel, the owner. He wasn't there.

"Excuse me," I leaned over to a thin, bright red-haired waitress carrying a tray of glasses filled with ice water. She couldn't have been more than eighteen. "Is Daniel here?"

She put the glasses in front of customers on a nearby table and responded over her shoulder. "He's in the back."

"Sorry to bother you, but when you get a chance, can you ask him to come out, please? I'd appreciate it."

She nodded then proceeded to take the order of the table she was serving. After repeating the order, the waitress disappeared through a door in the back of the restaurant. In a matter of moments she came back out, followed by the tall, lanky Daniel. I waved to him, and met him halfway.

"Hi. What's up?"

"Need your help. Do you have somewhere quiet?"

He tilted his head, indicating I should follow him. He walked to the entrance of the shop and out near the cars parked in front. "About as quiet as we can get. Is it about the kid who was shot in the dojo?"

"Daniel, you always surprise me. How..."

"It's a small community and cops come here all the time. We talk."

"So, the kid's name was Pavel Demirovsky."

Dave nodded.

"He was a member of a gang called *Shomrei Shamayim*, the Guardians of Heaven. Know anything about them?"

"Just that they've been around for about a year. They're kids who are sort of lost. Their parents don't know what to do about them. Drug issues sometimes...authority issues.

The kids put together this gang so they can hang out."

"Any particular places?"

"Well, here sometimes. Well, used to be here...Also in front of the convenience store about a mile up the road. But that may have changed." He paused for a moment. "Wait here."

With that he disappeared back into the restaurant. As I watched through the glass front, he went through the room and into the kitchen. He came out less that ten seconds later with the dark, scruffy-looking teenager in a white apron that Katie and I had seen him in earlier today.

"Sensei, this is Ronnie."

I shook his hand. "We met this morning. Hi."

Daniel continued. "Ronnie was a member of Guardians of Heaven for a few months."

"Tell me about the group." I looked at the young cook.

"Okay," his gaze went from me to Daniel and back to me. "Well, they started out as just a bunch of kids to hang out with. Y'know, we didn't like being at home...or school. We just sort-of did stuff together."

"You're not with them anymore?"

"No, they started breaking into people's houses and *shuls*, you know, synagogues."

"Synagogues? For the silver in the ark?" Torah scrolls typically had breast plates and crowns made of silver.

He shook his head. "For the liquor they had stored from weddings and bar mitzvahs and stuff."

I shook my head, thinking that was really low-life.

"I know. Pretty disgusting, robbing synagogues for the *shnapps*. I got out soon after that started happening. Daniel gave me a job."

Daniel looked at the boy. "Like I said earlier, he's the best chef we've ever had."

"Any problems leaving the group?"

"Not really. They just made me promise I wouldn't hang out with them." He laughed. "Not a problem. We were just kids trying to be bad-asses. "

I looked at him. Ronnie seemed like a good kid. "So, where's the hangout now?"

"Probably the main place is Blues Pool Hall and Game Center up near the Beltway on Reisterstown Road."

"I've driven by the place." I looked from Ronnie over to Daniel. "Any idea who's in charge of the group?"

The answer came from Ronnie. "Last I heard it was a kid named Joe something. Real name was Igar. He *was* a bad-ass. Liked hatchets. Heard he was taken out in a street fight yesterday."

I looked at Daniel. He didn't reveal if he knew the fight had been with me.

"So, who will take over now?" This from Daniel.

"Don't know."

"Anything else?" Daniel turned to me.

I shook my head. "Thanks. I appreciate the help."

"No problem." Ronnie headed back into the restaurant.

"Sensei, you think this group is involved with that kid's murder in the dojo?"

"Yup."

"And trying to kill that Israeli guy the other night?"

"Looks like."

"You're really pissed, aren't you."

"Yup." I let a moment go by. "What do you know about a boarding school here that teaches these kids."

"The New School?"

"New School?"

"That's what they're calling it. Man who's the principal is Dr. Aaron Cole. He's supposed to be really great. Turns these kids around."

"And Pavel went there, right?"

"I think so. Dr. Cole would be a great person to talk to."

That was a great idea. I definitely would like to hear Dr. Cole's take on Guardians of Heaven. Perhaps he could even point me in a direction. "Maybe I'll stop by tomorrow. Where is it?"

He gave me the address.

"Thanks for all the information." I shook Daniel's hand.

"It's a mess, isn't it?"

I nodded. "It'll get sorted out." I knew the kind of sorting out I wanted. "Thanks, again."

"Anytime, Sensei." He headed back into the shop and I went to my jeep.

I sat behind the wheel and looked through the windshield.

I was parked in front of the restaurant, so I had a clear view inside. The place was definitely busy. I watched as Daniel worked the patrons, stopping by one table, smiling and shaking customers' hands, then moving over to the next table and going through the same routine.

My thoughts wandered. I'd see the principal tomorrow. Tonight, though, there was one more lead to check out. The individual I had in mind knew me, but probably wouldn't cooperate since I put him in the hospital last night with a broken pubic bone and ruptured bladder. Didn't matter, because I wanted to know who sent the quartet after me.

I let out a deep breath. I was really tired. As I looked at the folks in the restaurant, I had what I hoped was a great idea. I pulled my cell phone from my pocket, dug out Katie's phone number, and dialed it. In a few seconds she answered.

"Hi. It's Gidon. I half didn't expect to find you home."

"Yeah, not a moment to spare in my busy social life." She laughed. "Actually, I was just sitting on my porch reading a book."

"Sounds great, actually."

"How are things going?"

"Well, no one's tried to kill me this afternoon."

"Always a good thing."

A moment went by and I wondered if I was intruding.

"Are you up for company?" I heard myself ask.

"Sure. That'd be great."

"Terrific. I have to make one stop and then I'll be over. Say about an hour?"

"That'll work. I need to run out to the food store, so that will be perfect."

"Great."

She gave me directions.

"I'll see you in an hour then," I said.

"Okay."

I hung up and smiled to myself. I should bring something. Wine?...Flowers?...Ice cream? Wine. Maybe ice cream next time, though.

Already I was feeling more energetic as I drove toward Sinai Hospital. By now, night had moved into the city, bringing with it a slower pace — or at least the illusion of a slower pace. Not only were there fewer cars on the road, but there wasn't that feeling of having to get somewhere quickly.

Sinai Hospital sat atop a small hill amid a park-like setting. The complex always seemed to be undergoing construction, with a crane and other equipment perpetually resting near the ER. I cruised the outdoor parking lot for a minute — it was tiered with the closest spots reserved for doctors — and found an opening on one of the lower levels. I parked and then walked up a small incline to the main entrance.

The kid Nate had told me about at the crack of dawn today, Gregory Segev, should be in a room by now.

The lobby of the hospital resembled that of a hotel,

with a mini-arboretum in the center and a gift shop and coffee pub to the sides. Instead of an information desk, there was a "concierge." I had to smile. No one would mistake this place for anything other than a hospital. I didn't get it.

The concierge informed me that my friend was on the third floor, room 325. The bank of elevators was opposite the desk, beyond the arboretum. I walked past the collection of oversized plants, past the elevators to a door guarding a stairwell. Without hesitating, I opened the door and took steps two at a time to the third floor.

The third floor landing deposited me in a waiting area fronting on a pair of elevators. Signs to the patients' rooms pointed to the left. Gone were the days of sterile-looking corridors. The third floor at Sinai was nicely wallpapered with a green-flowered motif complemented with red chair rail. Consistent with this homey design philosophy, the nurses' station had been turned into a kiosk with potted plants hanging from a suspended ceiling. At the moment there was only one scrub-attired nurse on duty, and she was entering data into a computer. She didn't look up as I walked by.

Room 325 was to the left, down a broad hallway. I walked past a pajama clad middle-aged man slowly pushing an intravenous pole. As I went by several open doorways I could hear a courtroom drama coming from televisions mounted high up on the walls. I peered into one of the darkened rooms while continuing to walk and almost tripped over a wheelchair parked against the chair rail. I none-too-graciously side stepped it, smiling at my own clumsiness.

After about ten rooms, the hall intersected another corridor and signs pointed me to the right. When I rounded the corner, I passed a teenager going the other way. He was dressed in a leather jacket and had long, stringy black hair parted in the middle. The boy continued walking, but looked back at me. I knew him. I had just seen his picture in the Demirovsky's apartment. He was Alex, Pavel's cousin...Pavel's cousin who was at Federal Hill last night, outside Alli's. He must've just visited his friend down the hall. The boy turned away, but then looked back at me again. Our eyes met...and he bolted.

Alex turned the corner and picked up speed as he tore down the long corridor, back the way I had just come. I ran after him.

He passed the man in pajamas pushing the IV pole. The boy hung a right and pushed the double doors open toward the elevators. The hallway doors were still open when I followed through. Pavel's cousin went past the waiting area, past the stairwell, and down a corridor marked "Radiology." He took a left and jumped over a small aluminum cart filled with pitchers, sending them flying. Three seconds later, I jumped over the small aluminum cart.

We passed examining rooms to either side. He rounded a corner to the right; I was ten feet behind him. Alex looked over his shoulder. I could see his frantic eyes.

At the end of the corridor, an orderly was helping a woman

into a wheelchair. Alex pulled the orderly off balance and into the middle of the hallway. A second later I moved the attendant as gently as I could. He hit the wall yelling at me.

Alex took a quick left and we found ourselves back in a patient hallway. Nurses looked at us as we ran by. A doctor, dressed in scrubs and a long white coat, stepped out of a patient's room and quickly jumped out of the way. The boy hung another left through familiar double doors. We had come full circle and were next to the stairwell that I had taken up to the third floor. Alex pushed open the door, swinging it wide. He took two steps down and jumped the remainder of the stairs to the second floor landing. He opened the door and ran out.

I took the stairs down more cautiously, taking *four* steps down and then jumped the rest. Coming out of the stairwell, I looked both ways. The second floor was not for patient rooms, but for out-patient care. Examining cubicles lined both sides of the hall. I looked left. He wasn't there. As I turned to my right, Pavel's cousin disappeared through a side door halfway down the hallway. I couldn't help but wonder if he had any idea where he was going. The door led down another flight of steps. I burst through the door to see him knock over two doctors on their way up. Alex, partially entangled with them, scrambled to his feet and pulled open the door on the next landing.

The doctors were still lying on the steps when I flew toward them. Their eyes went wide as I jumped over both of them, touched a stair with my right foot and pushed off to clear the remaining steps to the first floor level. I landed on both feet and caught the exit door just as it was about to close. I yanked it open and ran out into the lobby.

Alex ran past the arboretum and out past the concierge. He veered left through the sliding glass entry doors. As I followed him outside, I saw him running down the driveway, waving frantically. A motorcycle engine kicked to life. Alex shot another glance over his shoulder. He was too far ahead of me. A red Honda CRF dirtbike pulled up next to him and he jumped on back. The driver, clad in black leather and a white helmet, did a quick 180 and accelerated down the driveway incline. In a matter of moments, the motorcycle turned a corner and its throaty staccato roar was lost in city traffic.

12

I walked back into the hospital at a much slower pace than when I had exited. In the lobby, the concierge scowled at me, but I shook my head as if to say it was all the kid's fault. As I passed the bank of elevators to go to the steps, an elevator door opened to my left. It was a sign: angry doctors were probably still in the stairwell. I took the empty elevator.

When I stepped onto the third floor, I went through the double doors, past the nurses' kiosk, past the wheelchair against the right-hand wall, and past darkened rooms where patients were watching a courtroom drama.

So, letting my mind wander, what was Pavel's cousin doing here? Was his visit innocuous — was he just visiting his friend — or was something else going on? I rounded the corner without passing anyone I knew this time, and entered room 325.

Gregory Segev was inside. The question was, how much did he hate me and would that stop him from talking to me. I guess that was *two* questions.

Segev's room was "L" shaped, with a bathroom to the left and the room proper beyond it. The room itself was a standard private room: bare walls except for an unused bulletin board on one side, a long fluorescent fixture at the head of the room with oxygen and suction hook-ups next to it, an end table in a corner, and a television mounted from the ceiling on the far wall. Gregory Segev's bed, of course, filled the bulk of the floor space.

The young patient was supine in bed, covered up to his chest with a white sheet. His eyes were closed, and an IV ran into his left arm from a clear plastic bag hanging from an IV pole. Pain meds ran through a dosing device and down into his arm as well. The last time I saw this kid was almost 24 hours ago in Federal Hill. He had on a backwards Yankees cap and was reaching for something near his back pocket. I had kicked him just above his crotch before he had a chance to pull out whatever weapon he had. Now, looking the way he did, a smallish figure hooked up to tubes, it wouldn't be difficult for many visitors to have sympathy for him. I didn't have that problem. He was right where he should be.

There was someone else in the room who wasn't readily visible from the doorway. Sitting in a high-backed, cushioned chair next to the bed was a young nurse. She was probably in her mid to late twenties, with shoulder length brown hair. She was wearing scrubs but had on a purple zippered sweatshirt that had the words "Baltimore Ravens" across the front. I didn't know if she were a nurse from the unit or whether she was private duty. She stood up and came over to me.

As the nurse approached, I backed up and waved her to accompany me into the hallway, like I didn't want to disturb the patient. She looked at me more intently than I expected, but followed me out.

Her presence complicated matters. I could only imagine how the kid would react to me. I had put him in here, but then he tried to put *me* here — though bullies and attackers didn't think that way. If I had to terrorize him to get information, I would. I doubt a nurse would stand by if I threatened the kid. On the other hand, her presence was a good thing. Perhaps it would put off anyone trying to do him real harm. Right now, though, it would be helpful if she'd leave the room for a few minutes...get a snack or go to the bathroom...

"Hi," I said once we were outside the doorway. "I'm working with the police and I need to ask the patient a few questions. Is he up to it?"

The hallway to either side was empty and quiet. "He's still pretty out of it."

Perfect. Little resistance. "Are you with the hospital or private duty?"

"Today, I'm private. And you are...?"

"Gidon. I just need a few minutes with him." If she protested or if the kid reacted strongly to me, then I would just have to deal with her. That probably meant smiling and getting the hell out of there.

I began to move around her to go into the room, but she stepped to the side and blocked my way.

"I don't think so." She seemed very sure of herself.

"You're not going to let me in?"

"No."

"Even if I say 'please.'"

"No."

I looked at her for a moment then smiled. "You're a cop, aren't you?"

"You're Gidon Aronson, aren't you?"

"Yeah. And you're one of Nate D'Allesandro's."

She smiled. "Yes sir, I am."

"Nate told you I'd be here."

"Yes sir, and that I should give you a hard time."

"I was afraid I would have to use my charm, and that's always dangerous," I smiled.

"Don't worry, the Captain warned me. He also said I should cooperate with you fully. I'm Janie Marcus." She put out her hand and I shook it.

"So what's the deal here?"

"I hang out here and see who comes by."

"Friend or foe."

"Friend or foes," she repeated.

"Did the Captain tell you that someone might come in here and shoot this kid?"

"Yes, sir."

"Good."

I looked at Janie Marcus. She had a definite air of efficiency about her. I also assumed that she had a weapon concealed by her sweatshirt. I hoped she was fast.

"So, this kid had a visitor a little while ago?"

"Alex, I think I heard him say. Nothing much there. He just wanted to see how his friend was doing."

"Any names come up at all?"

"No. Their conversation was all very innocent. The kid, Gregory, apologized for screwing up."

"Did Alex talk about anyone being killed...a boy named Pavel?"

"No, sir. Like I said, it was very straightforward. After a few minutes of talking, Gregory drifted off and the Alex boy left."

"I have to talk to the patient."

"Of course."

I thought for a moment.

"You don't happen to know if there's any adhesive tape around, do you? And not that wimpy paper stuff."

"The good stuff that really sticks."

"Right."

"In the top drawer of the night table."

We headed back into the room where I retrieved the roll of tape. Gregory still had his eyes closed. I went over to his left arm, moved the appendage over to the bed rail, and wound layer upon layer of tape around both his wrist and the aluminum rail. After I was satisfied that his wrist was secure, I tossed the tape to Janie Marcus, who did the same thing to his right wrist.

When she finished she smiled, and tossed the tape back to me.

I moved to the head of the bed.

"Oh Gregory," I called softly.

A moment went by and he didn't open his eyes.

"Gregory," I repeated.

Nothing.

For the first time I realized that he was a red head. I guess I hadn't noticed it the night before because he was wearing his Yankees cap.

I leaned over and tapped his forehead. "Gregory, wake up."

This time he opened his eyes. He saw me and instantly jerked away in bed. Actually, he couldn't do more than move his head because his arms were taped to the guardrails. That and the fact that he was in a lot of pain.

"We need to talk," I said.

"Fuck you."

"No, actually, fuck you." Despite the epithet I kept my voice calm. "You and Igar came after me last night, remember? Igar had a hatchet, and you, what did you have, a gun? Probably a nice .357 or something."

He didn't say anything.

"Just so you know, Igar's dead."

I let that sink in.

"I also put you here, so that probably pisses you off, too."

"My friends will kill you."

"I don't think so. In fact, I wouldn't call your friends because one of them, maybe the person who sent you, killed Pavel."

He just looked at me.

"Someone he knew walked right up to him...someone he trusted got real close and shot him in the head." I left out the part that he was killed probably because he was talking to me. "The barrel of the gun was so close," I went on, "the shot burned his skin."

His face went white.

"Alex didn't tell you?"

Gregory just looked past me.

"That's probably because he's afraid. You and Alex are the last of the four from last night. Yesterday, somebody you trusted told you to come after me. That didn't work out too well, and now you know too much. Is that possible?"

"Fuck off," he said without too much energy in it, and turned away from me.

"I want you to picture Pavel. Picture him lying on the floor with a bullet hole in his head. His eyes were still open, by the way. I saw him. I don't want that to happen to you. Somebody doesn't trust you anymore."

Gregory turned back to me. His eyes seemed a little watery.

"Tell me who sent the four of you after me, and we'll keep you safe."

"Igar told me."

"Who told Igar?"

He turned away again.

"Okay, Gregory, don't say anything. Protect whoever it is who's going to walk in here with a nine millimeter and kill you."

I looked at Janie, but really spoke so Gregory could hear. "Better unwrap his wrists. Maybe he'll be able to put his hands up when his friends come to shoot him."

She nodded, "Okay."

Back to Gregory: "If you change your mind, just tell the nurse. She'll call me."

Gregory still didn't say anything. After a moment I moved away from the bed and motioned for Janie to come outside the room.

"What do you think?" I asked her once we were on the other side of the door.

"He's scared."

"Should be. Let him consider all this, and then we should have another conversation with him — maybe the Captain and me together."

Janie nodded.

I looked at her. "There are some bad people behind this. As you heard, Gregory's buddy tried to open my skull with a hatchet last night, and when one of the gang members came to me for help, he was killed."

"Point blank, you said. Is that true?"

"You could see the stippling on the kid's skin."

She just nodded. Nate wouldn't have picked this woman if she weren't up to the job. She definitely had an edge to her — I could tell — and I wouldn't want to be the one at the wrong end of her gun.

"Janie, some advice. Forgive me."

"Sure."

"I know you're carrying a piece. Don't wait too long to pull it out. And if someone comes in here and something doesn't feel right to you, don't let that person's hands disappear into a pocket or inside a jacket. Be safe."

"I know. Thanks."

"Also, we think it was a woman who shot this other boy, Pavel."

"Got it."

I nodded and turned back down the hallway.

As I continued back toward the nurses' station I made a mental note to ask Nate to assign a second person to the boy's room. Back-up was always welcome. Knowing Nate, though, it was already in his plans.

I rounded the final corner to the elevators and pushed the down button. I let out an audible breath. Time to move Alex out of my mind. Part two to the evening was ahead, and I was glad. With a smile on my face I entered the elevator.

Katie. Katie sitting on a porch swing in the cool evening. I had no idea if she had a swing, but it was a good image. Katie, me, and some wine. There was an unopened bottle of Cabernet in my kitchen this very moment. I walked out of the hospital without even noticing the concierge.

13

Katie lived in an area called Cedarcroft, a community west of York Road and just inside the city line. Homes were older, mostly shingled, and fairly large. All seemed to have a porch of one size or another, with huge, old trees lining both sides of the road. It really was a lovely, peaceful area.

I just wished I wasn't being followed.

As the neighborhood was filled with small streets and numerous turns, it wasn't difficult spotting the silver grey Taurus that stayed half a block back. I wasn't sure where he picked me up, and that annoyed me. Additionally, at this distance, and lighting being what it was, the driver was merely a silhouette. There was no telling who it might be.

I drove several intersections past Katie's block to park on another tree-lined street. Katie was expecting me, but this was going to take some time. I called her to beg for another fifteen minutes, then got out of my Jeep and started walking.

There was no destination in mind; I just wanted to see what my follower would do.

At the next corner I turned right, and surreptitiously noticed the driver had gotten out of his car. This person was definitely not a kid. He appeared to be in his late twenties and was dressed in dark pants and a white polo shirt. The shirt was not tucked in. Did the fact that he was older mean I had been upgraded? And if so, by whom?

By now, night had fully descended. Orange street lights flooded the area, turning the leaves and trees into otherworldly vegetation. Continuing up the block, I side-stepped a tricycle and moved a red wagon from my path near a driveway.

I took another right and went down a small street, heading back the way I had come, but on a parallel road. At the second house on the right a high hedge marked the property line along the right side. A good deal of the shrubbery was in shadow, thanks to ubiquitous thick trees. A quick glance backward confirmed that my follower hadn't turned the corner, so I walked onto the property, and moved close to the hedge. A big bungalow style house was just a few feet away on the left. The windows on the first floor were open, but any noise from inside was masked by a powerful window fan. I walked over to the deep shadow of the porch and disappeared into the blackness.

In a moment, the man in the white polo shirt passed by. He was looking up and down the block frantically. He may have had dark hair and a dark complexion, but I wasn't sure because of the lighting. His face wasn't familiar. As I watched him, I thought of Pavel. I also thought of a group of teenagers accosting me in Federal Hill.

The man turned around and walked back the way he had come, passing the front of the house. Without a sound, I moved behind him. He was half a head taller than me and on the thin side. With his back still turned, perhaps just two feet away, I spoke up.

"Excuse me."

The man spun around. His mouth was slightly open.

"Do you know what time it is?" I asked.

He just looked at me.

I hit him square in the face, breaking his nose. The man staggered back but stayed on his feet. Blood ran down his face and his eyes began tearing up — an involuntary response. He smiled, picked up his hands in a ready position, and then whipped up his right leg in a round kick to my head. Under other conditions he may have connected, but not now. I moved right into him so the kick couldn't come all the way up, and then swept his left leg out from under him. He fell straight onto his back. There was a distinctive *klunk* as the back of his head whiplashed into the cement sidewalk.

The smile was gone from his face. He was dazed — his eyes had a distant, unfocused look. With some effort, I grabbed him under the shoulders, and pulled him over the curb: his torso was in the street but his lower legs were still on the sidewalk. Both knees were now just above the gutter with clearance under them.

Leaning over him, I moved close to his right ear. "It's not polite to follow people." His eyes were refocusing. "By the way, it's 9:05."

I stamped down, first on one knee and then the other. Each time there was a distinct crack. The man passed out.

I bent over him and the first thing I found was a .45 Desert Eagle stuck in his waistband. That's why his shirt had been pulled out — to cover the gun. I stripped his shirt from him, avoiding the blood on his face, and used the polo to remove the pistol. Nate could check it for any matching ballistics. The man's wallet was next. His driver's license told me he was Arash el-Hanani. The rest of his wallet held some cash, credit cards, and several business cards. The business cards were in his name and noted that he was a chef at the Oasis restaurant. I put the business card back in his wallet and his wallet back in his pocket.

I stood over him for a moment, then dragged him by his belt into the middle of the street and left him there.

14

I didn't go far. In fact, I walked up the block a few hundred feet to a thick oak tree, growing next to the curb. Its roots had pushed up the sidewalk, creating a mini-pyramid of cracked concrete and earth. While that was an impressive feat of nature, more important to me was the generous cover the thick trunk provided.

The view down the block was unobstructed. I could see the motionless body in the middle of the road, as well as the entire street beyond. No one came by.

As I waited, I was very much aware that my pulse and breathing had picked up, stimulated by the sudden, yet controlled burst of energy that had flooded my body. Saliva had accumulated in my mouth and I swallowed slowly.

I waited for five minutes to be certain the man didn't have a friend nearby. Even as I thought about him, the man seemed to move ever-so-slightly on the macadam down the block. It was probably just some unconscious spasm. When he came to, one thing would be certain. In the days and weeks ahead, he would remember me. He would remember me every time the barometric pressure changed, or any time he had to climb stairs, or when he simply had to put one foot in front of the other.

Was breaking his legs really necessary? No. I could've followed him back to wherever he went, but that wasn't good enough. I wanted to send a message: *Enough*. And, *I'm coming for you*. Mainly, I realized the message was I was angry.

I waited another two minutes, then, satisfied the man had been alone, left him to be discovered by a passer-by.

By the time I drove the four blocks to Katie's, my system had begun to normalize. I stashed the man's .45 and shirt under my car seat and tried not to think about what had just happened. It was time to look forward to a more pleasant evening.

I pulled into a parking spot next to Katie's house, and no sooner had I locked my vehicle than I realized the wine I had intended to bring was still on the passenger seat. I shook my head, acknowledging that my mind wasn't totally at ease, and retrieved the Cabernet.

As I headed up to Katie's door, it opened in front of me.

"Hi," Katie said smiling. "I saw you coming up the walk."

"Hi." I kissed her on the lips. They were sweet.

For a brief moment, she looked at me, then said: "What happened?"

"What do you mean?"

"Your eyes. They're very...intense. And you're flushed."

So much for normalcy.

"Is everything okay?"

There was no sense in telling her about being followed or about breaking the guy's legs. "Just had a workout, that's all." I handed her the wine.

She took the bottle. "Are you sure you're okay?"

"I'm fine."

"If you say so." She thought for a second. "Let's go out."

"Go out?"

"Let me put this away for another time. Let's go out for a drink. Maybe someplace where we can walk around."

"Uhhh..."

"Yes?"

"Yeah, okay. That sounds good."

"I'll be right back." She kissed me lightly, then disappeared into the kitchen. "Where do you want to go?" she called from down the hall.

I thought about the man lying unconscious around the corner. Far away from here would be good. I did like the idea of walking around. "How about Fells Point?"

She emerged from the kitchen. "That'll be great. I haven't been there in a while."

"Good."

With that, I led her to the Jeep, and we headed out.

Fells Point is one of those areas around Baltimore that has a history going back to the 1700's. The area was a center for shipbuilding and commerce. Today, it's been reborn as both a residential district — off the main streets — and a neighborhood of Bohemian clothing shops, bars, restaurants, and more. While the area is busy during the day with shoppers and business people, the evening crowd leans toward sightseers and diners.

We mercifully found on-the-street parking near Aliceanna Street and then joined the late night masses on the sidewalk.

"So," Katie opened. "This is nice. Good choice."

I looked at her and smiled.

A moment went by as we strolled past an incense store.

"Fell's Point," I began in a mock tour guide voice, "was purchased in the 1720's by William Fell, an English land speculator. The area began as a major shipyard and ended up producing hundreds of sailing ships, including the famous Baltimore Clippers. The heyday of Fells Point was in the mid 1800's when more than 15 shipyards were operating at the same time."

I looked at Katie who was almost laughing at me.

"Fells Point," I went on, "in fact, served as the original Port of Baltimore, because the inner harbor basin was actually too shallow for bigger ships. Today, it's the home of a number of small theater companies, antique stores, eateries, and curio shops."

"Not bad."

"Remember, I'm a substitute history teacher, when I'm disguised as Clark Kent."

"How could I forget?" She let a moment go by. "So, how was the rest of Clark Kent's day after you dropped me off? Restful?... Productive?"

"Sometimes rest *is* productive."

"I'll agree with that."

"The afternoon wasn't restful. I went to Pavel's house to see how his folks were doing, followed up on some information, saw one of the gang members in the hospital." Broke a guy's legs. Left that out. "I've got a few leads, but I still don't know what's *really* happening."

"Do you want to talk it through?"

Talk about the guy who was following me to her house? How about the fact that he had an Arabic name and perhaps linked to an assassination attempt on an Israeli candidate? Or that I was now concerned there might be a terrorist cell here in Baltimore? That was my latest thinking.

"Let's talk about what to eat." I pulled her into a restaurant near the corner of Thames Street and Broadway called The Admiral's Sloop. It was a relatively small place, moderately lit, and was split between a bar in front and a restaurant in back. A wall separated the two rooms. The restaurant portion had small square tables throughout, and when we entered, we were directed to a meticulously set table in back.

"So," Katie said, "do you want to sit facing the room or facing the wall?"

I opened my mouth to answer, but she cut me off.

"You'll sit facing the room."

I smiled, shrugged and slipped into a chair with its back to the wall.

"So, where did we leave off with the Katie Harris story?

Tell me about your family. You were born in Massachusetts..."

"I have a younger brother living in New York. I think he works for a bank...or maybe it's a computer company."

"Maybe it's computers for a bank?"

"Could be."

"Parents?"

"Both live in Philadelphia. Retired. Dad was a car mechanic, mom was a school teacher..."

"Love life?"

"Thought you could slip that in, didn't you?"

"I'm smooth."

"Okay," she smiled. "I had been living with someone for five years. We broke up three month ago."

"Sorry."

"Yeah..."

I saw her look past me at nothing in particular. I didn't pursue it.

"And you like your job."

"I do. I love being with those kids. What about you?"

"Do I love being with those kids?"

"No, your life 'til now."

I began to say something, but our waiter — a young guy in a striped shirt, dark pants, and a green apron — came over with menus and to take our drink order. I ordered an ice coffee; Katie a Diet Coke.

After he disappeared, I looked at Katie. "My life. I think I mentioned I was born here, but went to college in New York."

"You went to Israel after graduation."

"That's the short version. The longer, more accurate version is that I left to do junior year in Israel. Stayed on a combined program with Tel Aviv University, then joined the army."

"That where you learned karate?"

"No. I've been doing it since I was about ten. First here, then in New York."

"You're very good. Very smooth. I could tell from before with the Israelis."

"Thanks. The martial arts and I have a symbiotic relationship. I treat them well and they treat me well."

The waiter came with our drinks. He asked if we were ready to order. We weren't. I poured the creamer into my ice coffee and dumped two packets of sugar into it.

"Anyway, I was pulled out of basic training for some...special opportunities and that kept me busy for about ten years."

I took a sip of my coffee. It was still bitter and I put another sugar in.

Katie didn't ask about the "special opportunities," though by the way she looked into my eyes I could tell she was wondering about them. I appreciated that she didn't ask. Instead, Katie moved the conversation forward. "What brought you back here?"

"It was time...I had to do something else."

Now it was my turn to look past her without focusing on anything specific.

"Maybe we ought to check the menu," she suggested.

We did, and after a moment I settled on a portabella mushroom sandwich with roasted peppers, onions, provolone, and Creole mayonnaise. Katie went for a salmon fillet.

"So," Katie said after we ordered, "would it help you figure this out if we laid out all the facts?"

I smiled. She had already asked me this.

"What? I shouldn't butt in?"

"You sound like a learning specialist."

"If you want I can draw a web of all the events so far."

"Maybe later." I smiled again. "Okay, this is what I've got so far. Eitan Lev, a leading candidate for the Prime Minister of Israel is almost killed by a gang member belonging to the Guardians of Heaven. They seem to be a group of kids, some Russian émigrés, some not."

"Why would they want to kill him?"

"Chances are they were hired by someone. But the name 'Guardians of Heaven' is bothersome because it sounds like it has religious connotations."

"Fanatics?"

"Don't know. These kids certainly aren't. Another curious thing: not all the gang members are kids...at least I don't think so. I came across a man tonight who may be part of the group... or not."

"What did he say?"

"Not much of anything."

She looked at me when I didn't elaborate.

"And then there's the 'Bella' connection. I need to find out who she is. Someone is definitely pulling these kids' strings, because they're terrified of talking."

"That may just be a gang mentality."

"Maybe, maybe not."

"So you're looking for a religious extremist group?"

"Perhaps. There is one thing that's really curious, though. The man I found tonight is an Arab. At least by the sound of his name."

"A Muslim extremist?"

"I don't know. This man may be Jewish for all I know...or an Israeli Arab. The problem is I have him on the one hand and the Guardians of Heaven, a gang of Jewish kids, on the other. I don't know if they're together, at odds with each other, or totally independent. I need more information."

"Maybe you need to speak to more gang members."

"That's in the process. One's in the hospital and he's not talking yet. There's also Pavel's cousin. He might be a good possibility, but he doesn't stay still long enough to talk to."

"So what's next?"

"Pavel's school. I'll speak to some people there. They may know something about the gang. I'll also put the word out that I'm looking for information."

"How do you do that?"

"I know where the gang hangs out."

"I don't think I would want to be there when you pay them a visit."

"I'll win them over with my sense of humor." I smiled.

Just as I finished my remark our entrées arrived, and we dug in. For me, the portabella-roasted pepper combination was perfect and Katie said her salmon was delicious. During the remainder of the meal we shifted the conversation to more mundane matters such as the different teacher personalities at school and the kids to keep an eye on. We also argued the merits of living in New York versus Baltimore. By the time the subject of culture came up, we were offered dessert menus. Katie and I looked at each other and then waived our rights to more calories — at least for the time being.

After paying the bill, we headed out of the restaurant and down toward the harbor area. As we crossed Thames Street we walked near the dock and could see a large schooner approaching the pier. We watched as the crew scurried about the deck, fastening lines and trimming the sails. They perfectly maneuvered in close to the dock and then jumped ashore to moor the vessel. It was impressive.

We headed back up Broadway on the other side of the street. At one point we passed a FedEx self-service stand, and I pulled out one of their large Tyvec courier envelopes...the kind that can't be torn, only cut. We then poked our heads into some of the galleries and marveled at some of the wrought iron modern art figures. For some of the more abstract sculptures we just looked at each other and shrugged.

By the time we got back to the car it was almost 11:00. Once behind the wheel, I pulled out the FedEx envelope and turned to Katie. "I have to make one stop before I take you back."

"Sure. FedEx? They're not open now."

"The police."

I grabbed a marker from my glove box and wrote Nate D'Allesandro's name on the envelope, and signed it simply with a "G." As Katie watched, I reached under my seat and pulled out the Desert Eagle stashed there. Handling it carefully by the man's shirt, I dropped it in the express pack, then peeled off the adhesive strip covering, and sealed the envelope.

Katie looked at me.

I smiled. "Don't ask."

She didn't.

We drove up Broadway, then cut over on Lombard Street and headed to the main police headquarters. The building was a huge structure with one-way tinted glass on all sides. I parked next to a hydrant and pulled out my cell phone. "I need to make a call," I said to Katie. She nodded and I phoned Nate. He answered on the second ring.

"Hi. It's Gidon. Sorry it's so late"

"Who'd you beat up this time?"

"Some old lady on Charles Street."

"What!?"

"Just kidding."

"So, this is a social call at...what time is it?"

I noted the clock on the dashboard. "Ten after eleven. Sorry." He must've been in bed.

"What's up?"

"I'm outside your office on Fayette Street and I have a present for you...a .45 Desert Eagle. Right now it's in a FedEx envelope and I want to drop it off without the desk officer inviting me to stay overnight." I looked at Katie and smiled.

"I'll call him. Is there a name that goes with the gun?"

"Arash el-Hanani."

"Wait a minute." I heard him scramble through a drawer. "Okay, spell it."

I did.

"So which hospital did you put this guy in...seriously?"

"Maybe St. Joe's. That'd be my guess." I was glad Katie couldn't hear the other half of the conversation.

"I'll check it out. By the way, Janie Marcus, my cop at Sinai Hospital, said you came by to talk to the gang banger."

"Yup. I gave the kid something to think about."

"That's what Janie said."

"She's good. I liked her. Could use some back-up though."

"Already done." There was another pause and I heard a muffled voice from the other end. "Rachel says hello."

"Hello back. Please apologize for the late call."

"I will.

"Talk to you tomorrow."

We hung up.

I turned to Katie: "Sorry 'bout the call. Didn't mean to be rude to you."

"I understand. Business first. Leave me the keys."

I handed her the keys, grabbed the FedEx envelope and went inside the police building. The entrance led to a small reception area and a uniformed African American officer behind a plate glass window. He was on the phone. When he finished, he turned his attention to me.

I leaned over to the two-way speaker above the glass. "Hi. I'm Gidon Aronson. I have a package for Captain D'Allesandro."

"Your driver's license, please."

I held up my ID to the glass.

"Put the package in the bin," he indicated a metal turntable under the glass window.

"Did the Captain call?" I didn't want to give him a package with a gun in it, unless Nate had cleared the way.

The officer nodded to the phone. "Yes, sir, he did."

"Great." I dropped the FedEx bag into the bin and the officer rotated the turntable so he could retrieve it.

"I'll see that the Captain get this, Mr. Aronson."

"Thank you." I waved and headed out.

The drive back to Katie's took fifteen minutes, and as I turned into her neighborhood off of York Road, I looked for signs of police or ambulances. I was thinking of an unconscious man in the middle of the street. But, all was quiet. I parked in front of Katie's house and walked her to the front door.

"Thank you for a great evening," she said looking into my eyes.

"My pleasure. Thanks for listening to me."

"My pleasure," she smiled.

I let a moment go by as I somehow seemed to have gotten closer to her. "I'll call you tomorrow."

"I hope so."

"But, there's something you need to know about me, and if you don't want to speak to me anymore, I'll understand."

"Truth in advertising?"

"Uh huh. I'm pretty much who you see. But there's the martial side of me that can get, um, not very nice, if you know what I mean. I like to think of it as violent but with style." I half smiled.

"I know what you mean. I saw you today in the dojo."

She said it, but I don't think she really understood the potential intensity. What happened this afternoon with the Israelis didn't compare to what Alli saw up close the other night. Or what I did mere hours ago to the guy who was following me.

"I just wanted to explain how I am sometimes."

"I understand."

My arms found their way around her and I kissed her softly on the lips. She returned the gentle pressure for more than a few heartbeats.

I pulled away to look into her eyes. "Well, I've got to go."

"Okay."

I smiled, not sure what that meant.

She leaned into me and kissed me again. "Good night."

"Good night."

She went inside and closed the door. After hearing the deadbolt slide into place, I headed back to the car.

On the way home, I thought about Katie. Her last kiss lingered on my lips. As I turned back onto York Road and headed downtown, I checked my mirror for any unwanted headlights, but all looked clear.

By the time I got home, I was ready for an epiphany. Perhaps the meaning of life was on my answering machine. In my office I flipped the rewind/playback switch on the phone's message system.

"Hi, this is Carol Cayhan calling. You substituted for me yesterday and today." Oh, God, not another request to teach. "I just wanted to say thank you. I heard you did a great job. Thanks again."

Well *that* was nice. Being appreciated is always appreciated.

Next message: "This is Amit. Call me." The Israeli agent's voice came on, snapping me back to the current world. Sounded urgent. Maybe he had some intel for me.

Next message: "Sifu, it's Jon. All I can say is one thing...Me, Evy ...*smokin'!* Just in case you were wondering."

I laughed.

Next message: "Hi, Gidon. It's Alli."

I stopped laughing.

"I'd like to talk to you tomorrow. Maybe we can meet for lunch or something. I miss you. Call when you can."

That was it, the last message, and I found myself staring at the answering machine, not sure what to do.

The phone rang and I scooped up the receiver, half expecting Alli.

"Gidon, David Amit. You just got home?"

"Just going over my messages. What's up?"

"Eitan Lev has been shot."

"What happened?"

"He was coming out of his hotel in New York when demonstrators across the street started shouting. It was a distraction, we think. There was a fight, and at that moment someone stepped up and shot Lev in the chest."

"And?"

"He was wearing body armor. He's okay."

"He's lucky it wasn't a head shot. Do you have the shooter?"

"Yes. *Shomrei Shamayim*. Guardians of Heaven."

"Interview the demonstrators."

"Done."

"All right, two things. Can you get me a dossier on Lev? As complete as possible. This group wants Lev dead. We need to know why."

"*Kain*. Yes. I'll call you when I have it."

"Use my cell phone number, if no one answers at the dojo." I gave him the number. "Also, I have a name for you to check. Arash el-Hanani."

"Who is this?"

"He was following me."

"I'll see what I can find out."

He hung up.

I called Nate. I didn't want to disturb him again, but it was necessary. This time he answered on the first ring.

"Hi. It's Gidon. Sorry, again. Eitan Lev has been shot. He's okay...he was wearing body armor."

"Lucky it wasn't a head shot."

"That's what I told the Israelis."

"This in Baltimore?" His voice was gravelly.

"New York. The *Shin Bet* guy said the shooter was from Guardians of Heaven."

"They must really want him."

"I'm getting a dossier on Lev tomorrow. Maybe we can spot the motive." I paused. "I really appreciate your help on this, Nate. I probably haven't said that enough."

"Anytime, anyplace," he repeated himself from when this whole thing started. "Talk to you tomorrow."

We hung up.

I sat in the room and rewound the day until my encounter with el-Hanani. That was enough. I headed upstairs, tucking it all away...Eitan Lev, Pavel, David Amit, and the rest. Instead, there was something else to focus on: Fells Point, dinner, walking around, a great smile.

At the top of the landing I paused for a moment. If I tried, and it really didn't take much, I could still feel Katie in my arms.

15

The Oasis Café was located in Mt. Vernon. In Baltimore, Mt. Vernon is not a former president's residence, but a park-like setting with benches, trees, a bronze statue of the Marquis de Lafayette on horseback, and a circular Washington Monument, the nation's first memorial to our earliest president. The buildings along the periphery of the park house The Walters Art Gallery and the Peabody Conservatory of Music. Mixed in with these famous institutions are book stores, boutiques, antique stores, and residences. In fact, I once checked out a tai chi class held on the top floor of a beautiful Victorian Gothic a block away.

The restaurant was located just west of the monument on Mt. Vernon Place. According to the eatery's web site, it was open for lunch, beginning at 11:30, so I got to the area by 9:30, and found an unobtrusive parking space that provided a clear line of sight to the front door. I took out a Nikon digital SLR with its attached telephoto zoom — borrowed from Jon — and waited.

Mount Vernon was such a beautiful area with its eclectic mix of structures and people that I didn't mind sitting and watching the goings on. On the southern part of the block was an antique store. Next to it was a bohemian boutique and next to that was an attorney's office. On the eastern part of the block were a Victorian-style apartment building, a used book store, and then a pricey tie and jacket-only establishment.

As I looked down the block at the quiet Oasis Café, I thought of Miyamoto Mushashi, the Japanese sword master who wrote *A Book of Five Rings*. In it, he tells a story about being challenged to a fight out in a field. He got to the site hours early, well before his challenger. He then waited in hiding beyond the appointed time. Only when his challenger was good and pissed off at his alleged non-appearance did Mushashi jump up and meet his opponent. The other swordsman was so emotionally bent out of shape, that Mushashi was able to take full advantage of his annoyance and surprise to best him in the ensuing fight — no doubt, slicing him into several pieces. I wasn't looking to slice and dice anybody, just arrive early enough to capture them in pixels.

By ten o'clock the climbing sun had cleared the buildings around me, and the shadows of early morning had disappeared, giving way to gorgeous spring sunlight. The streets became busy with pedestrians coming and going. At 10:15, the first person to arrive opened the front door of the restaurant. Through the long lens I could see that he was tall, perhaps six feet, dark-haired and dark complexioned, and wearing a solid blue shirt and black pants. I caught a profile shot as he fiddled with his keys, and then a full face when he pulled the door open. Once inside, he relocked the door and disappeared into the back.

Over the next ten minutes, three more people arrived, and the dark trousered man let each one in, in turn. Of the three, two were men, and one was a woman. The woman was probably in her early twenties, with long, straight black hair under a floppy straw hat, and wearing a flowered maroon and black wrap-around dress.

At 10:45, I got out of the car to stretch my legs and to find a different angle on the café. I planted myself next to a cement urn on the stoop of an apartment building. Across the street, the lights came on inside the restaurant, and the young woman plus one of the men began setting out goblets. Other than that, it looked like the tables had been set the night before.

As I sat on the steps, a young woman dressed in a halter and shorts walked by. She smiled at me with big expressive eyes and I automatically smiled back. Mt. Vernon was such a great place.

Movement inside the bistro supplanted thoughts of the great smile. I saw the black-haired girl put a small chalkboard in the corner of the front window. From my angle I couldn't make out the words, but the board probably listed the lunch specials. I wondered who was preparing them, as I knew the chef, el-Hanani, was in the hospital, probably heavily sedated. For a moment I considered how necessary it was for me to break both his knees last night, but then put any remorse out of my mind. The question to ask was, did the chef act alone or was he part of a larger group? If he were part of a group, were they awaiting an assignment...or was it already in motion?

As time passed, I meandered about and took photos of the Lafayette statue and the Washington Monument behind it. All the time, the front door of the restaurant was in sight.

At 11:15, fifteen minutes before the place was due to open, a tall man in a dark suit approached the door. I slipped next to the trunk of a tree and looked at him through my lens. He had great posture — he stood very straight — and had thinning salt-and-pepper hair. I zoomed in on his face. His complexion was pale, as if he hadn't been out in the sun for quite a while, and he wore plastic framed glasses. The man peered inside then knocked on the door. After a moment, one of the male employees, now wearing a white apron around his waist, let him in. Both disappeared into the back.

Suddenly, a car horn blasted from my right. It came from a red BMW convertible fifty feet away. The BMW with its college-age driver was honking at an older Ford and its even older driver in front of him. Apparently, the old man wasn't reacting quickly enough to a newly changed green light. The BMW, with one last shout of its horn, accelerated around the old guy. I looked back at the restaurant. Only a few seconds had passed, and I muttered to myself about being distracted.

It was five minutes before there was any further activity inside. When it came, the man with the straight posture exited quickly. He didn't look back, no one escorted him out, and he moved down the street with a focused, strong gait. I hung around for another thirty minutes, snapping shots of whoever entered the café. No one else stuck out. Patrons seemed mostly in pairs — pairs of men, pairs of women, and couples. I moved back to the stoop next to the urn for a final five minutes, hoping the woman in the halter and beautiful eyes would come back. When my magnetic good looks hadn't summoned her return, I stood up and left more disappointed than I would care to admit.

As I drove to the dojo, I considered the rest of my day. The mental list included a visit to The New School — Pavel's school — to see if the principal could shed any light on the Guardians of Heaven. There was also a meeting with Alli; Lord only knew how I felt about her at this point. There was David Amit — hopefully he had a dossier on Eitan Lev to share, and finally, there was Alex, Pavel's cousin. Leaning on him for some answers was definitely on the agenda.

Back at the karate studio, I entered to the sound of Jonathan teaching someone front kick: "The knee," his voice said, "comes up to waist level so that you could rest a tray on your thigh. Keep your supporting knee bent."

I rounded the corner to see him working with Evy. He was dressed in black gi pants and a red and black T-shirt with Chinese characters on it. Evy was in shorts and one of Jon's T-shirts — one of his white ones with a painted tidal wave on the front.

"Hi, kiddies," I said, approaching them.

"Hi, Sifu," Jon said.

"Make sure those toes are curled back," I said to Evy.

"Yes, Sensei," she said, with her supporting leg beginning to tremble from the strain of supporting her outstretched leg.

"Good response," I said to her, smiling.

Jon looked over. "I teach them right." He turned to Evy. "Work on this side some more and then work on the left side. Ten kicks slowly and then ten kicks regular speed."

"Okay," Evy said and she began to throw slow front kicks.

"So, Sifu," Jon said coming over to me, "what's going on?"

We walked into the office and I sat down at my desk, putting his camera down. I brought him up to date...the hospital chase, the guy following me, the phone call from Alli, Lev being shot, my intent to go to the school and talk to the principal. I purposefully left out Katie.

"Whoa baby. Alli called you?" He did pick out the important stuff.

"She left a message on the machine last night."

"Forget Guardians of Heaven, Sifu. What are you going to do about Alli?"

"I have no idea. Call her... meet. Talk."

'What if she wants to get back together?"

"She does, I think."

"Whoa, baby," he said again.

Evy came in from the main workout area. Sweat was running down the sides of her face. "Now what?" she asked Jon.

He took her hand and said, "Work on the basics I showed you, then I'll come over and I'll look at everything."

"Okay." She went back to her workout.

"So," Jon continued, "Alli?"

I loved Jon for his sense of priorities. "I'll talk to her. I'll be honest. Problem is, I don't know myself."

'And Katie?"

"Jon…" I trailed off with a look he knew well.

"Just asking."

"What are you doing later?"

"After I finish with Evy, I was going back to the office. What's up?"

"Two things. I need you to print the pictures I took this morning," I handed him his camera. "Thanks, by the way."

"Of course."

"And two, how would you like to help intimidate Pavel's cousin? I want to find out what he knows."

"I'd love to."

"I'll call and let you know what I have in mind."

"Okay."

"All right, I've got to make some phone calls, so if you don't mind…"

"Calling Alli?"

"Go teach your new protege, Jon. And if you don't leave me alone, I'll tell her about your *other* proteges."

He laughed and exited the office.

I would call Alli, but first I needed to speak to Pavel's principal, if I could get a hold of him. The New School was listed in the phone book, so in just a few minutes I had the school on the line. As I waited to be transferred to the principal's extension, I debated how to present myself – straightforward, or should I pose as a prospective parent. There was no reason not to be up front.

"Dr. Cole speaking."

"Hi, Dr. Cole. My name is Gidon Aronson. I'm investigating the death of one of your students, Pavel Demirovsky."

"Yes. Pavel. We're still in shock here."

"I understand and I'm sorry for bothering you, but is it at all possible for me to meet with you today? I have a number of questions, you may have the answers to that might help me figure out what happened."

"I'm sorry, but Pavel's funeral is this afternoon."

"I didn't know that. I'm sorry. "

"And I spoke to the police already."

"I'm sure you have." I paused a moment. "To tell you the truth, I have a personal interest in finding out what happened. Pavel reached out to me and he was actually at my place when he was shot."

There was silence at his end. I couldn't imagine what was going through his mind: Was I a friend?...a foe?...Was I involved in the murder?

"Can you come to the school now? I'll be here for another hour and a half before we have to leave. If you come soon, I'll make time for you."

"Thanks. That'll work."

He gave me directions and then we hung up.

That was the easy call. The next one made me nervous.

Alli answered on the first ring.

"Hello." Her voice sounded...great.

"Hi, it's Gidon."

"Hi."

"Got your message. How are you doing?"

"Okay." A moment went by. "I'd like to talk about what happened the other night. Maybe that'll help."

Talk about what happened? Did she mean what I did or her reaction?

"Can you meet me after I finish work?" she continued.

"Of course. I have a few appointments, so I don't know when exactly we can get together. I'll call you when I know the timing. Is that okay? Maybe we can hang out at the Inner Harbor?"

"Sounds like a plan. You'll call me?" She didn't sound sure of herself...or maybe she wasn't sure of me.

"I'll call."

"Okay.

We hung up and I just looked at the wall.

"So, what are you going to do?" Jon walked back in.

"Not a clue." After a moment: "Lock up for me, would you? I have to go to school."

The New School was about twenty minutes away, up Park Heights Avenue, not far from Pavel's parents' place. It was situated in a large converted house at the corner of a side street and a main road. I parked on the side street away from traffic and followed the sidewalk to the entrance.

The front yard occupied a double lot, and was populated with several tall oak trees that lent a quaint, residential feeling to the property. The house itself was tan stucco with black shutters and trim. To the left of the front cement staircase an iron railing led up to the front door. No signs announced that this was a school, and had I not double checked the address, this could have been an innocuous homeowner's front door I was about to walk into. With just a slight hesitation, I stepped inside.

The foyer was businesslike, yet warm. A Persian carpet covered the floor, a three-dimensional painting by the Israeli artist Agam hung on the narrow wall to my right, and a small Queen Anne table below it presented a display of school brochures. Straight ahead was a staircase, and to the right and left were larger rooms. I looked around, and heard "Can I help you?" coming from the right.

I followed the voice and walked into what once must have been a fairly large dining or living room. Two desks were in the center of the room, with a secretary behind each. Both ladies were busy at work. All four walls were lined with photos of teenagers in the midst of different activities: studiously working in classrooms, making presentations, playing soccer, shaking an adult's hand, wearing goggles and working in a chemistry lab...

The room itself was cluttered, filled with filing cabinets, supply cabinets, the secretaries' desks, and several chairs.

File folders were everywhere: on table tops, on chairs, on the floor. A teenager, dressed in a black T-shirt and black jeans, was working at a filing cabinet behind one of the desks. I turned to the secretary closest to the door who watched me as I entered. She was probably about thirty, had a round face and dark red hair, and was dressed in a high-necked lavender blouse and black skirt.

"Hi. I'm Gidon Aronson. I have a meeting with Dr. Cole."

"Which Dr. Cole?"

"I didn't know there was more than one."

"There's Dr. Aaron Cole, the headmaster, and Dr. Hannah Cole, the school psychologist."

"Dr. Aaron Cole." I smiled.

"One moment, please." She picked up her phone and dialed a two digit number. She announced my arrival, then turned back to me. "It'll be just a minute."

I looked around for a place to sit, but all the chairs had papers or file folders on them.

"Oh, just put those on the floor," the secretary said. "We're in the middle of shuffling file cabinets and we just don't have any place to put the folders."

A minute later, a woman, probably forty, came over to me. She was about five-seven and had tapered, jaw-length dark hair with some strands of gray mingled throughout. Her thin frame was flattered by a well tailored red blazer and navy pants.

"Mr. Aronson," she held out her hand, "I'm Hannah Cole. Pleased to meet you."

"Likewise." I shook her hand; she had a strong grasp. "I'm sorry to come here under such circumstances."

"We're just glad that someone besides the police is looking into what happened. Maybe an extra pair of eyes will help."

"I'll do what I can."

"My husband is wrapping up a conference call and asked me to show you around."

"That'd be great. I was really fascinated when I heard about this school. How long have you been around?"

"This is our second year."

As we chatted, Dr. Hannah Cole took me from room to room. On the first floor, off of the secretaries' area, was the kitchen. It seemed to have the original wood cabinets and they looked great.

"Refinished?" I asked, running my hand over one.

"Before school started this year. A private donor made some funds available. We have twenty young men here, and the kitchen, as you can imagine, is probably more important than the classrooms."

"Twenty teenagers? I hope you have a large pantry."

"Not large enough," she laughed. "We're constantly going to the store." She turned to two teenagers, who were sitting at a round kitchen table, eating sandwiches. "Right?"

They nodded.

She led me up a narrow back staircase to the second floor.

"This is where our classrooms are. We have six main classrooms here. With only twenty students, there's plenty of personal attention."

"How many staff members do you have?"

"We have seven part-time teachers who, thank God, have managed to balance their other teaching schedules around us."

"They sound dedicated."

"They are."

We poked our heads in a classroom. The floor was carpeted in a gray Berber, and the walls were off-white. Ten desks were set up in a circle, with the teacher's desk as part of the configuration. A dry erase white board dominated the front wall, while posters of ancient Greek ruins, China, Japan, England, and Israel filled the others.

We stepped into another classroom. For the most part the room had the same carpeting, colors, and shelving, but instead of a circle of desks, there were two rows of five desks facing each other, with a no-man's land of empty floor space in between — to allow for teacher pacing.

As we moved back into the hall, I looked around. There was a long flowery patterned couch against a side wall with a mop-haired blond student stretched out on it. He was reading a recent *Sports Illustrated*. For a school there didn't seem to be much teaching happening at the moment.

"Mr. Aronson?" I must have had a quizzical expression on my face.

"No classes?"

"We gave the students off for the day because of the funeral. We'll actually meet here in half an hour so we can all go as one group."

"Sounds like a very supportive thing to do."

"Thanks." She looked up and down the hall. "Well, the only rooms left are the basement — you don't want to see that — and the upstairs bedrooms. And you *really* don't want to see those. Trust me."

I laughed.

"Well, I think Aaron should be off the phone by now." She led me down the stairs and through an entryway cut into a former exterior wall that now led to a small vestibule. We walked just a few feet to a closed door. Hannah Cole knocked on it then poked her head inside. She looked back at me, waving me over.

Dr. Cole's office looked like an overgrown library, with floor-to-ceiling bookcases, two computers — one Mac, one PC — and a large wooden desk covered with textbooks, papers, and a baseball on a short pedestal mount. The baseball looked as if it had some signatures on it. The wall to the right had Judaica-themed photos and paintings. One painting was of a chasid holding a Torah surrounded by a ring of dancing students. To its right was a paper-cut of a phrase from *Song of Songs*: "I am to my beloved as my beloved is to me." Next to that, was a framed needlepoint of the Western Wall in Jerusalem. Straight ahead as I walked in, and directly behind Dr. Cole, was a bay window, allowing a full view of the expansive, manicured back yard.

Dr. Cole was sitting at his desk when I had entered, and he

rose to greet me. He was wearing a dark suit, and as he stood, I could see he had great posture. Dr. Cole had thinning salt-and-pepper hair, his complexion was light — as if he had been sequestered out of daylight for quite a while — and wore plastic-framed glasses. He held out his hand and I knew I had seen him before. At 11:15 this morning he had walked into the Oasis Café.

16

I didn't believe in coincidence. I didn't believe Jim Lovell happened to draw the Apollo 13 mission. Or that Ed Sullivan just happened to snag the Beatles for their first American appearance. I didn't believe that the Headmaster of a school with gang members as students just happened to visit a restaurant whose chef had been following me with unknown intent...and carrying a .45 Desert Eagle. I had no idea what the connection meant other than there was one.

Dr. Aaron Cole had his hand extended and I shook it. "Pleased to meet you," I said. "Thanks for seeing me on such a difficult day."

He waved me to a seat and Dr. Hannah Cole pulled up a chair next to me. "It's a tragedy. Nothing less."

The fact that Dr. Aaron Cole was involved in what was going on didn't negate the value of talking to him, even though he must have known about me.

I was now interested in his body language, what he said, how he said it, the direction his responses would take, and what he didn't say.

"Pavel was involved with a group called Guardians of Heaven," I began. "What can you tell me about them?"

Hannah Cole looked down, shaking her head slowly, sadly. "Until yesterday I didn't realize he was involved with them. I wish I had known."

"I didn't know either," Aaron Cole added from behind his desk. "We could have intervened. The group wasn't for him. He was a sensitive young man and it's a rowdy bunch sometimes. A good fit for some, but not for him."

"Tell me what you know about the group."

"The kids here formed this group out of a social need," Hannah said. "The boys feel out of place to begin with."

"They come from families where they are totally lost and their questioning of their parents is not tolerated," Aaron explained. "There are sections of this community, this Jewish community, that are very religious. The parents follow the letter of the law and don't, as we say, look right or left."

"In many cases, the parents grew up in the secular world and then turned very religious later in life," Hannah said.

"So," Aaron picked up, "in addition to being teenagers and rebelling against what teenagers normally rebel against, they're also faced with this religious rigidity."

"You have a lot of unhappy kids," I concluded.

"There are *some*," Hannah said.

"Not everyone is unyielding, of course. But the problem comes in when the parents don't know how to handle the kids and so they just lay down the law. Many children resent that."

"So these kids stay away from home, hang out, and get into trouble," I said. Considering I had some students of my own who were once in trouble, I understood that.

"Right. And that's where this school affects a change," Aaron Cole continued his wife's thought. "A proper environment that doesn't feed into their rebelliousness and anger is paramount."

"They are at such an important stage of their lives. Really at a juncture," Hannah put in.

"*All* these kids are important, and we in this community can't risk losing them. And that's exactly what would have happened with the kids here — if we hadn't come along."

"For example, we had students who, before they were with us, were involved in petty crimes," Hannah said. "We came along with an environment where there are rules, for sure, but also a certain amount of freedom."

As I listened to what they were saying, my eyes wandered to two diplomas hanging up near Aaron Cole's desk. One was a Ph.D. from Hebrew University and the other — all in Hebrew — was from a rabbinical seminary.

"And if you don't mind me asking, you're financially able to run this school because...?"

"Private donations," Hannah said.

"Private Donations," I repeated, smiling. "That name has come up before."

218 Stephen J. Gordon

"There are some very generous people in this town," Aaron Cole said seriously.

"Indeed."

"So, going back to Pavel," I refocused. "You feel he must have gravitated to the Guardians gang, because he was unsure of himself...or felt out of place?"

Just then, there was a knock on the office door and a tall lanky teen with an untucked, unbuttoned flannel shirt came in, carrying a slip of paper. He looked at Aaron Cole.

"Dr. Cole, I was wondering if—"

"*Excuse me,* Michael," Hannah turned to him, before her husband had a chance to respond. The tone of her voice had a sudden chill to it. "We're in a meeting. Can it wait?"

"Oh, I'm sorry. Yes, ma'am, it can wait. I'm sorry," he repeated, then began to exit.

Aaron Cole stopped him. "One minute, Michael. Have you finished the reading I assigned?"

"Uh..." he looked at his headmaster, then shifted his weight and looked out the window.

"Michael, studying happens before anything else. Nothing is more important."

"Yes, sir."

Aaron Cole nodded and when nothing else was said, the boy exited, quietly closing the door behind him.

Hannah turned to me. "I'm sorry, Mr. Aronson."

I smiled. "No need to apologize." Back to Pavel. "So you were saying that Pavel must have gravitated to the Guardians out of a social need?"

Hannah Cole responded: "He was somewhat lost and definitely looking to belong to a group. You could see that in him. I guess that's the only thing I can come up with."

I thought about the boy who had made himself comfortable at the dojo. He seemed to have a sense of humor and seemed fairly secure.

I looked at the baseball sitting on a mount on Aaron Cole's desk. I could make out the last name of a signature on the ball. *Ripkin.*

"You mentioned earlier that had you known Pavel was in the group, you could have intervened. What did you mean?"

Aaron answered: "Twice a week we have small discussion groups. Hannah, who is a psychologist, leads one, and I lead the other."

Hannah took over: "If from the discussion we see that there is an issue that needs more active attention, we have a one-on-one with the student and really get down to specifics. I have some psychologist friends who get involved and we try to break down whatever the problems are and help the student take an active role in changing the behavior pattern."

Sounded vague enough to me.

"Any idea how many of your students are involved with this gang?"

"I don't know if I'd call it a gang," Hannah said. "I guess there are, maybe, five students involved."

I thought, *five students*? If Aaron Cole and his wife were part of this, the veracity of their answers might be less that a hundred percent. So, five kids in the gang? I'd have to find out independently.

I turned to Aaron Cole. "Are all the students male and Jewish?" I was thinking of the name "Bella," the woman Pavel had called before he was killed. Again, the answer might not be truthful, but it was worth asking.

"Yes. For us, we're taking care of our own community, mainly because no one else does. And as far as only having male students, at this age, having the classes mixed would bring up more issues than we're prepared — or able — to handle at this time."

"I totally understand."

"So, you said on the phone that he was at your place at the time?" Aaron asked.

"Pavel must have gotten involved in the Guardians group and wanted out. He came to me, I think, for asylum and for help."

Hannah looked at me. "I don't mean to be rude, but why would Pavel come to you? Did he know you?"

"Well," I hesitated for effect, "his buddies tried to kill me, and he probably didn't realize what he had gotten into."

"Oh my God," Hannah said.

"Well, they weren't successful," I smiled.

"Thank God." Aaron Cole added.

"Do you know a kid, probably about 17, named Igar?" I had wanted to say "Hatchet Boy."

They both shook their heads.

"How about a Gregory Segev?"

Aaron Cole looked at his wife, then answered: "We have a student named Gregory *Fistel*. He's been missing for two days now."

"I don't know if it's the same kid, but this Gregory was part of the group that attacked me. He was Igar's partner."

Hannah turned to her husband. "Do you think...?"

"I don't know if it's our student. We'll have to find out."

They didn't ask more about what happened, or for a description of Gregory, or whether I knew where he was. Also, if this *were* the same Gregory and he was in Sinai Hospital, his parents would have been notified and they'd have contacted the school.

If it were the same Gregory.

Maybe the Doctors Cole and Cole were totally innocent and were preoccupied with their own communal loss to think clearly.

It was possible.

The fact of the matter was I didn't know who at the school was involved; just that Aaron Cole was at the café this morning where Arash el-Hanani worked. That had to indicate something.

At any rate, if they *were* connected, the Coles now saw I was actively involved. Of course, if they were on the inside, this was old news. Either way, maybe seeing me on their doorstep had to be unsettling...or maybe I was giving myself too much credit.

I stood up. "Well, I don't want to tie you up any more. I know you have a difficult afternoon ahead of you."

Both Hannah and Aaron Cole got to their feet.

"I'm glad you stopped by," Aaron said holding out his hand.

I shook it. "Thanks for filling in some of the details." I turned to Hannah Cole. "And thanks for the tour. The school is very impressive."

"Thank you," she shook my hand as well. "And you're welcome."

I headed out of the office, wondering whether the Coles were looking at the back of my head or at each other.

Once outside, I took the sidewalk around the house to the side street where I had parked. After settling behind the wheel, I turned on my cell phone to see if any messages had come in. There were two. I drove around the corner so as not to be on the Coles' doorstep, parked, then retrieved my voice mail.

The first message was from David Amit: "This is David Amit. I have the dossier." He meant the file on Eitan Lev. "Call and we'll meet." Short and to the point. Very Israeli.

The second message was from Nate: "Hi. Your circle of friends gets more and more interesting. The name you gave me, Arash el-Hanani, didn't come up in the database. But, when I ran the prints from the gun, all sorts of nice little flags and cute windows popped up. It seems that el-Hanani's real name is Mahmoud al-Sharif, and he's on every Watch List from here to Jerusalem. The Feds will want in on this one. We gotta talk. Call me."

So it *was* likely there was a terrorist cell here and it was most likely connected to Hannah and Aaron Cole and to the Guardians of Heaven. I thought about the house I had just come from: a school — a Jewish school — with students who were former drop-outs, who were now involved in a gang, a terrorist cell, and someone with a dislike for an Israeli candidate for Prime Minister. And somewhere in the mix, someone found a need to kill a boy named Pavel.

So a meeting with David Amit and Nate was next. We should confer and share what we knew.

The phone in my hand vibrated. I pushed the answer key.

"Hi. It's Alli."

"Hi."

"I was wondering how your day is going and when we could get together."

"The day is coming along. About getting together..." Would I be in the mood for Alli after meeting with Amit and Nate? Difficult to say. Also, I needed to see if Jon printed my Café Oasis pictures. So, after Jon but before Nate and Amit? "How soon are you free?" I asked.

"I'm out of the clinic in fifteen minutes." She worked in a physical therapy clinic not far from downtown.

"Are you still up for the Inner Harbor?"

"Sure."

"Okay. I have an errand to run and then some meetings after I see you, so instead of picking you up, can I just meet you there?"

"Sure."

"Let's say forty-five minutes. I'll meet you near the bow of the *Constellation*."

"Sounds good. How will I know you?"

I had to smile at her playfulness. She always brought a youthful energy with her. It was one of the traits that had attracted me.

"I'll be the man in front of the ship, with sunglasses, and probably sweating more than anyone else. My clothes may be a little out of style, but I'll be wearing them with confidence. Actually that might just be fashion ignorance."

She laughed. "I know that look. See you soon."

I disconnected the call and wondered what the hell I was doing. Alli had shut down on me before and now I was flirting with her? Wasn't I trying to walk away? Deal with this later.

I called David Amit. "It's Gidon."

"Yes."

"Let's meet down at the Inner Harbor at Rash Field. On the bleachers."

"Where?"

I described the location. Next to the merry-go-round beside the Science Center was a large field. Running the length of the field was a stretch of bleachers that faced the harbor.

"In an hour and a half," I added.

"Fine."

"Also, bring an extra copy of the dossier."

"Why?"

"For my friend, the cop."

"*Lo.* No."

"He already knows everything and he's my friend. Your man Yaron gave him a description of Pavel's killer."

There was silence on the other end. He was no doubt weighing the security issues.

"All right. Ninety minutes."

Next I dialed Nate. "Hi. Got your message."

"You've got an interesting party going on there, buddy."

"And I'll cry if I want to."

"Time to talk."

"Definitely. I'm meeting with the Israeli security chief in an hour at the Rash Field bleachers. We'll share."

"I'll be there."

I pulled away from the curb with all sorts of flashbacks running through my head. It was time to start talking everything through. If Katie were here, she'd probably take out some paper and we'd lay out all the events so far. Probably not a bad idea.

I called Jon to see if he had printed the Oasis Café shots. He had and they were at his office on St. Paul Street.

Jon's office — really his father's — was on the eighth floor of a twelve story building. The structure probably dated back to the '30's, but had been updated multiple times with new lighting fixtures, metal-framed windows, more efficient A/C, fresh carpet, and so on. Two part-time secretaries shared a single desk in a well-lit reception area, but neither of the ladies was present. Jon's open office door was behind the receptionist's desk and to the left. He came out just as I was walking over.

"Hi. Just finished these, Sifu. There are twenty prints." He handed them to me.

I shuffled through the stack...twenty pictures of people coming and going from the Oasis Café. Aaron Cole's photos were near the bottom of the pile. I had one of him entering and one of him leaving. The angles were more three-quarters than full face, but both were clear enough for an ID. I took the pictures and moved them to the top of the bunch.

"Thanks, Jon." I looked toward his open office and raised my voice slightly: "Hi, Evy."

"Hi, Sensei," she answered from inside.

I smiled at Jon, thanked him again then headed out.

Ten minutes later I was parking near the Inner Harbor at the base of Federal Hill... actually not far from Alli's townhouse. I crossed Light Street next to the Science Center and walked along the harbor promenade.

By now it was late afternoon and the pedestrians were out in force. More than once I had to weave through strolling tourists and meandering locals. One of the areas of congestion was opposite the Light Street pavilion. At the water's edge but in front of the pavilion was a visiting British frigate. Up close, it was a huge ship, with almost its entire superstructure contained in an envelope of grey plating. The frigate looked like a water-going bullet. A gangplank joined the port after-deck to the harbor walk and visitors were filing aboard.

After giving the ship an admiring scan, I continued along the cobblestoned promenade and around to another ship tied up at the Inner Harbor. This one was also a naval vessel, but considerably older: the *US Frigate Constellation*. The *Constellation*, sister ship to Boston's *Constitution*, was the last all-sail powered warship that the government had launched. I stopped near the bow and looked back toward the British vessel. It was an interesting juxtaposition: two ships of war from two different eras: one all wood with three masts, and one sleek and smooth, designed to incorporate stealth technology.

"Gidon," I heard a familiar voice and turned to see Alli approaching. She was wearing her work uniform of a dark green polo shirt and white pants.

"Hi." I leaned over and kissed her on the cheek.

"Well, you're kissing me. That's good," she smiled, a little unsure of herself.

"Are you kidding. I'll always kiss you."

We started walking.

She looked at me, "So, how're things?"

Well, let's see. Since she sent out vibes that I was not for her, I started a great relationship with Katie, Pavel was killed, I visited a *shiva* house, had a chase through a hospital, broke the legs of a probable terrorist, had a great dinner with Katie, staked-out a restaurant, met two educators who were somehow involved in all this, and discovered I really liked kissing Katie.

"Things are okay," I said.

She let a few seconds go by. "I was thinking of the other night...when you were attacked."

She jumped right into it. I was surprised. "Yes?"

"You did what you had to do."

I nodded.

"If you didn't, you would have been killed."

"And probably you."

"I had never seen anything like that before, I've watched you work out and throw Jon around and teach, but—"

"You weren't prepared for the real thing."

She shook her head. "Are you mad at me?"

"No," I said softly.

We turned around and starting walking back the way we had come.

"I don't know what to tell you," I looked at her. We continued in silence for a few more steps.

"Can you tell me what that attack was all about?...What's going on?"

I half smiled, knowing it would take too much out of me right now to explain it all. Funny, if Katie were here I would probably be happy to share my thoughts.

"I wish I knew," was the only thing I could say.

"It has to do with that assassination attempt at the banquet the other night."

I nodded.

"Do you want to tell me about it...over dinner?" she looked at me and I could feel she was genuinely interested. She pulled me closer and kissed me on the lips. I remembered her kisses, her taste.

"Okay," I smiled.

"Good choice."

"But I can't now."

She kissed me again.

"Really. I'm meeting with my police friend and an Israeli security guy. I can't."

"Okay."

"Maybe tomorrow night. How about for now, we wander into one of the pavilions and find something sweet."

"Mmm. Ben and Jerry's."

"I'll even buy."

She looked at my face, wiped the sweat that was running down my left cheek, then smiled.

"You're on."

Had any awkwardness been broken? I wasn't sure.

We headed into the Pratt Street pavilion, the one that housed The Cheesecake Factory, and found the ice cream stand. For whatever it was worth, talking and being with Alli was an effective reprieve from the reality that awaited me. We strolled some more and savored our ice cream. There were still moments of silence, but they seemed okay. Soon, it was time to meet Nate and Amit, so I said goodbye to Alli, and then walked in the direction of the Science Center.

The harborwalk went past the science museum and continued on to the other end of the harbor. A modest marina poked into the water on the left, adding a needed serenity to the commercial area, with its floating piers and quiet boats. Opposite the marina and on the other side of the promenade was a large rectangular open field. Beyond it was a stretch of bleachers. I headed over to them.

In the two minutes it took me to get there, I saw David Amit approaching from the opposite end, carrying two large manila envelopes. "*Shalom*, Gidon," he said when he was a few feet away. We sat down about halfway up the stands, in the middle section. "Here is the file on Eitan Lev." He handed me one of the large manila envelopes.

"Did you have a chance to go through it?

"I just looked very quickly. Meanwhile, you gave me a name to check...Arash el-Hanani? There is no such person in our files."

"That's because his real name is Mahmoud al-Sharif." He pulled out a pen and a slip of paper and wrote down the name. "Seems he's a major red flag."

"Not any more." We turned to see Nate making his way over to us. He, like me, was sweating.

I introduced them: "David Amit, Captain Nate D'Allesandro of the Baltimore City police. Nate, this is David Amit of..." Amit looked at me, concerned, as if I was about to give away a secret. "...of Israel's security services." That was vague enough, I suppose.

They shook hands.

"Arash el-Hanani a.k.a. Mahmoud al-Sharif has been killed." Nate continued to explain. "Someone went up to him in his hospital room, where he was in traction by the way..." he looked at me... "put a gun to his chest and shot him three times. And your young Gregory Segev, the one at Sinai Hospital, is dead, too."

"What happened?"

"Someone who had more finesse, poisoned his food."

I shook my head. Gregory seemed on the mend, both physically and emotionally. He wasn't like Igar. Gregory fell in with the wrong group, and was at the wrong place at the wrong time. It was really too bad. "And your officer?"

"Janie Marcus?...She's fine. Upset she couldn't have prevented it."

"Who is this Gregory?" Amit asked.

"He was one of the kids who attacked me the other night." I turned to Nate. "You still have the boy who tried to assassinate Eitan Lev at the banquet. What's he saying?"

"Just that he wanted to kill Lev because Lev wants to give too much land back to the Arabs."

"He's lying," Amit countered. "Lev is more conservative politically than a number of other politicians. He believes in returning minimal land, not very much. He also believes in troop deployment in areas under Arab control. That's the opposite of what the kid is saying." He paused. "There must be something else."

"Does he seem like a radical to you?" I asked Nate.

"No. He doesn't know anything about what's going on politically."

"Somebody has an agenda," I said. "Now that we know this, maybe you can lean on the kid some more."

"What about the two people who were killed?" Amit asked.

"Three," I corrected. "al-Sharif, Gregory, and Pavel."

Nate thought aloud: "Gregory and Pavel may mean more to our would-be assassin than al-Sharif. The kids may have been buddies."

A long moment went by. I looked out at the harbor across the way. From where we were I could see the two pavilions of Harbor Place, the British warship, and the *Constellation*. Directly across the harbor was the National Aquarium with its apex roof, capping the rainforest inside. In the water in front of the aquarium were numerous paddle-boats maneuvering in the mini inlet.

Amit looked from me to Nate: "Why would these people be killed now? Fear of them talking, I understand. But the overall timing..."

I reached into a pocket and pulled out my photos. "Mahmoud al-Sharif, who Nate says is on a terrorist Watch List, was the chef at a restaurant in Mt. Vernon called the Oasis Café. Earlier today I saw this man," I handed Nate and Amit a copy of Aaron Cole's photo, "go into al-Sharif's restaurant before it opened."

"Who is this, do you know?" Nate asked.

"Aaron Cole."

"I know that name," Amit said softly. I could see him reaching into his memory. "I don't know from where, though."

"He's the principal of a local Jewish school for kids who are life drop-outs. He takes them in and tries to bring them around. His wife works with him. Her name is Hannah."

"I know those names from somewhere," Amit repeated.

"That doesn't explain the timing of the murders today," Nate reasoned.

"Well, first of all I caught Mahmoud following me. Maybe they thought I was getting too close. Or, maybe because I paid the Coles a visit today, someone got worried."

"*Efshar*. It's possible," Amit said.

"Cole's kids may have formed the Guardians of Heaven."

"There's still no intent," Nate wondered, staring out at the harbor. "We don't know *why* they want to kill Lev in the first place."

"The answer may be in here." Amit handed Nate the envelope with Lev's dossier. "We all need to go through this. It's our file on Lev...biography, family, military service, political philosophies."

"An Arab terrorist and a Jewish school?" Nate wondered.

"I know. It's not like Aaron Cole hates the State of Israel...not with a diploma from Hebrew University or from a seminary in Jerusalem. That's not the impression I have."

"There are many *very* religious people in Israel, though, who are against the State," Amit commented.

Nate looked confused.

"I know, it's hard to believe," I said. "Many ultra, ultra religious don't believe in a secular state, only one that is totally religious."

"These people don't even serve in the army for mandatory service," Amit added.

"But, that's not the Coles," I said. "They don't fit that profile. They don't behave like extremists...they don't seem to teach like extremists."

"Unless," Nate said looking at me, "they're really good actors."

"I'll pass his name on to Tel Aviv," Amit said. "If there's an Israel connection, they might know his religious and political leanings."

Nate looked at the photo of Aaron Cole. He then flipped through the rest of the stack, depicting all who had entered the Oasis this morning.

I pointed to the shot of the man who had opened up. "This man was the first to arrive. He opened the place. These others," I pulled the photos of the three others who had arrived early, "must be waiters or other staff."

Nate tapped the edges of the stack of pictures, thinking. "If these guys are part of the restaurant where this al-Sharif worked, and he was killed to keep him silent..."

"Maybe they'll be killed, too, or..."

"Maybe they did the killing," Amit finished my thought.

"If this is a terrorist cell," Nate continued, "and they did do the killing, they may not hang around." He looked at Amit and me. "Want to go for a ride?"

We drove in Nate's old Jeep to the Mt. Vernon restaurant in less than five minutes. And that was without his siren; just Nate speeding and weaving. In the off chance that someone was still there, he parked up the block on Mt. Vernon Place in a bus stop. We were out of the vehicle before the motor was barely off.

As we approached the café we could see that the lights were on in the window, but couldn't make out much else. Pedestrians were walking up and down the sidewalk, but there was no traffic either in or out of the restaurant. In less than a minute we were in front of the entrance. We each looked through the window. No one was inside. In fact, the place was abandoned: the lights were on, but all the tables were left unbussed. Nobody had cleaned up...dirty plates were on the tables, drinking glasses stood partially filled, and napkins lay tossed onto tablecloths. Someone had left in a hurry. Nate tried the door just in case. It was locked.

I turned to the Israeli. "Where is Eitan Lev now?"

"Back in Jerusalem. I'll alert everyone."

I knew that Nate would see to it that airports and the FBI would be notified about these restaurateurs.

"We still have the Coles and their students." I said to both men. "Also, Hannah Cole mentioned more than once that an anonymous donor made major contributions to them. Maybe we can find out who this financial source is."

Nate nodded.

"And I don't want Pavel's killer to get lost in the shuffle here," I said. Frankly, that was the entire reason I was involved. Plus, I didn't like the idea of kids being manipulated for someone else's agenda.

"Speaking of which," Nate pulled out a paper. "This is the sketch based on your man's description of the woman Pavel let into the dojo." He handed it to Amit, and I looked over his shoulder. "It's not going to do us much good."

I saw what he meant. The composite was totally non specific: Female, with a round face, long straight dark hair, and a baseball cap. From the sketch, it was impossible to tell who it was beyond just a superficial impression.

After a final look at the deserted restaurant, we returned to Nate's Jeep. We rode back downtown in silence, each of us with our own thoughts. While Amit and Nate had more research to do — follow-up on photos, check Cole's finances, read Eitan Lev's dossier — I considered the one member of the gang we hadn't caught up with yet: Alex, Pavel's cousin. Thanks to my friend at the pizza shop, I had a pretty good idea where he might turn up. I would wait for him and then we would have a civilized conversation.

17

Jonathan and I sat patiently in my Jeep outside Blues Pool Hall and Game Center, waiting for Alex to come out. The billiards club, along with a hair salon and an electronics store, were on the left side of a hotel-shopping complex out Reisterstown Road, but tucked away from the high profile main entrance. In fact, hidden on this side of the building, the strip of shops was completely forlorn. The stores had no walk-in traffic; you had to know they were there. To the property owner's credit, there was a modest parking lot on this side — someone was an optimist — and Jon and I had a perfect view of all the shops. Fortunately, there were enough cars to park among so we didn't stand out.

We had staked out the pool hall for two hours, and now as dusk merged with night, the wayward Alex came out. He was dressed in a dark sport coat and khakis; he must've come here right after Pavel's funeral. No tie. At least he wore a jacket for the occasion.

He sauntered out of the pool hall alone, turned to his right and headed for the back of the complex around a tennis club building. I nodded to Jon, and we both got out of the Jeep.

The weather that evening continued to be warm and muggy, definitely unusual so early in the season. I hoped that this was not an indication of a non-existent spring. Alex continued to walk toward the rear of the building, keeping the wall of the tennis club to his right.

Pavel's cousin was the last of the quartet who had attacked me the night after the assassination attempt. The others were all dead now. Pavel, was killed for just showing up at my place, I took care of Hatchet Boy, Igar, and Gregory, his partner, was killed in the hospital by persons unknown. Alex, whether he knew it or not, was probably on somebody's short list. He needed to see the danger he was in so he would help me.

Before Alex rounded the corner I saw him reach into a pocket and pull out a cigarette. I silently followed him. When I turned the corner I saw that he had stopped behind the building to light his smoke.

"Do you really enjoy those?" I asked.

He spun around, saw me, and his eyes went wide for a second. It really was just a flash as he recognized me, but in that second I knew exactly what he was going to do. He turned and ran...

...right into Jonathan.

Pavel's cousin stopped in place, looked back at me, then at Jonathan, who now smiled at him. Alex reached into a pocket with his right hand and began to pull something out. Jon didn't let it happen. He punched Alex square in the bicep. It was a great move. I know because I had taught it to him.

Alex's arm, for all intents and purposes, would be useless for probably ten minutes, if not more. A folding knife fell from his hand.

"Not very sociable," I said.

He ran in my direction, trying to get around me, but I was prepared for that. I tripped him.

He looked up at me.

"You're such a difficult person to get a hold of, Alex."

He got to his feet.

"If you would just stand still for a few minutes, we could get this over with."

Jonathan closed the gap between the two us, with Alex in between. The boy turned to see Jon approach him.

"What do you want?" he turned back to me.

"For you to stay alive."

"Fuck you."

I looked at Jon and shrugged. I turned back to Alex and saw him watching me for a response. I gave him one. I punched him in the other bicep.

I think he said "shit" about four times.

"I need you to listen very carefully." I moved close to him. Alex was squeezing his eyes shut in pain and was trying to move his arms. I waited until his eyes opened. "I don't care about the other night when you guys attacked me. What I care about is why and who told you to do it."

Alex shook his head.

"Let me put this into context for you. Gregory is dead. Someone poisoned him in the hospital. Didn't know that?"

He just stared at me.

"You already know that your cousin Pavel was shot at close range in the head." I let a moment go by. "The people you're protecting are not nice people. They *will* kill you."

He turned away.

As we were behind one of the main buildings, the huge air conditioner fans were blowing hot air. Alex was sweating, but not because of this heat.

"They shot your cousin. Someone went right up to him and pulled the trigger. Pavel saw who did it, too. Can you imagine that? He thought he could trust this person. He had called for help. That's right, for help. And do you know what this "friend" did? This friend went right up to him...got right in his face and shot him," I repeated. "Do you understand? Pavel didn't know it was coming until it was too late. He was expecting help and what he got was a killer."

Alex continued to look past me.

"I can protect you. The police can protect you."

He responded quietly. "No."

I turned to Jon and sighed. "Do you know what this means, Jon?"

"No, Sifu, I don't."

I was taking a big risk on this one...going for the big bluff.

"I'll just have to call Bella."

"What?" Alex looked at me. "My sister has nothing to do with this."

"Your sister?"

I thought of the sweet young woman at the *shiva* house...the one who was kind and seemed thoughtful. Bella?

"No," I said. "She's not your sister."

"What are you, an idiot? She's my sister."

"Abby's not Russian." I remembered her name. Good thing.

"It's a joke...a nickname Pavel gave her, because she didn't have a Russian name. She has nothing to do with this. She loved Pavel."

That would explain why he called her. But she didn't kill him. I saw the hurt in her eyes. She also didn't match the general police sketch of the killer. As bad as it was, it didn't resemble her at all.

"So Pavel," Jon confirmed, "called Abby, and Abby innocently called someone else... someone who either directly killed Pavel or had..."

"...an associate do it." Another thought flashed through my mind and I had to suppress a shudder. All the loose ends in this case were disappearing...by sudden death. If Abby indeed called someone who then had Pavel killed, she was a loose end, too. I began to sweat.

I stared hard into Alex's eyes. "Your silence is not helping anyone, including your sister."

He just looked at me.

"Tell me who organized the Guardians of Heaven."

Alex shook his head. "If I don't say anything to anybody, no one else will get hurt."

"How about your sister?" This came from Jon, who was now next to Alex.

"No."

So much for intimidation.

"Bella, or Abby, had to have called someone," I reasoned. "You know that. And you know that whoever Abby called, probably arranged for Pavel to be killed, if he or she didn't do it personally. Abby knows who is responsible — though she doesn't realize it."

Alex remained silent.

"That puts Abby in danger. A lot of danger."

"So protect her."

"Tell me who's in charge."

A long moment went by. He looked down at the asphalt, then back to me. "Igar. Igar was in charge."

Igar, lover of hatchets. I looked at Alex. He seemed smaller than I had remembered. To his insulated perspective, Igar could have been in charge of his small group. But if Igar had controlled them, someone had to be controlling Igar. In structure, the system resembled a terrorist cell. The foot soldiers didn't really know who was up the ladder from them.

Nate could talk to Alex. The police captain might be able to lean on him harder than me.

I needed to find Abby and make certain she was okay. I didn't like the feeling in the base of my stomach.

"Igar wasn't making the decisions," I said to Alex, implying there was more to it than just Igar. It was also a warning for him to watch his ass. I pulled out my wallet and found my business card. "Call me, but don't wait until someone's at your door."

I turned to leave, but looked down at the folding knife that had fallen from Alex's hand. I scooped it up. "This will piss off the wrong person." I put it in my pocket and Jon and I left.

We walked back to the Jeep without saying anything. Before we got in, I turned to my favorite student. "We've got to find his sister."

We headed to the *shiva* house, hoping Abby would be there. There was a definite sense of dread in my mind. Abby was an important link, and if I knew that, so did someone else.

As we drove, I could visualize Pavel in my office, picking up the phone from my desk and calling Abby. He would say he was okay...He had gotten himself into something and that he was hanging out with this karate guy... He just needed time to think. Yes, don't worry. He was fine.

Then for some reason, Abby hung up and called somebody else. The now deceased Mahmoud al-Sharif? Someone at school? When I found that person...whoever was responsible...I'd ask him for the time of day, just like I had asked al-Sharif last night outside Katie's. But this time, I wouldn't stop at broken legs.

I just hoped Abby was around to talk to.

When we arrived at the *shiva* house, the Demirovskys were in the same position I had last seen them...on the couch. Now, however, the apartment was crammed with people, young as well as old. Lights were on all over the place and the room was filled with the sound of everyone talking — there were conversations in English, some in Russian. Jon and I walked through the crowd. No one was paying attention to us.

"Sifu," Jon asked, "what does Abby look like?"

"She's a very attractive young woman probably in her mid-twenties...short white blonde hair...dressed for the office."

We continued looking around, weaving our way through the visitors. I didn't see her, and the more faces I saw that were not hers, the more anxious I became. Maybe she was just not here and would be back later. Maybe she had to run to the supermarket for some food. Maybe she had to run home.

Or, maybe she was getting out of her car and someone had come up to her, put a gun behind her right ear, and pulled the trigger.

"She's not here," I said to Jon. "This isn't good. We'll have to find out where she lives."

"Do you know who to ask?"

I scanned the group and saw an older, weathered, dark-haired woman carrying a platter of bagels, cream cheese, and lox to the dining room table. As she moved it to the center of the table, I realized she was the woman who had interrupted Abby and me yesterday.

Motioning to Jon, we walked over to her.

"Hi. I'm Gidon Aronson."

The woman was now setting out a stack of paper plates and plastic cups. She looked up.

"We met yesterday," I continued. "I was talking to Abby near the door and you came over. Do you remember?"

Up close, the woman looked to be in her mid-sixties and had the dark, leathery skin of someone who has been out in the sun too often and too long.

"Yes, I'm her Aunt Sheila from Pompano." Her voice was raspy, like that of a smoker.

"I don't see Abby. Is she here?"

"No. She left last night at the end of the evening. She didn't come back today. Not yet."

That sinking feeling dropped further. I took Aunt Sheila by the elbow and gently led her to the side. "I'm investigating what happened to Pavel. I need to get a hold of Abby. Do you have her home phone number?"

"Yeah, wait a minute. It's written on the fridge."

She disappeared into the kitchen and a few moments later came out with a piece of paper in hand.

"Here you go. I wrote it down for you."

"Thanks." I looked at the number on the paper. "And this is in Baltimore?"

"Columbia." She named the planned community halfway between Baltimore and D.C.

"You don't happen to have her work number?"

"This is all I have, babe. But she works for some senator at the World Trade Center downtown."

"You don't know the name of the senator, do you?" If you don't ask, you'll never know.

Aunt Sheila turned to a group of older men hanging out in the center of the living room. "Hey, Sam," she called.

The group of men were in the midst of a heated discussion and ignored Aunt Sheila. I heard the name Joe Torres being bandied about, as well as Earl Weaver's.

"Sam," Aunt Sheila tried again.

This time, a tall silver-haired man who could have been in his seventies turned around.

"Where does Abby work?" Aunt Sheila called. "What's the name of that senator?"

"Daniels," the man answered and went back to his discussion.

"Daniels," Aunt Sheila rasped to me.

"Thanks." I reached for my wallet and a business card for the second time that night. "If Abby comes by, could you ask her to call me, please. Thanks."

Jon and I turned for the door.

"I hope you get the bastard who did this."

"I will."

As Jon and I stepped outside, he turned to me. "I'm sure she's okay."

I just looked at him.

"I mean, Sifu, she could be out shopping. She could be picking someone up at the airport. Maybe she had a doctor's appointment."

"All true."

"You don't think so."

"No."

"So what now?"

"We try Abby's number at home."

I dialed the number Aunt Sheila had given me. After three rings an answering machine came on. I left a message for her to call me.

"Now what?" Jon asked.

"Now we call Captain D'Allesandro and have him meet us in Columbia."

The community of Columbia lies halfway between Baltimore and Washington, off of Route 29. It was the sort of planned community where a GPS is almost essential, as so many of the streets and foliage look the same. Abby's apartment was in a complex adjacent to Little Patuxent Parkway and Columbia Road. Nate's old, dark green Cherokee was already parked in front when we arrived.

"So," Nate said stepping out of his Jeep to meet us, "how does it feel to have a police captain at your disposal?"

I patted him on the back. "I don't know. How does it feel?"

"I wish it were for other things."

"Indeed."

Nate pointed to a white CRV parked head-in next to us. "That's her car."

"You checked the registration?" Jon asked.

"Just now."

"How 'bout her apartment?" I asked.

"Didn't have the chance."

"I hope she's home," I said half to myself. Of course I had visions of her lying on the living room floor, shot in the chest.

We stepped inside Abby's building — a garden apartment building with dark cedar shake siding — and went up to the second floor. The lighting in the hallway was bright and the interior carpeted and clean. Four apartments were on this level; Abby's was straight ahead with an apartment to the left and two apartments to the right.

Nate rang the bell.

As the moments passed, we looked at each other. That image of her on the floor grew more vivid.

He knocked on the door.

Nothing.

"You don't have a magic document that says we can break in, do you?" I asked.

Nate shook his head.

"Neighbor?"

Nate turned to Jon. "Pick one."

Jon nodded to the left. Nate walked over to the door and rang the bell. After a moment, there were approaching footsteps and then the door opened. A man, probably 30, in a white shirt, tie, and dark pants looked out at us.

Nate had his badge ready. "I'm Captain D'Allesandro of the Baltimore City Police. We have reason to believe your neighbor Abby Moskowitz may be missing. When was the last time you saw her?"

"Maybe yesterday morning when we both left for work."

"Do you normally see her in the morning?" I asked from next to Nate.

"Not all the time."

"Her car's out front," I said.

The man in the shirt and tie shrugged.

"Did Ms. Moskowitz leave a spare apartment key with you, in case she was locked out?" I asked.

"No. Try Julie Gardner on the other side."

"Thanks."

He closed the door and we stepped over to the apartment across the way. Nate rang the bell. After about fifteen seconds, a dark-haired woman in her twenties, wearing a lavender T-shirt and white slacks answered the door.

Nate once again displayed his badge and went through the routine: "Miss Gardner?..."

Ten seconds later we got to the question I wanted answered: the last time the neighbor saw Abby.

"This morning. We were both outside. But I was going to my car and she was going back into the building."

"How did she look?" I asked.

"Fine. Like she was dressed for work."

"Did Ms. Moskowitz leave a spare key with you, in case she was locked out?" Nate asked.

"Yes, I have one. Give me a second."

She disappeared back into her apartment. My mind wandered again. Abby's car was out front and she wasn't answering her door.

"Here," Julie Gardner handed Nate a key on a green plastic Ocean City key ring. "Same key fits both locks."

"Thanks."

We walked over to Abby's door and Nate unlocked the dead-bolt and then the doorknob. The neighbor was still watching us when we stepped inside.

Abby's apartment was dark — it was already after nine o'clock — and Nate flicked a switch near the door. A halogen torchiere came on revealing a spacious living room with white walls, white couch, two matching upholstered armchairs, round glass coffee table and a wall unit with a large flatscreen television in the center. Abby was not lying on the floor in a pool of blood.

The living room opened onto a dining room and a hallway. We followed the hallway to the kitchen and then further down to two bedrooms. The master bedroom was at the end of the hall. A queen-size bed dominated the room, made up with a flowered comforter. Opposite the bed, were a dark wood dresser and framed mirror. A walk-in closet was on the left.

The three of us wandered about. No one was home. In the bathroom, a single toothbrush was in the holder and cosmetics were out on the counter. In the kitchen, countertops had been wiped, dishes were in the sink, and the small table had been cleared. Over in the dining room the *Washington Post* had been plopped near one end of the table. It looked like the front section of the paper had been pulled and read — it had been re-folded, but all the pages didn't line up.

"Well," Nate said coming over to me, "nothing seems disturbed. I checked her answering machine. Nothing unusual there — except your call."

"Most of her clothes are still there," Jon said.

"How could you tell?" I asked.

"Just one or two empty hangers."

I looked at Nate. "I don't know if that's bad or good."

"Either she's away and travels light, or she's just not home."

"With her car still here? I guess we just keep—"

My thought was interrupted by a cell phone ring. It was Nate's.

As he listened, he reached into his pocket and pulled out a folded piece of paper that was dog-eared and already written on. "Give me the number again?" he asked into the phone. He wrote something down. "Thanks. I'll call you back soon."

He hung up and turned to me.

"Well, just what you wanted to do right now."

"What?"

"Go to Israel."

Jon and I looked at him.

"Hannah and Aaron Cole are at this very moment boarding a British Airway flight to Tel Aviv."

"What does that mean — and how do you know that?" Jon asked.

"It could mean they're going on a simple trip, business or pleasure," Nate responded. "Or..."

"Or," I took over, "they could be running." A thought which didn't make me feel better about Abby's disappearance.

"I know this doesn't answer anything about Abby," Nate read my thoughts.

"I have visions of her lying in some park off the highway somewhere, shot in the chest."

"She'll turn up."

"I know." Alive or dead she'd turn up.

"How did you know about the flight?" Jon asked.

"We put an alert out to all airlines for the Coles. Not to stop them, but to contact us."

Nate still had the phone in hand. I pointed to it. "Any names to the faces on the Oasis staff?"

"Not yet. Your friend Amit may be more help there."

We turned off the lights in the apartment, locked the door, and returned the key to the neighbor. Nate took her phone number in case he needed to follow up.

Back in the parking lot, Nate leaned against my Jeep and I leaned against his. Jon was in the middle.

I went first: "I'll call Amit and ask that his people follow the Coles when they arrive."

No one said anything. We could hear the crickets.

"Shit," Nate said.

I looked at Abby's CRV parked five feet away. "Who did she call?"

"The answers are probably halfway around the world...between the Coles and the staff of the Oasis Café."

I let a few moments go by as I thought about Pavel and Abby. "Well, I've got some phone reservations to make and I've got to pack."

"You'll check in on Laurie," Nate said.

I smiled at the thought of seeing his daughter again. "She'll be the best part of the trip." After another moment: "Keep an eye on Alli and Katie while I'm gone."

"I'll try to not let them talk to each other," he smiled.

"Yeah, that'd be good."

He looked at me. "Be careful, my friend." He gave me a hug.

"I will. I'll call and let you know how to reach me."

He got into his Jeep, Jon and I got into mine, and we headed for home.

On the way back to Jon's place, I asked him to cover my karate classes and to keep an eye on the shop. When I finished going over those details, I added, "So, I expect that you'll be giving Evy a lot of personal attention while I'm gone."

"I've already started, you know. She's very talented."

"Hmmm. Just don't expect me to test her for black belt when I get back."

"C'mon, Sifu, of course not. Brown Belt, maybe." He smiled.

I dropped him off then went home to make reservations and pack. Online I found a flight to Kennedy and an El Al flight to Tel Aviv, both departing tomorrow. I didn't even want to think about the money. Next, I threw miscellaneous clothes into a carry-on. I also called Amit and told him about the Coles and that I was going to Israel to see what I could turn up there. He said he would arrange for agents to watch Hannah and Aaron Cole when they'd arrive in the morning. No doubt Amit would show up in Israel, too. It was where all this seemed to be heading.

There were two more calls I had to make. Before I did, though, I checked my voice mail in case there was something there that would affect my plans. I guess I should have done that before.

There was one message:

"Hi. It's Katie. It's about 10:00. I'm just sitting at home watching a DVD and reviewing some tests. I've got wine in the refrigerator...the bottle you brought last night we never got to share. If you feel so inclined and have the time, come by and we can open it. Call if you can. I'll be up late."

I had to smile. Katie was going to be my second call. The first one was to be Alli. I had to tell her I was leaving. If she were home, I could run by, talk to her, then head out again. Or maybe I could just say something over the phone. I actually didn't know how to respond to Alli's rekindled interest. With Katie now a presence, I felt awkward about her.

I dialed Alli's number. The phone rang five times and then her machine answered. My heart rate picked up.

"Hi, It's Gidon. I was hoping to come by." I felt uncomfortable with the half-truth. "I have to go to Israel tomorrow to follow up on what's been going on. Sorry about the last minute notice. I leave early, but won't get in until the next morning their time. I'll call first chance I get. Talk to you soon. Bye."

The anticipation of the next call made me nervous but for an entirely different reason.

Katie answered on the second ring.

"Hi, it's Gidon."

"Hi."

"So, you still there, working on papers and watching TV?"

"Yup. That's my exciting life...propped up in bed, working on a stack of assessments, and watching episodes of old shows." She paused for a millisecond. "So, are you going to rescue me from all this?"

"It's a thought."

"Don't think too hard."

"I'll be over in about half an hour."

I hung up and finished packing. I was glad I called. I was even more glad that Katie had called first.

Turning back to the carry-on, it seemed incomplete. In earlier years I would have packed some special paraphernalia — a knife, a gun — but now, as everything was X-rayed, particularly on El Al, even weapons in the checked baggage were a problem. Whatever I needed I could get at the other end.

It was after 11:00 by the time I got to Katie's. Traffic cross town had dwindled to the occasional driver, and this time, there were no recurring headlights in my mirror. I pulled into a spot in front of her house then headed up the walk. Katie opened the door and smiled that great smile of hers.

"Hi, is this the teacher who never rests?" I asked.

"No, she lives on the other side of town. This is the teacher who amuses herself with students' papers and inane romantic TV shows and movies."

"Good thing I'm here to distract you." I stepped in to the

house, wrapped my arms around her and kissed her.

After a moment, we separated enough to look into each other's eyes.

"Well," I said, "that was an eight on the lip-o-meter."

"Only an eight? Hmm..."

She kissed me again. I wasn't stupid. If I had said a ten the first time, we might not have had the encore.

"Not bad. Not bad." She smiled and I took her hand and led her to the couch. "So, how was your day?"

"Well, if you really want to know..."

"Oh, I do."

"The sixth and seventh grades are away on class trips, so the energy in the building was very different."

"Decibel level, too, I bet."

"Of course we had a staff meeting."

"So that countered not having the sixth and seventh grades."

"And what have you been up to?"

I sighed.

"That good?"

I gave her the abbreviated version of the day, but hit all the highlights...the Oasis Café, the Coles, the Gregory and al-Sharif murders, and Pavel's missing cousin.

I left out meeting Alli.

"So, what does it mean?"

"It means I need a glass of wine."

Katie smiled. "Wait here."

She disappeared into the kitchen and was back less than

twenty seconds later with two glasses of Cabernet. "I was ready for you."

After a few sips, I elaborated on the state of affairs.

"Pavel called his cousin from my dojo. My guess is she either called someone at the café or she phoned the Coles. Probably the Coles. Now whether the Coles called anyone else, I don't know. There's also this Guardians of Heaven group that has to be connected somewhere. Why they're involved in a political assassination attempt, I have no idea. I also don't know who is pulling their strings."

"There's something else."

"I have to go to Israel. It's the next step."

I saw her eyes darken for a moment. "You sure?"

"No. But with Alex's sister missing, and both the Coles and the Oasis Café people gone, it's the place to make connections."

"When are you leaving?"

"Tomorrow morning."

Katie just looked at me and I moved closer to her on the couch. I put my glass of wine on the floor and did the same for hers. Brushing the side of her face with my fingers, I kissed her briefly. She returned my kiss then put her head on my shoulder. I closed my eyes.

After a few seconds she asked quietly, "What happened in Lebanon?"

I let a moment go by. "I rescued a hostage."

"It was very dangerous, wasn't it?"

"Yes."

"It's never very far away from you, is it, what happened there."

"No." My response was barely audible.

Katie turned to me and I looked at her eyes that were so close to mine. I found the sweetness of her lips just inches away and I gently kissed her. In a few moments I moved from her mouth to the curve of her neck below her ear. She had a beautiful neck, too. From somewhere deep within her throat came a slight moan. Katie turned her head, and our lips met again. The tips of our tongues touched and a definite tingle went from my lips down to my groin where it lingered, and then to my knees. Her hands glided over to my chest and played with the buttons on my shirt, before unfastening them.

We found our way upstairs, undressing each other as we went. Our clothes, dropped to the floor, marking our path. With each step I could feel my heart quicken. At the top of the landing we pressed tightly to each other. Our apparel was long gone. I lost all sense of my surroundings. There was only Katie. I held her head gently and kissed her closed eyes. With my hands, I followed her curves, from the sides of her breasts down over her hips. Changing directions, I ran my hands up her back. Her skin was smooth and electric; I could have sworn I felt a vibration beneath my fingertips as they moved over her an inch at a time. Katie ran her fingers through my hair and then came down my back and over to my thighs. She caressed them and then moved over to the front. I stepped back slightly so she could touch me. My breath became irregular.

My hands found a spot just under the curve of her behind,

and I pulled her closer, if that were possible. With my left hand I reached up and caressed her right breast. She backed into her bedroom, but we didn't make it to her bed. I lifted Katie and she wrapped her legs around me. I lowered her to the floor and she directed me to her.

Sometime later we did make it to her bed. In the darkness of her room, with both of us now totally at ease, Katie lay partially across me, with her head on my chest. I had my eyes closed though I was awake, enjoying the warmth of her body and the feeling of her heart beating on my chest.

"I'd like to tell you a story," I said softly.

Katie shifted a little, so she could look into my eyes. She hadn't been sleeping either.

"It's not about Lebanon, but about a woman named Tamar."

"A beautiful name," Katie said softly.

I nodded, my mind already going somewhere else. "Tamar was born in Haifa, the granddaughter of *chalutzim*, early pioneers in the land of Israel. Her grandparents had immigrated in their youth to what was then Palestine, just after World War II. They wanted to settle the land and make a home for themselves there. They met and fell in love during the rough times after the State of Israel was declared, when Arab forces descended from all sides to destroy the country. Tamar's family survived the war intact, and continued their dedication to the land and to the people.

"Despite the inherent conflicts, Tamar's parents felt strongly about co-existence with the Arabs. Her mom was a teacher who taught in a mixed Arab-Jewish school, while her father sold farming equipment to whoever needed it, Jew or Arab.

"Time passed and Tamar was born. She grew up, becoming a beautiful girl, with dark hair and inviting dark eyes. She was petite and graceful and could easily have been a star dancer if she had wanted. But her passion was the outdoors. She loved hiking through Israel's many parks and nature reserves. By the end of high school, Tamar's hiking skills were so proficient that she often led youth groups on overnights that combined hiking and camping.

"After high school, she went into the army for mandatory service, and eventually became an instructor on survival in the wilderness. College followed, and in her sophomore year at Tel Aviv University, came across a very sure-of-himself American who was in Israel for a year or two."

Katie looked into my eyes. My gaze drifted off hers.

"The American finished his senior year with a degree in History. Graduate school called, but didn't really interest him. Instead of continuing along an academic route, the American joined a special army program for sixth months. He found he enjoyed military life and stayed on in the army. All the while, he and Tamar grew closer and spent all their free time together. The American officially moved to Israel, and established a dual citizenship so he could join a Special Forces program. He found he had an affinity for the work. He would disappear for weeks at a time, but the days passed quickly because he loved what he did and he knew that Tamar was waiting for him.

"Tamar, meanwhile, went into social work, to help families who were victims of terrorists. Her caring was limitless, as was her energy. When the American was off-duty, she brought him into her parents' and grandparents' homes. They were warm, vivacious people whose homes were always open to him. Tamar and the American started talking about a future together."

Katie put her head back on my chest.

"The American disappeared again on a cross-border operation, but before he left, he and Tamar agreed to meet for lunch upon his return. The operation was more difficult than expected, but a success nonetheless. He called her when he was back, and they planned to meet in a Jerusalem café near Zion Square."

Katie was back to looking into my eyes.

"It was a beautiful October day. It had rained the night before and the sky was cloudless. The American was early, taking into account the difficulty of finding a parking space in downtown Jerusalem. Miraculously, he only had to circle the block once before finding a spot about two blocks from the café. He parked at a meter and gave himself plenty of time. He had just left his car and was walking toward Zion Square when a sudden, deep explosion rumbled through the air. Black smoke billowed over the rooftops ahead of him."

Katie's eyes began to fill with tears.

"The American ran for those two blocks, not even remembering crossing streets or dodging cars. He rounded the corner to find that the café was nowhere to be found. Instead, there were just pieces of furniture and blackened wood, scattered all across the sidewalk and street. Cars that had been at the curb were blown onto their sides, their windows shattered and doors punctured by hundreds of flying nails that had been packed in the explosive.

"There were bodies everywhere and pools of blood. For the longest time — but probably it was only mere seconds — there was total silence. The American looked at the bodies. There were two young school girls, lying facing each other motion-less...and a grandmother staring up at heaven...a man, wearing a waiter's vest, face down in the street...a soldier was lying on his side."

I looked at Katie.

"Tamar wasn't there. The American looked over every per-son he could see, and Tamar wasn't there. The sirens came and ambulances pulled up. The American walked around where the café had been and then crossed the street. Windows on shops opposite the building were gone, leaving empty, cavernous holes where the glass had once been. And then he saw her. She was on her back on the sidewalk directly across from where the café had stood. Her eyes were open and there was not a mark on her. No blood, no bruises, not a scratch. She was alive...but ebbing away.

"I sat on the sidewalk and held her in my arms. She seemed very calm. I told her it would be all right...that the ambulances were there. I didn't know it then, but Tamar had been halfway across the street when the bomber detonated himself in front of the restaurant. The force blew her across the street, while the blast from the explosion ruptured her lungs. She was fine on the outside, but her organs had been destroyed. Tamar died in my arms as I was kissing her forehead."

There were tears streaming down Katie's face.

"Life goes on, you know. The American eventually came back to the United States, only in part because of what happened to Tamar. For now, he's at peace — at least a portion of him."

"I am so sorry."

"It's okay. There is still beauty in the world and people to love."

"And people to care for you."

"And people to care for you," I repeated.

Katie and I spent the remainder of the night holding each other.

18

The El Al flight from Kennedy left at 4:00 the next afternoon, but between flying up to New York in the morning, and then having to arrive 3 hours early for the security check, the day was basically a write off. Once aboard the Israel-bound plane, I took my aisle seat on the right side of the 747 so I could have more leg room and get out in a hurry if I needed to — though I hoped I didn't need to run up and down the aisle for any reason.

We took off on schedule and almost immediately began heading north and east. A small rectangular video screen was inset into the back of every seat, so with a graphic of our route on display, it was easy to follow along...up the coast to Newfoundland then arc across the Atlantic.

Twenty minutes after being airborne our angle of ascent flattened, signaling we had reached cruising altitude. I stood up and wandered about to get a sense of the plane's complement.

It was completely filled — a great sign of the confidence people had in the stability and security of Israel. A few years ago, a plane like this might only have been half or three-quarters filled.

As I looked around, travelers on our flight seemed to be mostly college kids, and professionals probably in the thirty-to-forty year age range. There were a few grandparents and a number of young families as well. Out of professional curiosity, I looked around to see if I could spot the undercover security people — young, fit, serious-looking men in their early twenties, probably just out of the army — and came up with a few possibilities. One man was sitting mid-plane on the aisle in the middle section; another in the rear near the back right.

Now that our climb had leveled off, the flight attendants got busy distributing dinner. While they made their way up and down the aisle, I swiped a bottle of water from a cart, then headed back to my seat. Before sitting down, I retrieved my carry-on from the overhead bin, and pulled out the large manila envelope David Amit had given me at the Inner Harbor. Inside was a dark blue, one-inch binder that was Eitan Lev's dossier. Bottle of water in hand, I settled back and opened the binder.

The first three pages were dedicated to current photographs: a formal head-and-shoulder shot, and then a series of candids: Lev in his office, at political functions with the Prime Minister and other dignitaries, at home with his family. I flipped the page and came to a write-up.

Eitan Lev biographical summary:

Eitan Lev was born in January 1948 on Kibbutz Yael just west of the Sea of Galilee. In February '66 he entered the Paratroop Corps and received high marks for his understanding of skills and tactics. In June 1967, during the Six Day War, Lev volunteered for a unit that went behind Jordanian lines to disrupt communications in Jordan's command and control centers. His superiors noted his initiative and calmness under fire. After his tour, Lev remained in the army, attended officer school and began studying at Tel Aviv University for a degree in counter-terrorism. Within a few years he moved up the ranks to captain in the elite Paratroop Reconnaissance/Commando division. As part of his training, he learned additional anti-terrorism tactics and helped form units to combat PLO incursions into the North. In 1973 he was stationed along the Syrian border in the Golan Heights where he again went behind enemy lines to disrupt communication and supply lines. His unit is credited as being instrumental in turning the Syrian advance.

In the following year, while still in the army, he continued his course work at Tel Aviv University and graduated with a double degree: one in history, one in counter-terrorism. As time progressed, he ultimately rose to colonel and became part of the inner circle at the Ministry of Defense. Due to his knowledge and expertise in counter-terrorism, he worked closely with the police departments of the major cities first as a security advisor and then to enhance their ability to fight grand thefts, burglaries, and the drug problem that was growing along with the metropolitan areas.

For a moment, I turned to my right and stared out the window into the night sky. The blackness was entrancing. There seemed to be no worries out there in the void...just the emptiness of the sky and our plane cutting its way through it. After a few more seconds, I turned back to the write-up.

Lev retired from the army in 1998 at the rank of Brigadier and successfully lobbied to be appointed as Police Commander of the Jerusalem District. Though he didn't come through the ranks of the police, his knowledge of strategy and tactics became his arsenal to counter the crime in Jerusalem. He earned many supporters within law enforcement circles for his initiatives.

At the behest of numerous friends, Lev retired from the police force in 2010 to run for the office of Prime Minister. His platform is based on expanding strategically placed towns to act as buffers between the Israeli and Palestinian controlled areas, and then to negotiate with the Palestinians from a position of strength. If elected, Lev's intention has been to expand the role of the country's police forces, plus increase the size of the army by disallowing military exemptions for higher religious study. He has a plan (see attached) to rebuild the economy that has been devastated

by the on-going fight with the Palestinians, and at the same time,
rebuild the trust between the peoples.

I took a few swallows of my water. What was it about Lev
that concerned someone enough to try to kill him? That's where
all this began.

I dug out a highlighter and marked recurring themes, such
as his areas of expertise. Several times the brief mentioned Lev
applying his knowledge of strategy and tactics. There was his
military life and then there was the police force. I reread his
political agendas.

The pages that followed were a mixed bag: fitness reports
and detailed evaluations from commanding officers, additional
photographs of family, copies of newspaper clippings, editorials
on his tenure as chief of police, copies of recent speeches...

After thirty minutes of reading, my eyes began to glaze over.
Nothing had indicated "This is why someone wants to kill me.
It's because..."

I tucked the dossier back into its folder and closed my eyes
just in time for the stewardess to ask me whether I wanted meat
or chicken for dinner. I summoned all my inner strength and
ordered the meat.

When it came, it wasn't bad; some sort of pepper steak con-
coction, with sweet potatoes and green beans on the side.

By the time the meal was over and the trays had been collected, I was ready for a distraction. I pulled out a paperback, a

review of American history, highlighting major events from the perspective of the ordinary citizen.

By page three I was asleep.

The ten and a half hour flight went by quickly, as I was more exhausted than I thought. I was actually able to stay asleep for an adequate stretch. In what seemed to be just a few hours, the night sky turned bright blue as we flew toward the next morning.

With the arrival of breakfast, the energy level in the plane picked up. Sleeping passengers stirred and then moved throughout the cabin — mostly in the direction of the bathrooms. By 7 AM we were descending over the coast of Israel, and many passengers were peering through the windows as the Mediterranean gave way to land. The sprawl that was Tel Aviv slipped underneath us and we headed southeast to Ben Gurion Airport. The flat coastal plain exhibited a lush checkerboard of farms and orchards.

Forty minutes later we touched down and the entire cabin broke out into spontaneous applause. Outside the window, the land was flat and the grass beside the runway was more like the wild grass of a field. The plane rolled to a stop at its gate, but it was another fifteen minutes before passenger off-loading commenced. Eventually, we walked off the plane and onto the upper level of the terminal. The long debarkation corridor briefly gave way to an open area where we could see duty free shops below, but then led to the large immigration hall.

All passengers from arriving flights were faced with a row of booths behind which passport control officers sat. I quickly moved off to the far right before the line there became too long. As I waited, I looked at the group that had just come off the plane with me. The eclectic crowd was dressed casually...a lot of jeans, Dockers, polo shirts, and some shorts. There was a definite conversational buzz in the air as we all waited.

Finally, I was next in line and came up to a serious, dark-eyed female officer of Passport Control. I handed her my Israeli passport, and then without much interaction, she stamped it and wished me a good day. After thanking her, I moved around the booth and on through to the baggage claim.

The baggage area was one huge open room. Luggage carousels were on one side and kiosk-style stands offering tourist information, newspapers, and currency exchange were on the other. I had a fair amount of cash, but would hold off on the exchange to shekels until I got to Jerusalem. As my only luggage was my carry-on, I was able to skirt the carousels and head for a kiosk selling pre-paid cell phones. I bought a moderately priced Nokia and immediately put it to work.

Stepping away from the booth, I faced a wall so no one could easily eavesdrop, then dialed a number I had memorized more than a year ago, hoping it was still active. It was, but an answering machine came on. In my best Arabic — which on my best days was pitiful — I left a message. It was all business: the time and a place for a possible rally. That was it. No name, no other information. Just a direct message. I just hoped that Ibrahim was still around to pick it up and that the phone line hadn't been compromised.

Compartmentalizing my concern, I continued on to Customs. Customs was located at the far end of the baggage claim area where there were two long stainless steel tables parallel to each other; a wide aisle between them. One side was for Israeli citizens, the other for everyone else. Being that I held dual citizenship and had an Israeli passport, the citizens' side was for me. The male guard unceremoniously waved me on, as I had nothing to declare. I walked through an open doorway, down a hall, and into the main receiving area.

The hall was everything you'd expect from an airline terminal...busy, somewhat noisy, and filled with greeters. Men and women were lined up where we had exited from customs. Friends rushed over to greet friends...relatives kissed relatives... and everyone seemed to hug.

Among the greeters was a line of people holding up small signs with names of passengers on them. I walked past the sign holders, but stopped when I saw a short, thin man, probably in his thirties with close cut hair. He was holding up a paper that said, "G.A." — and he didn't look as if he were having a good time.

"Guest American," I said to him, pointing to his sign.

"No." He stared past me and into the crowd.

"Gary Aronhime? He was my best friend in third grade."

He looked at me, then turned away again.

"How about Gidon Aronson?"

He looked me over. "Yes."

I showed him my passport. Without another word, he held out a large, bulky white envelope.

"And why should I accept a package from someone I don't know?" I looked into his eyes.

"Mr. Amit sends his regards and says you have a meeting with the Commander of the Jerusalem Police at 11:00."

So, Amit must've taken an earlier flight...or he made the arrangements from the States. I still hesitated, not totally sure this was Amit's messenger.

The thin man with close-cropped hair looked at me looking at him. He let out a breath as if bored. "Mr. Amit mentioned that he enjoyed speaking with you and your captain friend at the Inner Harbor."

"Good enough." I took the bulky envelope. "Will Mr. Amit be at the meeting?"

"He didn't say." He paused a moment. "Do you know where to go?"

"Jaffa Road."

He gave me the address just to be sure.

"Thanks."

The thin man nodded, then turned away and disappeared toward the main exit.

I hefted the package, but couldn't imagine what Amit would be giving me...more intel on the case? Maybe it was special soap from the Dead Sea? Peering into the envelope would have to wait until I was out of public view. I headed for the door.

Fifteen minutes later I was sitting in the driver's seat of my newly rented Mazda, parked on the ground level of a tiered, above-ground parking lot. I opened the package the humorless courier had given me. The first item, the largest, was a 9mm Glock in a clip-on belt-holster. Next to it were two fully loaded magazines. Along with the weapon was a military ID. Amit was thorough and definitely had a sense of humor. There was an old army photo of me on the identification card — he had been busy digging up my records — and some personal information. The ID would get me onto army bases and allow me to legally carry the handgun. But the personal information made me laugh. He had me ranked as a major; a promotion, because I had left the army as a captain.

Amit also provided a stack of cash. Paper-clipped together were 2000 shekels...a little over 530 dollars. A note card was tucked under the clip: "Welcome back. D.A." Below it was a phone number. The note card went in my pocket, as did the ID. The cash, gun, and ammo went back in the envelope.

By now it was 9:00 and traffic was still heavy along Route 1, the main highway that ran from Tel Aviv to Jerusalem and over to the northern end of the Dead Sea. The fascinating thing was, if you started on Route 1 in Tel Aviv and traveled the highway's entire length, you would go from the coastal plain, up to Jerusalem in the mountains, then take a relatively steep downgrade to below sea level and the Dead Sea.

Coming out of the airport, the land to either side of me was flat and beautiful. I passed orchards, wide open areas, houses, and forests. About thirty minutes into the drive the road began to gradually head uphill. The straight highway turned curvy as it made its lazy climb up to the capital. Along the side of the road every few kilometers, one could spot the rusted skeletal remains of trucks and armored vehicles left over from the War of Independence in 1948. They served as a testament and constant reminder of the country's violent birth.

As the road peaked, I was into the city limits and its constant congestion. Without leaning on the horn, I was able to weave my way between small cars and big trucks to scoot onto the streets that would take me to my hotel. The route was a little circuitous, but it would avoid the frustration of immovable downtown Jerusalem traffic.

The Dan Panorama, formerly the Moriah Hotel, was located at the base of Keren Ha-yesod, just above where it ran into King David Street. The exterior of the hotel was built from blocks of Jerusalem stone, a white-salmon stone that was ubiquitous in the city. I parked my car in front of the main entrance, informing the doorman that I would be back out in ten minutes after I checked in.

The lobby had a dozen people in it, milling about, talking excitedly...something about a family reunion here in Jerusalem. I smiled at their joy and turned my attention to the other side of the room.

The main desk was to the right, and behind the counter the young woman with eyes that hinted of the Orient, had me registered in moments. My room was on the fourth floor, and as I walked down the hall I passed a young couple headed the opposite way. We nodded to each other and kept moving.

Room 430 was a corner room: spacious, with modest sun exposure and an excellent view of the Yemin Moshe artists' colony a few blocks away. It was definitely great to be back in Jerusalem. I quickly walked through the room, checking out the bathroom and closets — not in any James Bondian fashion, probing for listening devices, but just to see what the facilities were. Back at the bed, I reopened the large white envelope and spilled out its contents. The gun, magazines of ammo, and the cash fell into a pile.

I scooped up the unloaded Glock, pulled back the hammer, held the gun out, and tested the trigger pull. It wasn't bad; a tad too resistant, but not bad. I dry-fired the gun two more times until I was satisfied with the feel. Next came the magazine. I inserted the clip, then pulled back the slide multiple times, pumping several rounds through the chamber and out the ejection port. It operated very smoothly. That was all I needed to do. I reloaded the magazine with the ejected ammo, then reinserted it back into the grip, put a round in the chamber, and set the safety. The gun and holster went under my waistband over my right back pocket. Next, the cash. That was divided into two groups and distributed in my front pockets. Finally, I pulled a windbreaker from my overnight bag and put it on to conceal the gun. Leaving a light on in the room, I headed out.

*   *   *

The central police station was located off of Jaffa Road, perhaps three miles away. I found a parking space in a small dedicated lot in back, then walked around front. The building looked new — a five story rectangular cube of stone and glass with multiple antennas and satellite dishes sprouting from the roof. I opened the main entrance door and came face-to-face with two young police officers manning a metal detector and x-ray machine. The officers were in their mid-20's and clad in their uniform of medium blue shirt and navy trousers. One officer carried a Jericho .41 handgun, while the other had an M-16 slung from his shoulder. In a moment they would ask me the common refrain: "Do you have a *neshek*, a weapon?"

Before they could ask, I pulled out my army ID and showed it to them. The soldier with the M-16 nodded, and waved me around the metal detector.

The Commander's office was on the top floor, and as I came off the elevator, I saw David Amit sitting on an upholstered chair outside a closed door.

"Shalom," he said. "How was your flight?"

"Smooth." I paused. "Thanks for the goodies."

He shrugged. "Whatever you don't use, I want back. Accountants, you know...they count every shekel and every bullet."

"I'll use everything judiciously."

He nodded.

"You're very thorough, Mr. Amit, but I'm disappointed in one thing." He looked at me, eyebrows raised. "You only made me a *major*? By now I should rate a colonel."

"On your next trip."

I smiled. "So," I nodded toward the office, "what's this all about?"

"As you've probably read — if the dossier didn't put you to sleep — Eitan Lev was Commander of the police district here. Ilan Dror, the current commander served under him. I thought he'd be able to fill in some details...maybe give us something we hadn't thought of."

Before I had a chance to concur, the door next to Amit opened and a uniformed officer invited us in. We were escorted to a corner office. The room, as one would expect from a corner, was large, but not overly so. The dominant feature of the room, however, was a huge window allowing a breathtaking view of the Old City. One could easily see the off-white weathered walls, ramparts, and domed structures and minarets that poked up in different quadrants of the city. Inside the office, the main feature was a large metal desk, not facing the window, but away from it. And behind the desk was a middle-aged man. He wore a Commander's police rank on his shoulders, but was physically unassuming: not husky or powerful, but of average build and balding. Without a doubt, though, if he were sitting in that chair, he was a sharp, intelligent man who knew his way around one of the toughest cities on Earth. Commander Dror stood as we approached; he was just slightly shorter than me.

"Come in, come in," Dror welcomed us. "David, how are you?"

Amit and Dror shook hands. "Except for this open investigation, just fine." He turned to introduce me. "This is Major Gidon Aronson. He's the one who stopped the assassination in Baltimore."

We shook hands. "I heard about it. We're all glad you were there."

"Thank you."

"So, you're a major in the IDF?" Dror looked from me to Amit, not truly clear on my relationship to the *Shin Bet*.

"My reserve duty," I responded. Amit didn't catch the inside joke. When he was trying to recruit me, he wanted me to accept the assignment as part of my army service.

"Yes. Now he works for us," Amit said.

I looked at Amit.

"*With* us," he corrected.

Dror let it go. He knew better that to ask what was going on, since it didn't involve his service; we were just here for background and context on Lev. The Commander got right to the point. "So, you want to know about Eitan," he said, sitting back in his chair.

"I understand you worked under him." I settled into a seat opposite him. Amit also sat in a nearby chair.

"I was with him for five years."

"Could you describe what he was like? What was he passionate about in his job?"

Amit added: "We're still looking for the assassin's motive."

"I understand." Commander Dror rotated his chair slightly so he could look out the window. He could've been gazing at the Old City in the distance, but more likely he was rummaging through his thoughts. "What was he passionate about?" He swung back around to us. "Easy. He hated crime."

"What do you mean?" I asked.

"He hated it and believed — still believes — that it is a plague. Jerusalem is a very beautiful city. There is not another like it on Earth. But it is also a difficult city: Jews, Arabs, the tourists from all over the world...religious, non-religious...my way is right, your way is wrong...the protests *for* building, the protests *against* building...demonstrations because we unearthed ancient pottery...demonstrations because there are demonstrations..." He paused for a second. "It's a huge task to keep everyone from killing each other — and we're not even talking about terrorist attempts."

"The city of God," I said, half to myself, sarcastically.

Dror looked at me. "But that's true. It *is* the city of God. That's why everyone feels so strongly here. There is a feeling of God's presence in this city."

"You had started to say something about crime," Amit said, refocusing the Commander.

"Yes. The major issues here are..." he held his thumb... "drugs and..." he held up his index finger, as if counting... "car thefts. Both are extremely profitable. For drugs, we are sitting at the corner of three continents. The old trade routes used to go right by this very spot...east to west, north to south...and back. The new drug routes still do. And car thefts...probably the only true cooperation here between Jews and Palestinians...is big business. The cars disappear from streets here and end up in Gaza or other Palestinian areas. A totally coordinated enterprise between Jews and Arabs. Very impressive, I must tell you."

"And Mr. Lev?" I interjected.

"Mr. Lev formed special anti-crime commando units. He put the pressure on whoever he could find: the little guy on the street corner with hashish in his pocket, or the big guy in charge of car thefts."

"I understand," I said. I still didn't see any possible link to either the Coles or to the Guardians of Heaven group. I pulled out a Guardians membership card and gave it to him. "Ever hear of this group, The Guardians of Heaven?"

"Yes. It's a gang here. The young ones just drink and go to places like Ben Yehuda Street. The older ones, though, push drugs."

"What about violence?" I was thinking of the assassination attempt and the subsequent attack on me.

"Usually not, but I can't say there isn't the occasional stabbing."

From Amit: "Do the kids have a home...and parents to talk to? In Baltimore, the kids were not welcome at home."

"It's a typical gang...the group is their family. And they operate out of several schools run by..."

"Aaron Cole," Amit and I said the name together.

"*Nachon*. Correct."

"So how 'bout this," Amit began. "The drug dealers — or whoever — hire the Guardians of Heaven to kill Lev because he's on their back."

"Why don't they do it themselves?" I countered.

"Maybe Cole is a partner, and by housing the gang, he gets some of the drug profits," the police chief suggested.

Amit continued: "If Lev becomes Prime Minister, he starts a whole operation against the drug dealers." He turned to me. "That was in his dossier...that he wants to expand the role of the police. If that happens, and he has all these people arrested, then the Coles' source of extra money will be gone."

"So Cole uses his influence on the gang to try to kill Lev? I don't know," I said. "Murder for profit, you think?"

"For power, " Dror said. He got up and sat on the edge of his desk, facing me. "Look, there are plenty of people in Jerusalem — some very religious people, or so they say — who will sell their virgin daughters if it means they can have more power or freedom to live the way they think is right."

"I don't know," I said. "I wish I knew more about the Coles."

"I may be able to help you. I know of a rabbi who knows Aaron Cole from their early post-seminary days."

"That would be great."

"I'll unearth his name and address and call you on your *pelephone*." Dror used the Hebrew for cell phone.

"One more thing, Ilan," Amit said to the Commander. "Do you recognize any of these people?" He pulled out the photos of the Oasis Café staff I had taken in Mount Vernon.

Dror looked at them for a moment, then shook his head. "No. But get me copies. And if I think of anything else..."

Amit nodded and rose to his feet. "Thanks. That fills in some more of the details."

The police commander began to head with us to the door. "Good. Eitan is a tough man. He feels very strongly about all of this. And the Coles...I'll call about them."

"*Todah rabba,*" I said, thanking him.

And with that we were outside of his door and walking to the elevator.

I turned to Amit. "He seems very good."

"Dror? He is. Very dedicated. Like Lev. In addition to being Commander of the Jerusalem District, he also has to be a peacemaker in this city."

"A job I wouldn't want."

"Right now, Gidon, I'm not crazy about my job either."

I smiled and we both headed out. Once in the parking lot, Amit climbed into a dirt-covered black Subaru and headed off into traffic toward the Old City. I, on the other hand, had some time to kill. My appointment, the one I had arranged at the airport, wasn't for several hours. First lunch, then call home, then...I'd figure something out.

Rather than driving around searching for another parking spot, I left the car in the police lot, and then walked toward the Machane Yehudah market. On one of the side streets adjacent to the market was a schwarma place with a small table nestled under an orange umbrella in front of the store. I could eat and people watch while out of the sun. I ordered a schwarma and a bottle of flavored water. In a matter of minutes, a young man brought out the order.

It was a beautiful day, and I enjoyed not only the food, but also observing those who walked by: young, old, Jews, Arabs, young mothers pushing strollers, ultra Orthodox men in long black coats, teenage girls — and not so teenage women — in colorful tube tops, boys in shorts and T-shirts; I heard Hebrew, Arabic, Yiddish, English, French, Spanish, and some languages I couldn't place. Regardless of culture, though, practically everyone was talking on a cell phone.

After taking the last bite of the schwarma/pita, I balled up the paper it came in and tossed it and the empty drink bottle into the trash. The man behind the counter waved to me as I headed out.

There was one final thing to do before going very far – call home. It was early morning in Baltimore — seven hours earlier — and I placed three quick calls: one each to Alli, Katie, and Nate. The calls were short and to the point: I arrived safely, my cell phone number was such-and-such, and I missed them. Okay, the last part I didn't say to Nate. He did tell me to kick some ass, though.

With some time left before my rendezvous, I wandered back along Jaffa Road toward the Old City and soon found myself near Zion Square. It hadn't taken me long to walk there, and in fact, I hadn't planned to meander that way. But there I was, close to the foot of Ben Yehudah, looking at all the stores beyond the moving wall of pedestrians. I could see a bank, some clothing stores, a camera shop, and a bagel place. There was also a rebuilt café where one had been blown apart some time ago. I just stared at it from across the busy street. All evidence of that horrific October day had been erased, at least to the eyes of most people. My eyes saw smoke, jagged pieces of metal, broken, torn bodies, pools of blood, lifeless forms — and one particular face. I swallowed hard and took a few long, deep breaths. I looked heavenward for a moment then moved on, trying to tuck that day back into its ever-opening compartment.

19

My appointment was scheduled to take place in Rehavia, a quiet residential area off one of the main streets; a neighborhood of old apartments in some areas and new high-rises in others. I headed for the older section, where even the main roads were narrow and not helped by cars parked on both sides of the street. In some places, the streets were so congested that cars parked *on* the sidewalks. Even though I knew this, and walkable for me, I elected to drive over.

The apartment building I wanted was sequestered on a lazy side street. The aging structure was on the left and set back about twenty-five feet from the road with a waist-high stone wall running the length of the front property line. An ancient carob tree stood over the yard, its thinning branches providing minimal shade. The apartment building itself was a boxy three stories.

I drove past the building looking for anyone loitering about, and then started searching for a parking spot. Two blocks away, as I approached a small corner flower shop, a blue Fiat pulled away, leaving just enough room for me. I pulled in, locked the car and began walking nonchalantly back down the street.

By now most people were on their way home from work, putting a fair amount of pedestrians on the sidewalks. Many people were young, perhaps in their mid-to-late twenties, and almost all were dressed casually — open collars for the men, comfortable dresses and slacks for the women. Almost everyone was carrying a shoulder bag or laptop case.

As I anticipated the meeting, my heart rate picked up. There was some potential danger ahead. The rendezvous location was old, so that meant it could easily be under surveillance by either the Israelis or the Palestinians. It could mean the person I was meeting, Ibrahim, might not come at all. He could be lying face down in a West Bank alley somewhere, and a less Gidon-friendly man might arrive in his place, semi-automatic pistol in hand. It was also possible that Ibrahim might have done away with this location months ago, and all I'd find is an old, toothless, gray-haired woman who came up to my navel.

The apartment house came up on the right, and I scanned the building across from it. No one in the widows...at least not in plain sight. I walked through the entry break in the stone wall, and then into the old lobby.

The vestibule was dim and stifling. Even though the front door was propped open, there were no windows for cross-ventilation. Adding to the oppressiveness, the foyer itself was dirty and in desperate need of a fresh coat of something. To the right against the wall was a small bank of mailboxes. Straight ahead were the stairs. I pulled out the Glock and took off the safety. Hopefully, no one was waiting for me. Silently, I made my way up two flights. This visit was my third ever up these stairs, but this was the only time I felt uneasy. Fortunately, I was early, and if someone meant me harm, at least I would be waiting for him. Outside Apartment 7, I took out a key I had brought from Baltimore and opened the deadbolt lock.

As I stepped inside, stagnant air filled my nose. It wasn't a bad smell, just not fresh. A window hadn't been opened here in months. The apartment was also gloomy. It was filled with dull, early evening light that would soon be gone altogether. I took a step toward the light switch on the right-hand wall, but froze mid-stride. A gun barrel touched the back of my head.

There was no sense wondering how I let this happen. Too late for that. I remained very still, my own gun pointing at empty space. Without moving — not even my eyes — I took in the room. Straight ahead was a small den, with an off-white slip-covered sofa against the wall. To my left was a living room; to the right was an open kitchen area with an orange countertop. A ceiling fan was motionless overhead.

The person behind me didn't say a word. I didn't say a word either.

With my gun still in my right hand, I could always whip around as nimbly as possible. Who knows, I might be fast enough. And if there was someone else in that room with a weapon I could be shot from *two* directions. Not that it'd matter, with a bullet entering the back of my head at more than 800 feet per second.

More silence. Probably all of two seconds passed.

I closed my eyes then re-opened them.

"I see you like getting to an appointment early also," I said.

No response. The gun was still pressed into my head

"But don't you think that this is *too* early, Ibrahim?"

The barrel of the gun backed off of my head.

"Not to catch you, my friend." There were very few people on the planet who called me "My friend." One was Nate. The other was Ibrahim.

I turned to see a tall, dark-skinned man. He had a round face, but a neatly-trimmed gray mustache added a little length to his countenance. His eyes were bright and full of energy. We smiled at one another then gave each other a bear hug.

"How are you? How are you?" Ibrahim kept asking.

"Fine. Fine."

We let go and took a good look at what we each saw.

"You've put on some weight," he said.

"You've gotten gray."

We laughed and hugged each other again. We both put away our weapons.

"How are you?" I asked. "How is your family?"

"We are fine...today. Life here..."

"I know. I know."

"And with you? All is well?"

"I'm healthy...and better than I was a year ago."

"I hope so. You were not good then."

I nodded in agreement.

"So what brings you back? I thought we had lost you for good."

"I've got a story, but it's not for bedtime, my *chaver*." I told him. We sat in a darkening corner of the living room and I told him all that had happened since that evening when I stopped the boy from trying to kill Eitan Lev at the banquet.

"So, all roads lead back here," he said finally.

"It seems so." A moment went by, and then I asked, "Are you still Security Chief?"

"Yes, yes." Ibrahim looked down as he said it. "But life here for us in Gaza or the Territories has become even more insane — and dangerous — since you left. On the one side, Hamas and the Palestinian Authority are only interested in their own political and religious agenda. There is nothing else to them. They have been very successful in poisoning the people against both the Israelis and peace. It will be generations before people like us can stand together. And if someone wants change and stands up...well you know what happens."

I knew. Any moderate voice from the Palestinian side got suddenly silenced. Usually by being dragged through the streets of the town, then hanged...or beheaded...or carved up...or just shot.

"Then there is the corruption."

"I know."

"And the Israelis don't make life easy, either."

I nodded. After a moment I looked back at him. "Are *you* safe...you your family?"

"For now. But I have to tell you, the younger ones today are out for blood — and not just Israeli blood. *Anyone* around the Palestinian inner circle can suddenly find himself dead — if someone doesn't like what you're doing, or if they just want your job."

"Your instincts have always been good."

He let out a deep breath. "I'm afraid they won't last forever and then..." he trailed off.

The last time we met in this very room I had suggested he get out of the line of fire...that I could help him either find a quiet place in the beautiful north of the country, or even come to the United States with his family. Ibrahim, of course, declined. And in the year since I last saw him, he had aged quite a bit. There were more lines on his face, and he was indeed grayer. His eyes, though, still had the same vibrancy.

"So, what can I do for you, Gidon, that you've come all this way?"

I reached into my pocket and pulled out the pictures of the Oasis Café staff. "Do you know any of these people?"

Ibrahim looked over the snapshots. Almost immediately he nodded.

"This one." He showed me the shot of the café's owner. "His name is Aziz el-Hadam, but he's known here as The Iraqi. You would call him a gangster, a pure mercenary out for himself. No ideologies. Only business. I saw him in Gaza maybe six months ago brokering stolen Israeli weapons. He takes the money he makes and gives some to Hamas, some to Al-Aqsa Brigades, some to this group, some to that group."

"So he stays in everyone's good graces."

"Yes. In the middle of war there is always business for some."

"So why would he be in Baltimore and what would his connection be to Aaron Cole."

"I don't know, but I guarantee that whatever it is, it will be so he can continue to make money. Your Mr. Lev would not be good news for him if he's elected." He paused. "I don't know if he would be good news for me either."

I smiled weakly. I didn't have an answer for that. I let another moment go by. "This Iraqi, maybe he was helping the Guardians gang. But you know, even as I say that, I can't believe that Aaron Cole or Mrs. Cole would go along with that."

"You are still naive, I see."

"Maybe. But I don't see a motive for the Coles or a connection."

Ibrahim shrugged. "Business? Money? Even some of the Israeli soldiers are selling equipment to us."

I didn't say anything.

"I'll ask around. See if el-Hadam is back. Maybe I can have a friendly chat with him."

I could only imagine what an intimate conversation was like with Ibrahim if he wanted information. "If he's doing business with some Israelis — even if they are teachers — then perhaps we can all be part of it — and find out what's going on. After all, if Lev is killed and it points back to us, then the results will not be in our best interest."

"So, you'll be in touch if you find out anything."

He nodded.

"Let me give you a friend's name here, just in case something happens to me." I gave him David Amit's name.

Ibrahim stood up. "So, let me change the subject and ask you...how is your heart? Have you found anyone to fill it?"

The second time we had met here was after Tamar had been killed and I had decided to leave. I looked at him. "Someone to fill my heart? Perhaps. We'll see." I thought of Katie. I let a moment go by. "Maybe next time I come I'll bring her and we can all walk along the Mediterranean."

"May that time come soon."

"May that time come soon," I repeated.

With that, I hugged Ibrahim and watched as he left the apartment. As the door closed I said a silent prayer, asking that God watch over my friend.

After a long minute, I left the apartment as well. For Ibrahim's safety we couldn't leave at the same time; one never knew who was watching. I left the place the way I had found it, and walked down the dimly lit stairs and then outside.

By now, early evening was settling in. Up in the heavens, the western sky still had some remnants of blue left. I paused on the stoop to adjust to the decreased light, and then turned right to take the long way around to my car. Halfway up the street in front of me, Ibrahim was approaching an intersection. A traffic light hung from overhead wires. Ibrahim paused in front of a flower shop to look over some outdoor displays. Even from fifty feet away I could see how colorful and lush the arrangements were. As my friend looked at the flowers, I noticed an old, dark green Mercedez had slowed to a stop perhaps twenty feet behind him. Ibrahim's back was to the car. From where I stood, I could see that the car's license plate was orange with black letters and numbers — a standard Israeli plate. Nothing unusual there. While Palestinians' were green and white, something still didn't fit. Old model Mercedez sedans were typically Arab taxis.

Ibrahim continued inspecting the flowers and the Mercedez began to creep closer to him.

A young woman with a Golden Lab walked past me on the left. Two young boys, each probably ten or twelve, cut across my path, forcing me to stop short. They were arguing about a soccer match.

Before I was actually aware of it, the Glock was in my right hand. I began to run forward. The boys were looking at me.

The Mercedez was now ten feet behind Ibrahim and to his left. There were two figures in the car — the driver and someone in the passenger side. The passenger's arm was leaning out the window.

The light above the intersection turned green. The flower shop owner — a small, balding man wearing a green apron — came out to talk with his new customer.

I continued to run forward. There was a gun — I could see it clearly — in the passenger's right hand and he was bringing it up toward Ibrahim. In the distance there was a siren.

The tail lights on the Mercedez glowed red as the car came to a stop next to my Palestinian friend. Ibrahim turned to the car. Either he sensed the change in movement to his side or perhaps his peripheral vision had picked up the car. His right hand went inside his jacket but he would be too late.

The Mercedez was barely moving and the line of fire was clear. I shot the man in the passenger seat three times from twenty feet out. The back windshield of the sedan shattered.

The man in the passenger seat was propelled forward and the gun in his hand flew from his grip. The boys who were talking about soccer looked at me and dropped to the ground, covering their ears. The flower shop owner ran back into the shop. Pedestrians across the street ducked behind parked cars.

I saw the tail lights on the Mercedez go out and there was a throaty roar from the engine as the car began to accelerate. I fired once at the driver. For several seconds I didn't know if I had hit him. Then the car, already picking up speed, plowed into a lamppost at the corner of the intersection.

I went over to the passenger side, gun still leveled. Ibrahim joined me. The passenger was definitely dead. He was slumped forward over the dashboard with a dark red splotch high up in his back. We moved around to the driver's side. This one was still alive. As we approached from the rear of the car, the driver shoved open his door and spilled onto the ground. He was probably in his early twenties, with short straight black hair, and dressed in jeans and a dark T-shirt. His left shoulder was a mess, with blood saturating the shirt.

"Do you know him?" I asked Ibrahim as we looked down at the driver.

"Yes."

The driver began cursing at Ibrahim in Arabic. I could only catch every third word or so...something about Ibrahim being a traitor and then something disparaging about his lineage — all in very colorful Arabic. Then he began to talk about Ibrahim's wife.

"Ask him if he knows what time it is."

Ibrahim looked at me.

"Your Arabic is better than mine. Ask him."

Ibrahim asked him. The driver looked over at me, suddenly confused.

"It's seven o'clock," I said. I brought my gun up and shot him in the other shoulder.

The man passed out.

I turned to my friend. "You better go. Will you be all right? Do you have to move your family?"

"No. This one just wants my job. He doesn't know anything. Probably just wanted to impress someone."

"You sure?"

Ibrahim nodded. "As long as he stays as a guest of Israel then I'll be fine."

"I'll take care of that. Be careful."

Ibrahim turned, crossed the street, and disappeared into the next block.

I put away the Glock and called David Amit.

Ten minutes later, Ilan Dror, the Police Commander, was first to arrive. I explained I couldn't say much about who I was meeting, but just that the men in the Mercedez had tried to kill him. Dror didn't press for more information, knowing that I might be more open at another time.

Amit showed up shortly thereafter and I filled him in, particularly about the Iraqi Ibrahim had mentioned.

We walked over to the flower shop, out of the way of the commotion that had started. By now there were ambulances and more police.

"Well," Amit looked at me, "at least we have a face to give some of this. Aziz el-Hadam," he repeated the Iraqi's name.

"But still no connection to the Coles."

"You don't accept money as a connection?"

"No." I looked over at the police, going over the Mercedez that was still half on the sidewalk. "I wish we could find something concrete to link the two."

"That, my good major, would make life too easy."

I smiled, mostly at the reference to "major."

"Go back to your hotel. Relax. I know how to reach you. I'll check on this Iraqi and we'll talk."

"Call me," I emphasized.

I took a last look at the excitement in the intersection, then headed for my car.

In a matter of minutes I was back at the Dan Panorama, parking my car in the lot behind the hotel. Rather than go up to my room, though, I walked out on the main street, Keren Ha-yesod and turned right. Jerusalem was built on a series of rolling mountains and most streets went uphill and down eventually. Keren Ha-yesod was no different. As I walked, the street indeed began to climb. I passed a number of hotels. Near the top of the incline, the high-rise Leonardo Plaza Hotel was set back on the right in a park-like setting. On the left, also set back from the road was the central synagogue for the city. Though it was after 9 PM, many people were strolling about on both sides of the street.

I continued up the block, then crossed the street for no specific reason. Images of the last few days filled my mind. I could see Pavel, the Coles; I re-ran my chase through the hospital, the Oasis Café chef following me, my meeting with Ibrahim, my last night with Katie.

We weren't moving quickly enough, and I wasn't sure what to do next. Maybe that was fatigue settling in. I hadn't really slept in more than 24 hours. There was a solution of course: my bed was half a mile away. Fresh ideas would hopefully come in the morning.

On the way back to the hotel, I spotted a used book store — which was surprisingly still open. A squeaky, rotating bookrack filled with Shakespeare's works stopped me. I was just considering a copy of *Julius Caesar* when my cell phone rang.

"Gidon, it's Nate."

"Nate, how are you? What's up? Everything okay?" I looked at my watch. It was mid-afternoon in Baltimore.

"Yeah, I just got some news. You know Abby, your 'Bella' who disappeared?"

I could feel the pounding in my chest. Pavel's cousin from the *shiva* house. Pavel had called her from my place and now she had vanished. I fully expected her to be in a gully somewhere.

"We found her."

Nate's voice betrayed nothing...I couldn't tell whether the news was good or not.

"Apparently she had gone to New York for a late meeting right from the *shiva* house. She got a ride to the train station and that's why her car was in front of her house."

"So she's okay?"

"She's fine. Her cell phone had died so no one could get through."

I let a moment go by. "So that was important enough for you to call me half way around the world?"

I could hear him laugh.

"Yeah. I thought you could use some good news."

"Just in time, too."

In front of me, near the entrance of the book store, I saw a teenager put down a black backpack and walk over to a table filled with stacks of books. The backpack was left unattended fifteen feet away.

"So," I went on, "did you ask her if she called anyone after Pavel reached her from the dojo?"

"Of course I did. I wouldn't be a captain in this fine police force if I hadn't."

"Nate."

"She called Hannah Cole."

There was silence as I let the thought sink in.

"Hannah Cole," I repeated. "Do you think she's the shooter... that she came over to the dojo and shot Pavel? He would definitely have opened the door for her."

"Ask David Amit to show her picture to the agent who watched your place, the one who saw the woman at your door."

"Will do."

Hannah Cole. I could see it, I guess. I recalled sitting down with Hannah and her husband in the latter's office. She had quite a strong reaction when a student interrupted us. Did she have it in her to shoot Pavel?

"So how are things going on your end?"

I heard Nate ask the question, but my eyes were on a soldier walking in my direction. He was dressed in his olive uniform and was wearing a black beret. A Tavor assault rifle was hanging across his abdomen. He spotted the lone backpack near the curb, and in one fluid move, wrapped his right hand around the trigger housing of the rifle, brought his left hand over for an assist, and swung the weapon up.

"Gidon?..." Nate's voice was in my ear.

The soldier looked around. "Does this belong to anybody?" he shouted, pointing to the backpack.

Images of parcels exploding, hurling nails and spikes must've filled everyone's mind. Pedestrians nearby, turned and ran the other way. Three shoppers — two elderly men and one woman — hurried from the shop.

"It's mine," came a shout to my right. It was the teenager who had gone over to look at the table of books.

The Israeli soldier fired questions at him: *Who are you?... Where are you from?...Why are you here?...Do you have identification?...*

When the hapless teenager stuttered his responses, the soldier continued to shout at him: *What's the matter with you?...Why did you leave the bag there?...Don't ever leave a bag around...Don't you know that?... What's the matter with you?* he repeated.

"Gidon? Are you there?" Nate was asking in my ear.

"Yes, yes, Nate, I'm here. I was just watching some excitement."

"Did you have anything to do with it?"

"No."

"Good."

"But you'll be happy to know I've been busy."

"Oh, God."

I told him not about the shooting, but about the Iraqi who brokered stolen guns and greased palms with his money.

"I'll see what we have on this end on the guy, but you're right at the source for this stuff."

"I know. That's it for now, buddy. By the way, I expect to pop in on Laurie tomorrow, if I get a chance."

"I won't ruin the surprise."

"Talk to you later."

We hung up, but I immediately dialed David Amit. An idea had occurred to me while I was talking to Nate as to how we might be able to get some concrete information on the Coles. Maybe even something linking them to the Iraqi. That would be helpful.

Amit liked the idea. He liked it a lot. But it would have to wait until morning before we could put it into effect.

I walked back to the hotel, less tired than before.

20

At 8:00 the next morning I was sitting next to Amit in his dirt covered black Subaru. We were in the quiet Jerusalem suburb of Ramot, and parked up the street from the Israel branch of Coles' school. Ramot was a beautiful area northwest of Jerusalem, just off a main highway. This particular neighborhood was relatively new and had an open feel to it, with clean, new streets and young trees planted along the sidewalks. The Coles' school itself was nondescript, built box-like with a facade of Jerusalem stone that added to its clean, new appearance. To the right of the building was a fenced-in recreation area, probably for recess. From where we sat diagonally up the block, we could see the entire street — schoolyard and school — and had an unobstructed view of the main glass entry doors and the security man in front.

I looked at the guard. Like so many of the security people here, this man also seemed post-army. He had close-cut hair, sunglasses rotated up to the crown of his head, and alert eyes. In case there was any doubt as to his role, he wore a lightweight black tunic over his shirt, which all Israelis recognized as a security guard's unofficial uniform. They also knew it concealed a holstered pistol and a walkie-talkie.

Based on the information Amit had researched — he had called the school office posing as a prospective parent — the school ranged from kindergarten through high school. Obviously much more was involved here than at the Coles' Baltimore school. The question was, did he also have a special class for at-risk kids here like the one back in the States? Probably so, as Commander Dror said, they had run-ins with some Guardians kids.

For now, the block was quiet. School had started thirty minutes ago and only a late-comer or two walked past the guard to be buzzed in. There were other entrances to the building — around the side and back — but not only were these probably locked, they were of no interest to us at the moment. I looked up at the sky. It was a cloudless, radiant blue and the air still had an early morning crispness to it. I knew that come ten o'clock, the heat would settle in. By then, we'd be long gone — hopefully.

Amit and I continued to watch the block. In addition to tardy students hustling down the sidewalk, there were also a few young couples out for a jog, several senior citizens ambling along, and the occasional young mother walking a toddler. Traffic in the street next to us was minimal.

"So how does it feel to be back here?" Amit asked randomly, as we watched the building.

I let a moment go by before answering. It was a question

that had crossed my mind more than once since arriving yesterday. "How does it feel?" I repeated. "Wonderful, and at the same time, sad."

He looked at me.

"I've never been more at home than here, doing both the work I was good at, and a job that I felt was important."

Amit nodded.

"But there's a price."

He nodded again, adding, "You were very young and very..." he paused looking for the word... "intense. Or so I was told."

I let the "Or so I was told" comment go by. "I don't remember being young." I smiled. "I do remember being intense."

There was a rumble overhead and we looked up to see a pair of Israeli F-16's streak across the sky.

"You're still intense, my friend. But calmer, I think. And in a way, that's more dangerous, I would imagine."

"It's an illusion," I laughed.

A deep motor sound came from behind us and we turned to see a white mini-van pull up to the front door. A man wearing a delivery service uniform jumped out carrying a large envelope. The guard stepped forward and felt the weight and general shape of the envelope's contents. Satisfied with his assessment, he let the messenger push the door buzzer. The messenger looked toward a corner of the doorway — there must have been a camera out of my sight line — and in a moment the door unlocked.

"We are becoming more and more like the United States," Amit lamented after watching the delivery man run into the school. "We have overnight deliveries, shopping malls, sandwich stores, buyer's clubs, even pollution. The tightened security for you, however, is more recent."

"Progress."

"But this is Israel, not the U.S. God told us to live with our neighbors in peace...then He surrounded us with enemies."

"A divine joke."

"I don't think we're laughing anymore."

The delivery fellow came out of the school building and climbed back into his mini van. A moment went by as he checked on something we couldn't see, and then he pulled away.

"It's very hard work that you do," I added.

"As you probably once said, 'If not me, then who?'"

I smiled. "I did say that." After another moment: "You know that I'm not here because of Eitan Lev."

"You're here because of the boy. I understand."

"And the Coles are involved," I nodded to the school building. "Have your men been following them?"

"Yes."

Before Amit could elaborate, he pointed to three women across the street, but still up the block from the school. The woman in the center was quite curvy — really had an amazing figure — while her companions were more slender. They were all in their mid-twenties, dressed fashionably with clothes that did each of them justice. The curvy woman wore a form-fitting tank top that up close would turn the head of anyone with a pulse. Her right-hand friend was dark-complexioned, perhaps

Yemenite, and wore an off-the-shoulder top. On the other side, the third woman could have been a model with long legs accented by a short hip-hugging skirt. They were easily three of the most eye-catching women I had ever seen. The Yemenite woman was carrying a black backpack trimmed in bright orange; all three women were in the middle of an animated conversation as they walked along the sidewalk.

Down the street, movement to our left caught my attention. A lone uniformed police officer was walking up the block when he spotted a scruffy-looking teenager leaning against a signpost and talking on a cell phone. The teenager was in a green soccer jersey with a Brazilian flag logo in the center. The cop began questioning him.

Though we were carefully tucked away in a driveway, we could easily see both the trio of women across from us and the policeman and teenager to our left. While we watched both scenes, a familiar deep motor sound approached. It was the delivery van once again. The driver pulled his vehicle forward of the security guard and climbed out. Based on his hand gestures, he needed to get back inside. Perhaps he forgot something, or maybe he had a pick-up to make. The guard nodded, the delivery man pressed the buzzer and soon disappeared inside.

The three women, meanwhile, had stopped in front of the playground fence. They moved closer to each other to share a private thought. Then, all three turned to the guard. The woman in the tank-top took a step toward him, but stopped and went back to her friends. The security man watched the three of them for half a second then went back to watching the street.

"He's trained well," I said, "not allowing the women to distract him."

Just then there was shouting down the sidewalk from us, across from the guard. The teenager was yelling at the cop. The cop yelled back.

As the shouting got louder, the guard took a step toward them — for just a moment. He stepped back to his post. He'd wait to see if his help were needed.

The three women, oblivious to all this, continued past the guard, who moved clear of them. The ladies went by, still in animated conversation.

The shouting down from us continued, and the security man called to the officer, asking if he needed help. The policeman responded in the negative. After a few more seconds the policeman and the teenager moved off together, apparently having resolved whatever conflict they had.

The guard at the school's entrance visibly relaxed. Again, he looked to his left then to his right. The three women, who he would have been interested in under other conditions, were now thirty feet past him.

Suddenly, the security man turned to his left. In front of the playground fence sat a black backpack trimmed in orange. The Yemenite woman had been carrying a black backpack trimmed in orange.

Amit handed me a pair of binoculars. As he had a pair for himself, we were both able to look at the abandoned bag. Two wires were sticking out where the zipper hadn't been completely closed. An image of a café near Zion Square filled my head.

The scene vanished as quickly as it had come, leaving me to stare at the black backpack trimmed in orange. With wires sticking out of it.

"Careless of the woman, leaving those wires hanging out," Amit said without lowering his binoculars. "Sloppy work."

"Very sloppy," I agreed.

By now the guard was bent over the backpack. He easily spotted the wires, and then stood up, reaching inside his tunic for his walkie-talkie.

Within seconds we could hear the muffled sound of an alarm going off inside the school. Moments later, students began to file out the far side of the building and over to another structure. Teachers directed them to move quickly. In less than a minute, kids of all sizes had exited the main building, from little kindergartners through the tall kids from the high school. As we watched the students we could see teachers reprimanding some kids for jumping around and misbehaving. Using my binoculars, I scanned the adults for the Coles. They weren't in the yard.

"The Coles came to school this morning, right?" I asked without lowering the binocs.

"Yes. They arrived together at 7:15. They're here. The question is, will they come out?"

A siren gradually grew louder from our right and in less than a minute a medium sized army truck pulled over to the front of the school followed by a number of police cars. The bomb sappers had arrived.

"By the way," I said as the bomb squad vehicle came to a halt, "I liked the idea of adding the cop and the teenager."

"Thank you. Just having three beautiful women would have been too obvious. By itself, it never would have worked."

While the police officers began to establish a safe perimeter, two men jumped out of the army truck. One was tall, the other slightly shorter. Both wore heavy body armor and helmets with plastic face shields lowered. Without a word between them, the smaller man threw a heavy-looking blanket over the backpack. I knew it was made of Kevlar and other highly dense material. The men wanted to minimize the explosion in case the bomb went off before they could defuse it. They needn't have worried. I knew exactly how much explosive was in the pack: enough to take out the side of the school, even from this distance. The explosion would also blow out windows of the surrounding buildings and probably blast the cars opposite the yard with pieces of shrapnel.

Fortunately for all of us, a crucial connection between the battery and the detonator was not made. That was my suggestion. I had also recommended that we let the bomb sappers know what was going on, but the bomb squad commander wanted his men out of the loop. That way, he said, they would handle the call as if it were an active bomb. It'd be good training.

Amit and I watched the two sappers continue their work. By now they had lowered a rolling robot from their truck. The robot had two long mechanical arms, and from a safe distance, the tall agent worked at a remote control to guide the robot over to the backpack.

"The Coles are out," Amit said.

I looked over at him to see that he still had his binoculars trained on the school yard, not on the sappers. "Where?"

"Side door."

Through my binoculars I saw both Hannah and Aaron Cole as they were walking next to other adults and away from the building.

"Now," I said to Amit.

He picked up a walkie-talkie. "*Lech.* Go!" he spoke into it.

Ten seconds later a car pulled in front of the sapper's truck. Two men, each carrying a large briefcase, jumped out of the car and went to the front door. The express delivery man, who had been inside waiting, opened the door as they approached. No one saw them; the bomb had everyone's attention.

The two men who were just let into the building each carried the electronic equipment needed to image any computer's hard drive. Imaging a hard drive usually took hours. The Israelis had perfected a means of doing it in minutes. The question was, did they have minutes? They knew exactly where the Coles' offices were within the building, but, still, it all took time.

The tall bomb sapper had moved the robot into place. Now, he carefully guided it to pick up the blanket-covered backpack. This was a two mechanical-arm process: one arm slid a rigid metal plate under the pack, while the other grabbed and secured the backpack from on top. The officer maneuvered the two arms simultaneously, so there was no shaking of the bomb.

We looked over at the school yard. The Coles were still outside, but they had separated. Hannah had moved over to the lower school children filing into the shelter, and Aaron was talking with his staff.

Out front, the police had blocked off the street and were in the process of evacuating an apartment building opposite the school. As people poured out of the building, they were quickly shunted a safe distance away, behind hastily erected barricades. The police, the bomb squad, and the populace were all moving so efficiently, it somewhat sadly spoke of an informed, trained public.

I refocused on the bomb sappers. The robot had the backpack securely in its sandwich grasp, and was moving toward a large armored containment vessel. In a well rehearsed maneuver, the officers lowered the backpack into the vessel and then began to place it in the back of their vehicle. In another 60 seconds the backpack would be loaded aboard and the truck would pull away. Once that was accomplished, the students and staff would re-enter the main building. I could picture the two technicians inside frantically working to copy the hard drives.

Amit and I watched as the sappers made their last move into the truck. The robot and its cargo were loaded aboard. Heavy rear doors closed and the officers climbed into the cab. Over at the playground adults were giving directions; we watched as the students were ushered back inside the school building from the shelter. Hannah Cole was still with the kindergartners, and she filed inside with them. Aaron was just behind her, talking to some of the high school kids.

Amit looked at me then picked up his walkie-talkie. "Time to go," he said in Hebrew.

There was no response.

The bomb squad truck pulled away from the curb. The last of the children and staff were heading in from the outer building. Did the electronics team not hear Amit? If they were at the computers when the Coles arrived, there'd be some fancy footwork to do.

"My friends, where are you?" Amit asked into the unit in his hand.

After a very long minute, the double glass doors at the front entrance opened and out scrambled the electronics guys and the delivery man. As they hustled to their car, the electronics guys hoisted the briefcases.

"They enjoy doing that, don't they?" I asked. "Playing it so close."

"Of course they do." We watched as their car pulled away, followed by the delivery van. "It'll take a little while before we can tell if there's any record of a connection between the Coles and the Iraqi."

I nodded. "I still need that name from Commander Dror about the rabbi who knew Cole way back when."

"I'll remind him. Where will you be?"

"I want to pay a visit to a friend."

"I'll drop you back at the hotel."

"Are your men still watching the Coles?"

"Yes."

"Alert your team that the Coles might be on the move."

Amit looked at me, inquiringly.

"If you were the Coles and a terrorist left a bomb on your doorstep, wouldn't you like to speak with your Iraqi contact to see if he knows anything?"

"They'll want to talk in person of course."

"*If* we've made the Coles paranoid enough to visit him. Maybe the Coles now think the Iraqi wants to dump them — permanently."

"Was that part of your plan, Gidon...use the bomb to also scare the Coles?"

I smiled. "No. I just thought of that possibility a minute ago. But, it may work."

21

By midday I was heading west from Jerusalem to a *moshav*, a collective community, outside the city of Rehovot. Within fifteen minutes of leaving the capital, the Judean hills flattened out into open spaces with fields on either side of the highway. For part of the trip I retraced my route in from the airport, but then turned off onto well traveled side roads. With the windows rolled down and the bright blue sky above, the drive was refreshing.

As I approached Rehovot, the dual lane highway became more and more congested with commercial traffic. Fields gave way to new high rises and then to busy city streets. I had just passed an industrial park when my cell phone rang. It was David Amit.

"I have the name of the rabbi you wanted, the one who knew the Coles. His name is Ari Goldman and he lives near Gush Etzion." Amit gave me his address and phone number.

"On the opposite side of Jerusalem from me, of course."

"The drive will do you good. Soak in as much of the holy air as you can."

"I always do." I popped on a pair of sunglasses as a curve in the road put the sun in my eyes. "The rabbi will be my next stop after this. Does he know I'm coming?"

"Dror told him."

"Fine. And any word on the Coles' computer files?"

"No. It'll be another few hours."

"Keep me up to date." I needn't have said that, but I did.

"Of course." He paused. "By the way, my man checked Hannah Cole's picture to see if he recognized her from outside your place."

"And?"

"He couldn't say for sure. Remember, the woman he saw had long dark hair and she was wearing a baseball cap. But we're playing with the picture to get variations on her looks."

"Let me know what happens."

"I will. Where are you?"

"Rehovot. I'll be back in Jerusalem in a couple of hours."

"Okay."

We hung up and I continued my trip to the community west of town.

In a matter of minutes, I had skirted the town and was outside the city limits once again. The road became rural, with low shrubs and trees all around. My mind drifted to Laurie, the woman I was hoping to see. My visit would definitely be a surprise; hopefully, *I* wouldn't be surprised by Laurie not being there. The last time I had seen her, about a year ago, she had recently been released from the hospital and was settling into her cousin's house in the *moshav* to recuperate more fully. She remained there ever since. My mind brought up her image: a slender woman of medium height with wavy dark hair and a brightness in her eyes that her ordeal couldn't suppress.

After driving about two miles on the rural road, there was a break in the foliage to the right. I pulled onto a small access road and came up to a gate that had a small, one-person guardhouse next to it. The last time I was here, the gate was kept open all day.

I slowed to a stop and the guard, a round-shouldered thirty-something civilian in a striped shirt and jeans, came out to look me over. His hands rested on an Uzi, slung from his shoulders. The young man noted my Israeli license plate, sized me up, then waved me on. The gate opened and I pulled through.

The *moshav* was a community unto itself, almost like a gated community in the States. The roads were laid out grid-style and the homes in each block varied in size. This was not a new community, though there were some areas where new housing was going up. In a way, the land was very flat, similar to Florida, plus it had the typical tropical foliage of palm trees and sharp-leafed shrubs. To keep cars from speeding down the long road, speed humps were positioned in every block. There were no gutters or sidewalks; the sides of the roads just ended and lawns began. I drove past a new community recreation building, turned left, and headed for an elementary school.

Halfway up the block was a single story school building. I pulled off the road onto the grass and got out. Across the street, a tractor rumbled down the road, hauling a wooden trailer filled with farm equipment. A pair of gold and white cats scooted into the street immediately behind the two-wheeled rig.

Once the roar of the tractor had faded, sounds of children playing filled the air. The sounds were coming from the other side of the school. I walked past the main entrance to the far side of the building where a waist-high, chain link fence enclosed a playground. Within its perimeter, there were, perhaps, twenty third-grade boys and girls playing on the dirt and scruff-covered grounds; some were on see-saws, others were climbing in and out of a plastic house, and others were on swings. Supervising the mini-horde were two women halfway across the modest playground. One was blonde and thin, perhaps thirty, wearing a red and white summer dress and sandals. The other was younger, about twenty, in a sleeveless white top and khaki shorts. Her hair was dark with a feathered pixie cut that gave her face and cheekbones a sculpted appearance. With her dimples and dangling earrings, I could see it was a great look for Laurie.

Feeling a little nervous, I walked through the gate.

At first, the women didn't seem to notice me, but as I made my way closer, there was a pause in their conversation as they looked my way. I stopped about fifteen feet from them and took off my sunglasses.

"Hi."

A good three seconds went by as the women looked at me. Then Laurie's eyes widened.

"Oh my God. Gidon!!!"

She came running over to me and I opened my arms. She jumped into them and we hugged tightly.

"Gidon, Gidon," she repeated. "Oh my God, oh my God, you're here." She squeezed me.

I laughed. "I was in the neighborhood."

She pulled away from me and there were tears running down her cheeks. She wiped them away with her fingers.

"You look great," I said looking into her eyes.

Laurie hugged me again. I looked over her shoulder to see the other woman approaching. Laurie pulled back a little, but still holding onto me, turned to her co-worker. "Liat, this is my hero...Gidon."

I laughed at the mention of hero. "*Shalom*. Hi." I smiled to the other teacher.

"*Shalom*," she smiled back and held out her hand which I shook.

"I can't believe you're here," Laurie said, tears coming again. She turned to her friend. "This is *Gidon*," she repeated, probably more for her own acceptance.

"Would you like me to watch the kids for a little while?" Liat offered.

"That would be perfect."

Laurie walked me over to a small pavilion that had been set up to provide some shade. We pulled two plastic patio chairs over and she sat next to me, her hand firmly holding mine.

"Okay, I'll be calm. I'll be calm," she said to herself out loud. "Oh my God, how *are* you?"

"Fine. Very well. And your folks send their love."

"They know you're here?"

"I spoke to your dad last night. He's probably jealous of me, but won't say it."

"I also spoke to them last night. He didn't say anything."

"Naturally."

Laurie suddenly jumped up. "Okay, I can't sit still. C'mon."

She put her arm through mine, and we started to stroll around the building.

"So, is this a pleasure trip or are you moving back?"

"Business...actually."

"Same old business? No, I shouldn't ask that."

"You can ask."

"Same old business?"

"Don't ask." She looked at me and I cracked up. "Just kidding. No, it's not the same business. Some people may think it's related, that's all." I paused. "So, tell me about you. What's going on? Are you okay?"

In the distance, three helicopters crossed the sky, their collective percussion reaching us as a dull rumble.

"I'm fine. My cousins, you know, took me in. I'm still living with them. And I'm teaching school here. I can't believe you stayed with me in the hospital the whole time."

I shrugged, like "Of course."

"Your turn," she smiled, looking into my eyes. "How are *you*...really?"

"Really?...I'm doing okay. Your dad has probably told you. I have my dojo, I teach in a middle school from time to time. And there may be someone waiting for me when I get back."

"Awesome. *That* he didn't tell me."

"We'll see where it goes. And you...really?"

Her voice dropped and I could sense her energy come down. As I looked at the base of her neck below her right ear I saw the remains of cigarette burns. I remembered finding her in the make-shift cell, burned and bleeding and barely conscious. Plastic surgery had taken care of most of the scars, but there was still some disfigured skin.

"I should never have gone so far north, you know," she said quietly.

I looked up at her, but Laurie was staring past me, off toward a memory that wouldn't fade. I knew where her mind was. It was on a trip she should never have taken...leaving the archeological dig in Caesarea to sightsee with a girl friend up near the Lebanese border. I've often imagined what it must have been like for her, suddenly realizing how late it had become... grasping that the darkness that surrounded them wasn't benevolent... Not knowing until it was too late that it hid four terrorists, planning to enter a kibbutz. Laurie, I knew, still heard her friend's scream and the gunfire that cut it short.

I took her hand, but didn't say anything.

Her eyes came back into focus. "Am I okay? I still get an occasional nightmare."

I looked at her. "So do I."

I let a moment go by. It was time for something else.

"How about men in your life? The folks back home will want to know."

She smiled. "Oh, just the *folks* want to know? You're not curious at all."

"No, not at all."

"In that case, I'll go with mmm...maybe. There may be someone. Like you said: we'll see."

"Awesome," I mimicked her words.

"So how long are you here?"

"Don't know. Depends how quickly things come together."

"So, tell me about this friend of yours."

"Katie," I smiled, "is terrific."

I told her how we met and what was going on. I also mentioned how strained my relationship with Alli had become. Laurie then told me about her life here, halfway around the world, plus the on-going arguments with her mom about staying here after the rescue — and conversely, how supportive her dad was.

Laurie asked me about my leaving after Tamar was killed. I explained, and she said she understood my reasons. I told her she was one of the few who did.

We had walked along the outside of the building, coming almost full circle.

"I just want you to know," I said to Laurie, coming to a stop, "that you look great."

"You too. You too."

"And I thought your eyes were good."

"Can't take a compliment, huh?"

Before I could think of a comeback, my cell phone rang. It was Amit again.

"They've left school. They're heading out of Jerusalem. North."

"I'm on my way." I hung up.

Laurie was looking at me. "Be careful. Please"

"I will be."

"And come back to see me."

"I promise."

I kissed her on the cheek, gave her a long hug, and then took off, looking back once.

The Coles, apparently, exited the school building, and then drove northward in a hurry. They could've just randomly left school in the middle of the day for a picnic in one of the country's many parks, or perhaps they had a specific rendezvous in mind — alongside the road for instance, or at a gas station, or even in a beautiful forest setting.

I traveled eastward at considerably greater-than-speed-limit-speeds. What were the Coles involved in?...Creating the Guardians of Heaven, assassination attempts, murder of a young man...dealing with a known terrorist and mercenary?

And what stimulated this sudden excursion in the middle of the school day? They were nervous about something...perhaps it was the bomb on their doorstep. That would do it...or maybe they were just worried and running away.

I rendezvoused with David Amit ten minutes later at a gas station near the town of Modi'in. I parked in back and climbed into his Subaru. We took off even before exchanging pleasantries. Amit and his team were tailing the Coles using a three vehicle "tail that car" strategy. The lead vehicle, a green Hyundai, had a man and a woman in it, the second car, a silver Nissan, had two women, and then there was us. The idea was leapfrog: one of the three cars would keep an eye on the Coles for a short time then would drift back to be replaced by car number two. After a few minutes, we'd take over. Then the rotation would repeat.

As we loosely caravanned northward, Amit moved us into the number two spot.

"Well, this is pleasant...a nice scenic ride," I commented, looking out my window.

"It is, isn't it. So good of the Coles to provide this diversion."

"Did I ever tell you, Mr. Amit, your English is very good."

"Thank you."

"Of course, that's why you have this job."

He smiled. "So how was your visit to Rehovot?"

"Too short."

"You'd like this to be over, wouldn't you?"

"I'd like to find the person who shot Pavel, yes."

A small, white late model car passed us on the single lane road and pulled in front of us. The Coles were probably half a mile ahead in a maroon mini-van. They were truly easy to follow.

"*Savlanute*, patience. This is detective work, my friend, not that other stuff where you disappear into the night with the enemy all around."

"Well, if I don't do that every so often I get crabby."

"Crabby?"

"You know... bitchy."

"Ah, I know bitchy."

"Your English isn't as good as I thought."

A walkie-talkie in the space between our seats came to life. The car behind us wanted to move to the front position. In a few moments, the silver Nissan with the two women agents passed us and began to leapfrog forward.

"I've been thinking," Amit looked at me, "it may just be time for you and a small group to take a little hike tonight. We could use some more information and we're not getting anything here. Interested?"

"Definitely. It will do wonders for my attitude. Where?"

"Not sure. Perhaps Ramallah."

"Why Ramallah?"

He nodded forward. A green sign ahead of us with white lettering in three languages — Hebrew, Arabic, and English — noted that Ramallah was five kilometers ahead.

"The Coles are going to Ramallah?" I thought aloud.

What was so interesting was that Ramallah was under Palestinian control. It generally would be unwise for Israelis to travel there, depending on how hot the political climate was. And the Coles were not lost, that was certain — which indicated they had been here before. Maybe I had been right, and they were seeing somebody about the "bomb" that had been placed on their doorstep.

As we approached the town, the ample foliage that had been on either side of us had thinned out, leaving only a shrubless, rocky terrain. Traffic began to slow down as well. We were approaching an army checkpoint where concrete barriers were funneling vehicles past soldiers and a small guard tower.

Amit picked up the walkie-talkie and ordered the other cars to turn around and head back. We would stay behind to see what happened to the maroon van in front of us.

Up ahead, in fact, were two checkpoints: first the Israeli, and then fifty feet beyond that, the Palestinian. We pulled to the side of the road out of traffic, well before the Israeli checkpoint.

"Let's see what will be," Amit said as he kept his eyes on the Coles' van.

All sorts of vehicles were now stopped at the checkpoint: regular cars, taxis, trucks, even a maroon mini-van. All were waiting to be cleared by the Israelis. The Coles were the fourth vehicle in line, and in a matter of minutes came to the quartet of soldiers manning the roadblock. Two of the four soldiers stood to either side of the van — no doubt to look over the occupants. Their partners remained fifteen feet further to the side to get an overview of the stopped vehicle. Each of the four soldiers had a rifle slung across his front. To my right, I also noticed that a guard was manning the short tower, overseeing the entire area.

As the Coles pulled up, the soldier on the driver's side leaned slightly forward and spoke to Aaron Cole, who was behind the wheel. The conversation lasted perhaps fifteen seconds and then the guard stepped back. The maroon van continued straight. The Coles went another fifty yards and came to a stop at the Palestinian checkpoint. The set-up was similar, with armed soldiers to either side and concrete barriers beyond them.

"Here," Amit handed me the binoculars I had used earlier today in front of the Coles' school. He grabbed a second pair for himself.

We watched as the Palestinian soldier questioned Aaron Cole. Cole pulled out a folded paper and handed it to the guard. The soldier looked from the paper to the man who handed it to him, then back to the paper. Finally, he returned the paper to Cole, then pointed to an area over to the left behind the barricades. The guard stepped back and the mini-van pulled forward. Once beyond the checkpoint, Aaron Cole pulled his vehicle to the left and parked behind a black Mercedez that had already stopped beside the road.

For a long moment nothing happened. The maroon mini-van remained where it was — no one getting out — and the Mercedez remained where it was — no one getting out. Finally, the doors to the Mercedez opened and four men emerged.

I turned the center focus ring on the binoculars to get a sharper view.

The four men approaching the Coles' vehicle were a mixed

330 Stephen J. Gordon

bunch: two were on the small side — one bald and one with a full head of gray hair — and two were taller. Both of the taller men were dark complexioned, but one was clean shaven while the other had a neatly-trimmed gray mustache. As they approached the mini-van, Aaron and Hannah Cole got out to meet them.

"Well, well," I said.

"Well, well," Amit repeated.

I trained my binoculars on the two taller men who had come from the Mercedez.

"Do you see the tall, clean shaven man?" I asked.

"*Kain*. Yes."

"Does he look familiar?"

"Perhaps."

"The last time I saw him, he was opening a restaurant in Baltimore."

"The Iraqi. So there is a connection."

"We just don't know what."

"Do you recognize anyone else?" Amit asked, binoculars still to his eyes.

I looked at the tall man who had the gray mustache. If I had been up close to him I knew that his eyes would be bright and full of energy. My friend Ibrahim was no doubt there on official business.

"Anyone else look familiar?" he repeated.

I let a second go by.

"No." I lowered the binoculars and handed them back to Amit. "Let's go back."

"What is it?" Amit looked at me. "What's bothering you?"

"I want to know more about the Coles. I don't buy that they're doing business with the Iraqi or anyone else for money. Maybe I'm wrong, but there has to be another reason."

"If you have a question, perhaps it's time to ask a rabbi."

After a moment, I understood what he meant. It was definitely time to see the rabbi.

22

"I have to tell you, Mr. Aronson, this conversation makes me very uncomfortable."

I was sitting in Rabbi Ari Goldman's living room in the community of Alon Shvut about twenty minutes south of Jerusalem. The community and those nearby were strategically established decades ago, for they were along the main road to Jerusalem coming up from Hebron. If an army wanted to take Jerusalem from the south, they had to come this way first. The communities were an important buffer. They were historically significant as well, as they were part of the traditional pilgrimage routes; ruins of ancient homes were still scattered in the area.

"You understand the importance of this information," I replied evenly.

Rabbi Goldman, a thin man in his sixties who I was told walked three miles a day, stood up, obviously agitated. I looked around his living room. One wall was lined with bookcases, containing Judaic texts but also a selection of best sellers. Another wall had family portraits. Off to the side was a baby grand piano.

"I do understand, but I don't believe in gossiping about someone else."

"This isn't gossip, Rabbi. We're talking about someone who may have committed and may be committing major crimes."

"I don't want to hear that, if you don't mind."

"Okay. Let me be more specific as to what I'm looking for. I'm trying to get some insight into Aaron and Hannah Cole. I know they care a great deal about their students, but what else are they passionate about?"

Rabbi Goldman sat down and for several moments, lost in thought, as if he were going through some sort of internal debate. As he searched for what to say, I looked at him, putting together what I had learned about him.

The man in front of me had been raised in England, but came to Israel in the 70's. He was highly regarded across the religious spectrum, and as such, was the Chief Rabbi for this entire area of the country. Whatever I did, I was not going to push him into answering something he didn't want to answer. Maybe I could nudge him a little, though.

"Rabbi, why don't you just tell me about the man you know. That's all I want."

"All right. But everything I tell you will be facts, not speculation. That wouldn't be appropriate."

"Fair enough."

"First of all, you know that he is a bit younger than me. In fact, he was a student of mine in our seminary many years ago. At the time, his name wasn't Aaron Cole. It was Aaron Kolevski. I think he changed it when he went to the United States."

"Why do you think he did that?" I was asking him to speculate, but it was a natural question.

"He probably thought he could reach more kids that way. I don't know. I do know that he's from a very distinguished family and has always put the study of our laws and customs before anything else. Maybe that's why he changed his name...perhaps to appeal to a broader audience."

"His name change must not have sat well with his family."

"I really don't know about that. Don't ask me to speculate again, Mr. Aronson."

I had to smile.

"But I do know that he always jealously guarded his time."

"What do you mean?"

"I mean that study for him came before anything else. That's what motivated him to build all his schools...to reach out to as many young people as he could."

"So they could learn *Torah*."

"That's right."

Interesting laws he taught his students, I thought but didn't say: How to be a gang — the Guardians of Heaven — and that it was okay to come after someone with a hatchet. I hadn't forgotten about that one.

"I know he has been very successful at attracting all sorts of children."

"Very much so. Children from abusive homes, new immigrants, and just anyone who wanted to learn ."

"As far as you know, was he ever political?" I was thinking of why he would want to kill Eitan Lev.

"Generally not." He paused for a moment. "In this country, as you know, there are political parties for every occasion. Even religious beliefs. Aaron was always quiet about such matters."

"Did he serve in the army?"

"No. Like many seminary students, he was exempted so he could study. I know he feels strongly about that."

"Not serving in the army?"

"There is a philosophy: if we don't learn, who will?"

"But there are some seminary students who *do* go into the army. I know, I served with some of them."

"Of course there are, and they're highly motivated. Many times, though, it depends on what religious group you're in." He let a moment go by. "Come with me." He got up and brought me over to a sliding patio door in the dining room. Rabbi Goldman opened the slider and we stepped out onto a deck that had an amazing view of the countryside from the high vantage point of his house. Rabbi Goldman's home, and his community, were up in the hills, so our view had a grand quality to it. We could see for miles. "You know this country, Mr. Aronson. What do you see?"

I looked to my right and left, plus at the sun to get my bearings. "We're looking west. The Mediterranean is off in the distance straight ahead."

"You can see it sometimes on a clear day."

"Jerusalem is off to the right and Beersheva and the desert are to the left."

"In this community, let me tell you what *we* see. We see a need for education in all directions. By educating our own people and by educating our Arab neighbors we can break down the walls keeping us apart."

"But you must have a willing audience on both sides."

"Of course. And we also need to be safe."

"Tough combination sometimes." I looked out toward the land in front of me, then shifted my line of questions. "What can you tell me about Mrs. Cole?"

"Not very much. My impression is that she's more all business than Aaron. My son, who was in one of their schools, said that she was always very strict. But you know, strict to a young student may be a teacher holding to his or her standards. So, I don't know if I'd give much weight to that. I do know that she tends to be more political than her husband...to make sure they have the funds they need."

There was that magic word again — "funds." We had discussed it in Baltimore.

"Any idea how Aaron Cole's schools are doing financially?"

"Sorry. Can't help you with that one, Mr. Aronson."

I didn't know if he was not being cooperative, or if he just didn't know.

"Anything else come to mind about the Coles that you might think is helpful?"

"Just that their schools reach a lot of kids."

"Well, that's all I've got, Rabbi." I began to move off the deck to the inside of the house. "Thank you for your time."

"I hope I wasn't too evasive."

"Not at all. I understand. It's also good to be reminded that facts are important, not just hearsay."

"Take care. You know how to get back to Jerusalem from here?"

"I was stationed nearby for six weeks."

"Drive safely."

With that, I walked back outside and into the bright sunlight again. As I headed to my car, which I had parked under a nearby tree, I turned on my cell phone. By the time I was in the driver's seat and had the windows down, the phone beeped, indicating messages. There were two.

"Gidon, this is Nate. We had talked about locating the Coles' anonymous benefactor here. Just wanted you to know I got a hold of the school treasurer and he told me a good portion of their operating money comes from a local philanthropist. He assured me there were no foreign investors. I don't know if that convinces me or not. There may be money he's unaware of."

If it were true, then there were no financial ties to the Iraqi.

"Or," Nate went on, "if it's true, then there are no financial ties to the Iraqi. And there goes our connection. The question is, is that accurate? More ambiguity to figure out. Talk to you later." He hung up.

Well, there *was* a connection to the Iraqi; we just hadn't found it yet. Perhaps a second read of Eitan Lev's dossier would turn up something. He was the common factor in all this.

The second message followed. It was Ibrahim. "Salaam, my friend. You asked for the name of the book. It's *The Caravan Stop*. You'll enjoy it." He hung up. I checked the time of the call. Ten minutes ago. He must have just gotten back from Ramallah. *"The Caravan Stop."* It sounded like something from an old spy movie, but the cryptic message was necessary in case anyone overheard him. He had left a package or a letter for me at our safe drop.

I came out of the Rabbi's housing development and headed up Route 60, the main avenue into Jerusalem from the south. The road was a single lane in each direction, with rocky terrain to either side. As I approached Bethlehem, an Israeli checkpoint slowed the flow of trucks and cars, but the soldiers for the most part were moving everyone along. I was now leaving the West Bank. On the other side of the checkpoint Route 60 went through two tunnels. Originally, another road led to Jerusalem from this region, but Jewish travelers came under fire from nearby villages. To keep its citizens safe, the government skirted the old road and cut tunnels under the Arab village of Beit Jala.

Fifteen minutes later, and with the tunnels behind me, I was back in the neighborhood where I had rendezvoused with

Ibrahim. The streets were once again lined with cars, some parked in legitimate spaces, others on the sidewalk. The florist shop where Ibrahim stopped to look at flowers was open for business, and there was no evidence a drive-by shooting had been prevented right there. Pedestrians, mostly older men and women, were perambulating, dressed in lightweight clothing and hats. In another hour or so, rush hour would hit the city and a younger generation would dominate the streets and sidewalks.

Instead of looking for a parking space, I double parked in front of the familiar boxy apartment building that had the thinning carob tree in the yard. Key in hand I ran into the lobby.

It was as stuffy and as airless as it had been yesterday. The staircase was straight ahead, but I was more interested in the bank of mailboxes on the right. The ambient light was still dim, so I had to look carefully at each handwritten label to find the box for Apartment 7. It was the third from the right. Inside the narrow space was a single folded piece of paper.

The note was written in black ink: "Your friends are meeting tonight at 2:00 with my guest." There was a Ramallah address at the bottom.

Hopefully, Ibrahim hadn't put himself in danger getting the note to me. I smiled introspectively. Everything Ibrahim did put him in danger. I pocketed the note, knowing that before I could take action on it, I needed to review Lev's file again.

The Dan Panorama was five minutes away, and would be a welcome place to pause and think. As I walked through the lobby, the attractive woman who had checked me in — and who had eyes with a hint of the Orient in them — smiled at me from across the counter. I smiled back before realizing what my cheek muscles were doing.

Back in my room, I pulled out Eitan Lev's dossier, collapsed onto the bed, and began reading.

Eitan Lev biographical summary:

Eitan Lev was born in January 1948 on Kibbutz Yael just west of the Sea of Galilee...

When I finished, I stared up at the ceiling for a moment, then grabbed my cell phone to call Amit. He answered on the second ring.

23

I waited for the Shin Bet man in a courtyard near the Cardo, the excavated Roman thoroughfare, in the Old City's Jewish Quarter. By now it was early evening, but the Old City was still busy with tourists and residents. The heat of the day had passed, and the coolness brought a new vibrancy to the streets.

Amit found me sitting atop a short wall near the renovated Hurva Synagogue. I pointed to a pedestrian space between two nearby buildings. "Let's walk."

"So what did you discover?" Amit asked, as we headed up the alleyway.

"I met with Rabbi Goldman, as you suggested."

"As Commander Dror suggested."

I smiled. "Yes. And what he told me was that Aaron Cole put study above all else...that he jealously guarded his time so he could teach."

"Not unusual in this country."

"And not ignoble either. But what if all your hard work,

which you probably thought was a Divine duty, would be un-
done by someone in power...someone who had a very different
philosophy?"

"Eitan Lev?"

A middle-aged couple, the man wearing an Orioles cap,
walked toward us then stepped to the side to get past us in the
narrow passageway.

"What do you remember about his politics...specifically
about his view on religion?" I asked.

"That he wants to..."

"He wants to remove army exemptions for students who are
in seminaries."

"Correct. It's a hot issue."

"I'm sure the kids aren't crazy about it, but can you imagine someone like Aaron Cole, whose whole life is being able to
control these kids...how *he* feels about it? Going into the army
would be like a major perversion for him."

"I can tell you something else...If Lev is elected, he wants to
examine whether these schools are unfairly taking advantage of
government subsidies."

We stopped next to a private residence. I leaned against a
wall next to the front door. "That would be a problem for the
Coles and anyone else in that position. Would they go as far as
assassination?"

"This is sometimes a country of zealots who do things for
what they believe is a higher purpose."

"But still," I began to play the other side, "there's no evidence that this is what Cole is doing. He seemed genuine enough when I spoke to him. Maybe he'd simply not vote for Lev."

"No. Not good enough for him. Let me soothe your conscience. My agent identified Hannah Cole as the woman outside your dojo before Pavel was killed. We altered her hair and removed the cap from the composite image. My man is certain it was her."

I just looked at him.

"We have no weapon or ballistics, of course, saying she pulled the trigger."

"But we know she was the last one to see Pavel. Your man didn't see anyone else come in, right?"

"Correct."

I thought of Pavel opening the door, letting Hannah Cole in because he trusted her. I could feel the heat in my face begin to rise.

Amit continued: "And the Iraqi is in this because—"

"Lev is a tough guy when it comes to crime. Commander Dror said it himself — and it was in the dossier. Lev will do everything he can to stop people like the Iraqi, whether he's a street thug or an arms supplier to terrorists."

"So both the Coles and the Iraqi want to kill Lev but for different reasons." He absent-mindedly looked down the alley at a young couple walking hand in hand. "We still don't know how they got together."

"We'll ask them tonight."

Amit looked at me.

"You're sending a team into Ramallah tonight, aren't you?"

"Yes."

"The Coles and the Iraqi are meeting at 2 AM. I have an address."

"You have a friend who knows these things?"

"I have a very good friend who knows lot of things."

24

It was just after midnight and there were six people in the briefing room: Amit, myself, and four soldiers. We were all in uniform with the exception of Amit, and collectively we bent over a table, covered with aerial photos of our target site. Earlier this evening, after I had given Amit the Ramallah address, he made some calls, and the air force sent a drone over the location for photographic reconnaissance. The address, it seemed, was actually a series of connected buildings in an industrial area of town. From the detailed shots, we could see that the buildings were in a "U" shape with a courtyard in the center. As of ten o'clock this evening, there was no activity in any of the buildings and the courtyard was empty.

"Looks quiet," Amit looked at me.

"For now."

A tall blond soldier leaned over: "We leave in forty-five minutes."

I scanned the four men in uniform around the table.

Over each of their left shoulders hung the tree emblem of the Golani Brigade. I knew additionally that these four men were part of the brigade's commando unit, *Sayeret Golani*. By comparison, I was under-dressed. My uniform had no markings of any kind except for my rank.

I turned to the blond soldier who was watching the time. He was Dov, the commander of the squad. "You know," I said, "before both our times, my unit and your unit worked together."

"I know. In Africa." The Entebbe rescue. "No casualties tonight, though."

I nodded and looked at his three men. To Dov's right was a red-headed, bespectacled soldier named Yury. On the other side of the table were Idan and Yoni. The oldest among the four of them was probably Dov in his mid-20's.

Once we had gone over the photos, Amit and I pulled Dov aside. With my major's rank I was senior man in the group, so I needed to address that, plus the fact that I was an outsider. Most units didn't welcome outsiders. They didn't know the personalities of the team, plus no one really knew what to expect of them. They had no shared history.

"Dov," I began, "This is your squad. I'm not here to take over."

"Don't worry," he said matter-of-factly. "Everything will be okay. I'm pleased you'll be with us. There is no problem."

"Has Mr. Amit explained our objectives?"

"Yes, mostly reconnaissance. If we catch your people under the right circumstances, we will take them back with us."

I wasn't sure what "the right circumstances" would be, but

the fact that the Coles were associating with a man on the Israel's target list was sufficient to bring them all in for interrogation. I wanted more, though, particularly of Hannah Cole. She had to pay for Pavel.

As Dov walked away, one of the other soldiers, the red-headed Yury, came over to me. "Glad you're here." That's all he said, and then turned and went back to the photos.

"That's nice," Amit said to me. "They seem to trust you."

"What did you say to them before I arrived?"

"Not much. Maybe I mentioned Lebanon."

"You mentioned Lebanon."

"I wanted to make sure they knew you'd be able to handle yourself."

"Uh huh. Thanks."

"I have to tell you," Amit continued, "I'm very curious to see what the Iraqi is up to."

"There are some missing pieces."

"Whatever they are, you'll check them out and put an end to them tonight."

I nodded.

"Do you think your friend will be there?" Amit was always thinking. I, too, had been wondering about Ibrahim.

"I don't know. I hope he's at home with his family."

The Shin Bet man nodded.

I watched the *Sayeret* team ready their packs. At the moment, the four soldiers were putting civilian clothing into their bags.

I turned to Amit. "Do you still have your phone on you?"

He handed it to me.

"Mind an overseas call?" I was already dialing.

"Not at all."

I moved to the corner of the room, for the illusion of privacy.

"Hello?" Katie's voice came on the other end.

It was seven hours earlier in Baltimore — a little after 5 PM.

"Hi," I said casually.

"Gidon, hi. How are you?"

"Doing okay." I paused. "I'm glad you're home. I wanted to hear your voice."

"Yeah, I was hoping you'd call. How are things going?"

I surveyed the Golani soldiers packing their gear. "Moving along."

"Good. You're satisfied then?"

"Ask me tomorrow." I half-laughed.

"Call and tell me."

"I will. You're okay?"

"Fine. Had a teachers' meeting today. Exciting stuff.... Reviewing how to write constructive report card comments." Katie sounded a universe away. She was.

"Hmmm...fascinating."

"So, how much longer do you think you'll be there?"

"Don't know. Couple of days. I'll let you know. When I get back, I'll take you to dinner and then we can work on another bottle of wine."

"Mmm. That'll give me something to look forward to."

"Me, too. I'll call you when I can."

I hung up and returned the phone to Amit.

"Time to pack up," he said.

I moved over to where the soldiers had gathered around a pile of equipment and began to check and load my gear: night vision equipment, water, some energy bars, miscellaneous electronics and radios, extra clips of ammo. My Glock went into a holster at my waist and then I picked up my M4 carbine. The M4 was a lightweight, more compact version of the M16. It was a shoulder-fired weapon with a collapsible stock, and several interesting options: a grenade launcher that fired a 40mm grenade, a laser sight, an infrared pointer/illuminator used in conjunction with night vision goggles, and a sound suppressor to reduce noise and muzzle flash. The M4 was a primary weapon for Special Ops teams, and as I looked at the rest of the squad, I saw that each soldier had one.

I loaded a clip into the weapon and set it aside.

"Major," Dov called to me.

I looked over and he tossed me a tube of camouflage cream. I opened it and proceeded to blacken my face and hands. Additionally, any shiny surface on personal paraphernalia was blackened as well. Yury spread cream on his wire-rimmed glasses and on the clasp of his watch. In a matter of minutes, the five of us lost our individual features. We each donned an ear piece and mini-microphone, which would remain off until we were closer to our target.

"Let's go," Dov said.

He left the room followed by Yury, Idan, and Yoni. Amit and I were last. I looked at him.

"You don't know of any other operations in Ramallah tonight, do you? I'd hate to run into a group of friends."

"I checked. No other operations in Ramallah tonight."

I nodded, grabbed my equipment, and exited the room.

We left the army base and rode eastward to Ramallah in two covered, specially muffled jeeps. For fifteen minutes we used single lane rural roads, but when Ramallah appeared in the distance, we turned off and began traveling across open country. The drivers extinguished their headlights and put on night vision goggles. The sky was moonless, and with no competition the stars were out in full bloom. As we drove across the rolling terrain, we had become merely a shapeless presence moving across a black field.

We drove with one vehicle in front of the other to minimize tracks. I sat in the back of the lead jeep with Yury, while Dov sat up front next to the driver. No one spoke. I tried to imagine what greeted us in the Palestinian controlled city. Hopefully, nothing. If all went well, the streets would be deserted and we could slip over to where the Cole-Iraqi meeting would be taking place without coming across insomniacs, Palestinian police, or army units. We'd watch any business that transpired, and then move in.

We drove to within a mile of the outskirts of Ramallah and then came to a stop. Ahead of us was the southeastern part of the city. From where we were, we could see darkened houses and some paved streets. Fortunately, the industrial area we wanted was just on the other side of this outer neighborhood. In another minute, the jeeps slowed to a stop. Without a word, we climbed out of the vehicles, waved to the drivers, and watched them disappear into the darkness. If all went well, small armored trucks would pick us up at the target area within five minutes of our call. At that point we might have several guests in tow. If the night went badly, there was always cover fire from a helicopter and extraction via a vacant parking lot a block away.

The squad fell into two parallel groups. I held my M4 in front of me as we walked silently forward, my right hand on the pistol grip behind the trigger and my left holding a ridged dowel-like handle projecting down off the barrel. The night air was still, but cool.

As we got closer to the residential area we could see both one-story and two-story homes. The houses were quite stark — cement or stone walls, flat or slightly pitched roofs. Some of the doors and windows were trimmed in turquoise to chase away the "evil eye." Dov motioned and we slipped behind the houses, keeping to the shadows. No one was about. The streets were abandoned, everyone hopefully asleep. We continued toward the center of town, keeping to the side streets.

As we moved a few blocks west, the neighborhood immediately changed. All that was here was rubble. These piles of debris were once houses...there were pieces of furniture, pipes, even toilets mixed in with smashed concrete. The homes might have been part of a Ramallah demolition project. It was impossible to tell, but even the street seemed torn up, with large chunks of rock and concrete scattered across a dirt road.

The earpiece in my left ear came to life. It was Dov. "Move to the right. Late night walkers ahead." We instantly obeyed and disappeared into the shadow of a stone wall.

As we waited in the darkness I looked from Dov to Yury, from Idan to Yoni. Their faces behind their masks of camouflage paint showed no emotion.

The voices of two men drifted over to us. They were speaking in Arabic and what I could make out sounded like a friendly argument about a soccer game they had just watched. The men were probably in their forties. They were dressed in jeans and button-down shirts, and one of them had what looked like new white tennis shoes. The soccer fans passed under the only streetlight on the block, and in the stark white light, the white tennis shoes stood out.

They walked down the street looking only straight ahead, thoroughly engaged in their discussion. As they approached us, I could feel myself pressing into the wall. It wasn't necessary. We were black forms hiding in a blackened space. The men passed within twenty feet of our squad without even a sideways glance.

We waited until they rounded a corner and then held off another thirty seconds before moving on. Dov took point and I took the second position. Yury was behind me, Idan and Yoni behind him. Dov knew exactly where to go. We silently moved from shadow to shadow as we proceeded through the neighborhood of houses and demolished buildings.

In another two blocks, Dov ordered us to the side once again. We were mid-block, pressed against a large structure that could have housed anything from offices to machinery. The collection of buildings we needed to get to was around the corner to the right. The problem was a Palestinian police car was parked in the middle of the street ahead of us. Four officers were standing around the vehicle, two on each side, talking across to each other. All were armed with AK-47's. Dov looked at me. I pointed to a break between the buildings we had just passed. The idea was to head between the two buildings and bypass the policemen. Dov nodded and we moved toward the break.

No sooner had we silently stepped between the buildings then we heard moaning. We stopped. There were buildings on either side of us now, and the moaning came from the left, near a doorway. The squad moved into a loose semi-circle to see a young man, perhaps nineteen, kissing a dark-haired older woman. They were standing, pressed up against the wall of the building. His hands were under her shirt and her hands were on his butt. They were very close together. She was moaning louder and louder as he kissed her neck.

She saw us first and suddenly pulled back from the boy. He followed her look and turned to see us. His pants were only partially unbuckled; we must've interrupted him. The woman, as she looked at us, was frozen. But the boy quickly scanned our squad and I could see his mind racing. All he had to do was shout and the Palestinian policemen would come running. Two scenarios flashed through my mind. If he screamed, both would silently die right there and we'd feel badly, but disappear into the night, then decide whether to abort the mission. Or, more likely, we would just disappear into the night, abort the mission, and try to avoid a firefight with the Palestinian policemen. Not good for us either way. Really bad for the lovers the first way.

Maybe they wouldn't say anything. Not a chance.

The boy took a deep breath, prelude to a yell.

I sprung forward and grabbed him by the throat — actually between his windpipe and the neck muscles to either side of it — and squeezed hard. He couldn't breathe, let alone scream.

Yoni, the soldier who was at the rear, stepped next to me and spoke in clear, fast Arabic.

"Do not scream, do not breathe, if either of you want to live."

The man's face was turning dark. His lady friend just stared at us.

Now what? There was no doubt in anyone's mind that if we just left the man and woman there, they'd go right to the Palestinian authorities.

"Yury, Idan, cover them," Dov's voice said in my earpiece.

Silenced Sig Sauers appeared inches from the lovers' faces. I let go of the boy who immediately started gasping for air. Yoni, the Golani who had spoken Arabic, wrapped a big hand around the kid's mouth until he settled down.

Again, now what? We hadn't gained anything. We needed to move on and we couldn't let them go.

"Yoni..." Dov nodded to his man. Yoni let the boy go. While

Yury and Idan kept their Sigs on the couple, Yoni began fishing in a jacket pocket for something.

"We don't want another Gush Etzion 35, so we came up with a workable option," Dov said quietly to me.

Almost all Israelis knew of the Gush Etzion 35. In 1948, thirty-five Haganah soldiers had set out to re-supply four blockaded kibbutzim south of Jerusalem. They were discovered enroute by Arab civilians. The Haganah unit released the civilians unharmed, but they sounded the alarm. All thirty-five soldiers were killed after a battle that lasted most of the day.

"Ketamine," Yoni said, pulling two syringes from his pocket. Each had been pre-filled with a clear liquid. "It'll keep them unconscious for 4-6 hours. "

Dov spoke to the couple in quiet Hebrew. "Lie down."

The young man and older woman just looked at him.

"I don't want you to fall. This drug will not hurt you, but it works quickly."

The couple didn't move.

"We need to get going," Yury said, behind his pistol.

I looked at the frozen boy and woman. "Live to make love another day," I said. "Do you understand?"

They each nodded. Language wasn't an issue. They sat on the ground.

"On your sides," Yoni said. "It'll be easier for you to breathe."

They stretched out, facing each other. Yoni made a quick adjustment in the doses, then plunged one syringe into the boy's thigh, and the second into the woman's. In a minute they were unconscious, but their eyes remained open.

"Okay," Dov commanded, "let's go."

"Wait," I said. The four Golani soldiers looked at me. "Yoni, leave the syringes next to them. In case they are discovered."

Yoni nodded and dropped the syringes between the couple. It looked like they injected themselves. The squad continued on.

Our target, the "U"-shaped building complex, was three blocks away. Keeping to the shadows as we had before, we covered the next two blocks without further distraction. Before moving any closer, we paused for a first-hand look at our objective. The complex was two stories, had a flat roof and nondescript walls — with the exception of some Arabic graffiti scrawled along its western length. Outside a back entrance, abandoned cars lined the street. There were two sets of windows that we could see — one pair on the left-hand wall and another pair on the back wall. Floodlights lit the perimeter of the building, and, as far as we could tell from our angle, lit the courtyard as well. Two sentries were already in place on the roof. Both were wearing army fatigues and had their heads and faces wrapped in *kaffiyahs*. Each man carried a Kalashnikov.

From where we were crouching at ground level, we couldn't see what was happening in the courtyard. The only building close enough to provide us with some height was an adjacent structure under construction. For now, there was a skeletal framework of iron beams, some flooring, and partially completed walls. Interestingly, there was no building equipment around, so the building site could have been abandoned. Its best feature was that it was two stories taller than the warehouse next to it.

Dov motioned and the five of us headed into the building. Night vision goggles came on and we walked up to the third floor. Without a sound or direction between us, we took up positions in openings along the wall, facing our target building. Then we waited. And watched.

The warehouse looked very much the same up close as it had in the drone's pictures of two hours ago. The building complex was indeed "U"-shaped, with its open end to the left. A sliding metal gate closed off street access. The big difference between the drone's photos and the present view was that now the compound was lined with cars; earlier it had been empty. I took out night vision binoculars and checked out the cars.

"Israeli license plates," I said in my mic, to no one in particular. "All of them."

Dov's voice came on softly: "Stolen cars."

That's why the sentries are here, I thought. Protection.

So, this was what the Iraqi was probably up to. Car thefts. Police Commander Dror said that besides drugs, it was one of the major, most successful criminal activities in Israel. If indeed the Iraqi was involved, then Lev's political platform of anti-crime commando units would not be welcome here. In fact, they would do considerable damage to a major income producing activity. Now, to make me happy, I just needed to see the Coles working with him.

"Yoni, Idan," Dov interrupted my thoughts, "time to change."

They nodded and moved away from the window. I watched as the two soldiers pulled out a small collection of *kaffiyahs* from their packs. They chose checkered ones and wrapped them around their heads. With the two men already in fatigues, and now with the heads and faces wrapped, it would be difficult from a distance to tell them apart from the Palestinian sentries. At least that was the hope. With a nod from Dov, Yoni and Idan disappeared the way we had come.

While they were gone, two men came out of the right-hand building and started walking among the cars. They were both dressed in well tailored pants and shirts, and strolled around as if on a car lot, nonchalantly shopping for a good deal. The fact that multiple flood lights bathed the entire compound in a harsh white light gave the area an arena-like feel. It wouldn't be difficult to just watch the activity, detached from the impact of the action. But it was all very real and personal. There were sentries five hundred yards from us and each carried an assault rifle that could fire 600 rounds a minute. We were Israeli troops in enemy territory, trying to capture the planners behind a series of attempted assassinations and successful murders.

Beneath the moonless sky, the early morning air was cool and clear. A light breeze flowed through the partially completed building where we had established our position. At the moment, I was lying prone on the floor in front of an opening in the wall, watching through night glasses. To my left was Dov and to his left was Yury. Both of them had their M4s in hand, as they too were prone on the floor. But they were looking through their nightscopes, not binoculars.

As I continued to watch the two men in the compound below, my earpiece came on. It was Idan. All he said was two words: "In position."

A moment later, Yoni: "In position."

Before Dov could respond, a white BMW pulled up to the long gate at the end of the compound. Without moving his eyes from his nightscope, Dov replied. "Wait."

The two men in the compound who were perusing the stolen cars, looked up to the sentry nearest the gate. The sentry, Kalashnikov in hand, pumped his arm in the air twice. One of the men who was watching for this signal, walked over to the right end of the gate and pushed a button. The gate began to slide open, pocket-door style.

Through the binoculars, I watched the men on the ground. Their attention was on the BMW. If I wanted to take the sentries out, now would be the time.

Dov, apparently, realized the opportunity as well. He spoke into his mic to Yury, even though the red-headed soldier was next to him. "Yury, take the man on the left. Ready?"

"Yes."

I looked from Dov to Yury. They were totally focused on what they had to do. I could imagine looking through the nightscope, centering the crosshairs on a sentry's heart. There were two dull popping sounds as Dov and Yury fired. Each sentry was instantly thrown backward, but no sooner had they been knocked to the ground, then Idan and Yoni, in their *kaffiyahs* were standing in their place. They even had picked up the guards' weapons. I turned back to the people on the ground. The two men were still watching the gate slide open. From their angle, due to the short safety wall on the roof, they would never see the bodies at Yoni's and Idan's feet.

The BMW drove into the compound, and as the gate slid closed, pulled over to the side closer to us. Three men got out of the car: the Iraqi came out from the front passenger side, a young man, probably twenty, came out from the back seat, and then the driver. The driver was tall, wearing a navy blue Yankees windbreaker, and had a mustache that I knew was well kept and handsome. Ibrahim hadn't gotten my mental message to stay home tonight. More than likely, he needed to be here. But if shooting began, he could easily get hit.

After putting away the binocs, I picked up my M4, looked through the nightscope, and spoke softly into the microphone. "The man in a Yankees jacket standing near the line of cars...the big man with the mustache, he's mine. No one targets him."

When I finished, Dov assigned each of his men, including Yoni and Idan a target. If fighting broke out, the men below would be killed immediately.

Ibrahim and the Iraqi waited in the center of the compound. After a minute, a maroon mini-van pulled up to the gate. The attendant looked up at his sentry to make sure all was clear. Yoni — or was it Idan — lifted his Kalashnikov into the air twice. The men on the ground accepted it, and rolled back the fence.

Hannah and Aaron Cole pulled to a stop next to the BMW. They got out of the van and started walking toward the Iraqi and Ibrahim. From where we were, all we could do was watch the interaction, not hear it. The Coles, Ibrahim, and the Iraqi just walked and talked for five minutes. In all that time, not a *shekel* passed from one hand to another.

After another moment, Ibrahim led Aaron Cole inside, leaving behind the Iraqi and Hannah. The two of them walked around for a few moments, only half looking at the stolen cars. As I watched, Hannah looked to where Aaron had gone into the building, then moved closer to the Iraqi, and kissed him.

He didn't push her away; he didn't move away. He put one arm around her waist and held her close. Just for a moment, but it was enough.

Hannah Cole and the Iraqi. I wondered who initiated the relationship. Did it matter?

They separated and went back to the distance that had been between them earlier. They continued their walk through the compound.

That's all I needed to see. We had the Iraqi and the stolen cars — and now a connection to the Coles. I just wasn't sure if one were just using the other. It could have been true love. It's possible.

I thought back to the first time I saw the Iraqi. I was looking through the lens of my camera as I staked out the Oasis Café in Mount Vernon. He had opened the restaurant. The question was, and maybe it was academic, did Aaron Cole know what was going on between the Iraqi and his wife? Was that the reason for his visit to the café? Or was it all business?

"Dov, let's move in."

"Wait."

I looked at him, but he was looking through his scope at something. Then I heard it...a low rumble. I turned to see a truck approach the gate.

"Shit," my voice said.

The vehicle was an Israeli army truck, here in a Palestinian-controlled area.

"Look at the driver," Yoni said in my ear.

I moved my weapon to target the driver. The man behind the wheel was wearing dark clothes and a *kaffiyah*. He pulled the truck into the compound then made a three point turn and backed the truck up to a loading dock. As soon as the truck stopped, two men climbed out of the back. Both men were dressed like the driver, in black, and had the scarf head covering.

"Yoni, Idan," I said, "can you see what's in the truck? Is anything there?"

"Crates," Idan said.

The men began to unload the large wooden containers with a forklift and moved them into the warehouse.

"Shit." Now it was Dov's turn.

The crates had Hebrew markings and the name of a destination, an army base up north. There was no doubt the crates contained weapons...Israeli weapons.

If a truckload of weapons had been hijacked, the military had kept it quiet. It appeared that the Iraqi had a hand in it; perhaps he masterminded the operation. Whether he did or not, these weapons would make it easier for terrorists to disguise themselves as Israeli soldiers. They could walk over to a bus stop crowded with army personnel, press a switch on a suicide belt, and kill as many people as possible. Or, the armaments themselves could be used as weapons against Israeli civilians and soldiers alike. Aaron Cole and Ibrahim came back outside.

"Let's take out the men," I said. I gave the Golani men their targets. As far as Ibrahim, I had planned on wounding him — a clean shot with a full metal jacket to the outside of his thigh. The bullet would pass right through his leg. He'd be wounded "as part of his attempt to fight us off," but the wound would be clean and he should recuperate without difficulty. Once he was taken out of action, we would pick up the Coles as well as the Iraqi. For any prosecutors, this was even better than the stolen cars. These stolen Israeli weapons put all of them in the realm of terrorists.

"No," Dov commanded. "Wait. No one do anything."

He began to radio for air support.

"What are you doing?" I turned from the nightscope to look at him.

He ignored me. And kept calling for air support.

The Coles, the Iraqi, and Ibrahim walked over to the truck to watch the off-loading, oblivious to what was going on up here — or what was about to happen.

As we watched, more crates came off the truck.

I heard myself shout silently: Now! Take out the guards. Now!

Instead, there was the roar of a helicopter. God, he must've been close.

"Yoni, Idan, withdraw immediately!" Dov ordered.

The people on the ground began to run for cover. The Iraqi turned to the sentries — to Yoni and Idan — but they were no longer on the roof. Two of the men — the ones we saw first who were well dressed — jumped into a car, a dark green Toyota, and hit the accelerator.

I turned to Dov. "What the hell are you doing?"

He looked at me. "It's not your mission. Sorry."

"What?"

The two well-dressed men pulled away, heading toward the open gate. The helicopter fired a missile. Upon impact, there was a flash of searing white light within the vehicle, followed by a concussive boom. The car with its two occupants was propelled off the ground. It hung about five feet in the air, exploded further in a ball of yellow flame, then crashed back to earth.

The Coles ran back to their mini-van, while Ibrahim crouched next to the army truck. He was looking around the periphery to see if he could spot us. I brought my crosshairs to the edge of his left leg. And squeezed the trigger.

Ibrahim fell to the ground immediately.

"Sorry, my friend," I said to myself.

Hannah and Aaron Cole were back at their van. He got behind the wheel, while she pulled open the passenger door. The roar of the helicopter was deafening. Another car exploded about twenty feet away, but not from a missile. The cars in the compound were parked too closely together for this sort of action. This car, a black Acura, was next to the Toyota when its gas tank ignited.

A man, the passenger in the Iraqi's BMW, came running out of the building behind the army truck. He was carrying an RPG launcher. The man brought it up to his shoulder. Next to me, Dov and Yury fired. The man was thrown backward as his chest took the hits. The grenade launcher was flung to the side.

The Iraqi watched all this near Ibrahim then ran for the warehouse building. Hannah Cole paused while getting into her van. She looked at the Iraqi, then ran after him, leaving the van door open.

She had gone about thirty feet when there was a huge explosion behind her. She turned to see her maroon mini-van erupt in smoke and flame. Her husband was inside.

The Iraqi turned to her for a moment. It was just for a moment, and Dov next to me, took his shot. The Iraqi was hit in his upper right shoulder. Dov could have hit him dead center if he had wanted, but that wasn't the idea. The Iraqi was knocked backwards, but he wasn't dead.

From our elevation next door, I looked at the compound and all the exploding vehicles. Oily, thick smoke billowed up into the black sky beyond the range of the floodlights. In the middle of the compound, Hannah Cole collapsed to the ground and put her head in her hands.

25

The twelve year old blond boy wearing a white gi and a yellow belt stood motionless in the center of my dojo while his classmates sat on the floor behind him. We were in the middle of the boy's green belt test and the room was silent. Sweat was running down both sides of his face. Despite the pressure, the boy looked calm. Jonathan sat in a chair next to me, perhaps twelve feet in front of the student.

Jeffrey, the yellow belt, had performed perfectly so far. He had run through his basic techniques — kicking, blocking, and punching while moving in stance, and now was waiting to begin the next portion, the *katas*. These were a series of techniques organized into choreographed forms that tested coordination, strength, understanding, and diligence. Jeff was one of the stars of the class, a solid worker, with more than some talent. His techniques were strong and clean within the context of his age.

"Very good so far, Jeffrey. Now let's see Kata Number One."

Without hesitation, he bowed to me, then moved into

the first form, turning, blocking, kicking. As he continued his moves, I leaned over to Jonathan.

"He's pretty good, wouldn't you say?" I whispered.

"Very solid."

"No hesitation." I paused. "Now, you know that he probably sees us out of the corner of his eye, and he's got to be wondering what the hell we're talking about."

Jonathan nodded pensively.

"This little conversation I'm having with you drives the students nuts. They think I'm discussing their mistakes."

"It's just a mind game."

"Sometimes."

"You're an evil man."

I nodded and turned back to Jeff who was almost finished. He had covered a fair amount of distance across the dojo floor, but now the form had brought him back to where he had started. He finished with a kick and a series of rudimentary crane movements, then concluded the form.

I waited a long few seconds before saying anything. "That wasn't bad. What do you think, Jon?"

He shrugged. "It was good."

"All right, Jeff, relax and then when you're ready, begin the next form."

Out of breath, he nodded.

As he paused, I scanned the rest of the dojo. There was a mixture of all belt colors here this evening, from white all the way through brown. Roughly three times a year we had major belt testings, where we spent several hours looking at students individually. It was a time of great anticipation for some, and great anxiety for others. I was pleased to see Jon's girlfriend, Evy, there as well, sitting with her back against the wall, watching the proceedings seriously.

Jeff continued his strong performance. I did, however, make him repeat a few sections of the form so the rest of the students could see how competent he was. He was clearly ready for the next belt color. When the time came at the conclusion of his forms, I had the entire room stand and I addressed Jeff, saying how solid a student he was, and how impressed I was at his diligence. As he let the sweat roll down his face, he looked at me, smiling. I walked over to him, untied his yellow belt and gave it to Jon to hold. I then tied a new green belt around Jeffrey's waist. Jonathan started clapping and the rest of the dojo enthusiastically joined him.

We continued for the next hour and a half, testing nine more students. Toward the last half hour, as two teenage purple belts — one boy and one girl — were demonstrating a fighting routine, Katie walked in and tried to unobtrusively sit off to the side. As far as I was concerned, Katie was too attractive to be unobtrusive anywhere. We caught each other's eyes immediately. I smiled, but didn't let her interrupt my train of thought.

"Where was I?" I leaned over to Jon.

"You weren't saying anything."

"I knew that."

I watched the remainder of the purple belts' program — a series of attacks and defensive moves — while in the back of my mind thought about Katie. She had picked me up at the airport last night and then we had gone back to her place. We talked for about thirty seconds before pulling each other's clothes off. At some point we found ourselves in her kitchen, finishing off the promised bottle of wine. We really hadn't discussed the trip in detail, just that it was a success from someone's point of view.

The two purple belts finished their routine, turned to me, and bowed, bringing me back to the present. I complimented them, made some suggestions, and thanked them for their demonstration and effort. The final event of the evening was to have the entire dojo line up and perform all the forms, from yellow belt on up to brown, with each rank dropping out upon completion of their own level. There were thirty students in the room starting out, and watching them move in unison, up and down across the dojo floor, was something to see. The coordinated kicks, punches, and fluid movement was impressive. When the forms were over, I thanked everyone for coming and congratulated the students who had been awarded new ranks tonight.

As the group broke up, Katie came over. "Very striking. No pun intended."

Jonathan leaned over: "I'd say it was the fine preparation by their substitute teacher that made all the difference."

"But of course," I smiled. I looked around the dojo for Evy.

Jon's friend was socializing with some college buddies who were part of the group. "So, why hasn't Evy run over here and congratulated you for something or other?"

"She doesn't want to make a big scene."

I looked at Katie. "She likes the private attention."

"Understandable. *I* like the private attention, too," Katie said, looking at me.

"Hmm. It's time to lock up." I turned to the students who hadn't left yet. "Go home everyone. Congratulations. See you next time."

While the dojo emptied, I went into my office and changed from my gi into a casual print shirt and black pants. Jon, Evy, and Katie were waiting for me. We exited the dojo, stepping down to Charles Street.

"See you tomorrow, Sifu," Jon said.

"Goodnight, children."

Jon and Evy moved off, heading up the block. Katie and I turned to the right, in the opposite direction and began strolling. She put her arm through mine.

After a few long moments, I said, "I made the right decision a year ago."

"What's that?"

"To leave the army."

She looked at me, not sure where that had come from. Smart woman that she was, she let me go on.

"I was on all these missions and they just got muddled."

"How do you mean?"

"The missions were important — I felt strongly about that — but different people in charge had their own reasons for having us do what we did."

"You're thinking of Ramallah?"

"It should have been straight-forward. It *was* straight-forward. Survey the situation, and if the circumstances warranted it, move in and capture the Coles and their contact. That way they could be interrogated and we could unravel all the details."

"But that didn't happen."

"Not the way I wanted."

We reached the end of the block, turned right, and kept walking. An occasional lone man or woman coming from the opposite direction passed us, usually without looking our way.

"Well at least you got to see friends."

"That I did." I thought of Laurie and Ibrahim. "I saw Nate's daughter and I shot a friend of mine."

Katie turned to me.

"He's okay. I had to do it to save his life."

Katie still looked at me.

I shrugged. "It's a crazy place."

My mind went back to the second floor of Hadassah hospital. I had handed a note to a nurse to give to my friend. It was an apology and a wish for his quick recovery, but I had to laugh. I had written it in Arabic just in case Ibrahim was being watched, and it was probably phrased on a third grade level. I would've loved to have seen Ibrahim's reaction.

"I still don't know about Amit." My mind had shifted to our pre-op briefing.

"Do you think he knew what was going on?"

"He said he didn't. I don't know." I took a breath. "People lose their way sometimes, I guess. A kid like Pavel. An adult in a position of authority. Me."

"Sometimes we don't know we're lost."

"The operation was a success, according to the government. We stopped a shipment of stolen arms, and caught those responsible." I looked at Katie. "But I don't know."

"Aaron Cole is dead."

"He is. So we can't talk to him. We caught Hannah Cole and the Iraqi. He was only wounded. We found documentation linking him to the hijacking, but there's no physical link to connect the Coles. Same with their computer files. At least that's what Amit told me."

"So what happened to Hannah?"

"There's no evidence against her. The Iraqi wasn't saying anything. We lost Aaron Cole, and Hannah didn't have much to say about any of this. They let her go for now."

"Do you know where Hannah is?"

"She's here."

"You've seen her?"

I nodded.

"But she hasn't seen you." Katie knew me pretty well already.

I nodded again.

We crossed the street and kept walking.

"She and her husband set up their Guardians of Heaven as a hit squad — probably with the Iraqi's help or influence — because they didn't like Lev's intentions, if he were elected. And for whatever reason, the army didn't let us gather the intelligence to make a case against them. The Iraqi will be held a long time — and questioned. That's for sure. He's guilty of many things without the Lev assassination attempts."

"What about Pavel? You're convinced Hannah killed him?"

"Amit's man positively identified her as the last person coming to the dojo before he was killed. But do we have the weapon? No. Do we have an actual witness? No."

"But you know she did it."

I nodded.

"So what are you going to do?"

I shrugged, but didn't say anything.

Pavel had come to me for help and Hannah Cole had killed him. Shot him, point blank. He trusted her, and she walked up to him and shot him, coldly, and probably without hesitation.

"So, how was your life while I was gone?" I asked.

Katie looked at me for a brief moment, then answered my question. She told me about school, about going out with her friends, and about missing me. Eventually that evening, we made it to a restaurant — an Italian gem of a place off of Boston Street in Canton — and then went back to her house.

And so it went. We resumed our routines. I slipped back into the dojo work — after all, I had a fresh crop of newly transitioned students to teach. And there was the occasional substitute teaching job at the middle school. There were just a few weeks left to the school year, but there was work for me.

I finally made it over to Nate's house one evening and allowed Rachel to cook me dinner. We talked about how well Laurie was doing. I did get back to see her again before leaving the country...and had the foresight to bring a camera. "I knew you'd want pictures," I told Nate and Rachel.

Then there was Alli. Over the next few weeks we continued to talk, but my interest truly wasn't there. We never really went out after I returned; we met for coffee a few times. Alli wanted to resume where we'd left off, but that time had passed. I resolved to tell her how I felt. I just had to pick the right moment.

And lastly, there was Hannah Cole. She and her husband were linked in the press to an Iraqi terrorist. That cost them in the Jewish community. Parents and community leaders were in shock when they heard about the weapons theft and the Coles being involved. They wasted no time in pulling their kids — and their funding — from her institution. When Hannah finally returned after the Israelis released her, she found the school already closed. She had become a pariah.

I watched Hannah Cole and waited. As June turned into July and then August, I made mental notes of her habits...where she liked to eat, where she liked to exercise — at a health center in the neighboring community of Towson — where she got her hair cut, where she went food shopping. In the humid nights of the Baltimore summer I watched as Hannah came home and as she went to her office at the abandoned school. Late at night I took particular notice of the shadows in front of her house and in front of the school.

By the end of October enough time had gone by since the evening in Ramallah. The news wasn't fresh anymore and the community had moved on. There was too much else to be concerned with than a woman many saw as a traitor.

Late one Thursday night I followed Hannah as she stopped by the school. From across the street, I watched as she went into the building. The institution itself was closed, but the building hadn't been sold yet. Hannah still went back from time to time to work in her office.

When I saw the light on the second floor go on, I took out a 9mm Beretta that I had brought from Israel. As I watched the lit window, I attached a silencer to the muzzle of the barrel. I put the pistol under my belt near my left pants pocket and stepped out of the car.

The air had a chill to it. Baltimore usually didn't see snow so soon in the season, but this year might be different. I crossed the street. A deep shadow near the school's front walk invited me and I disappeared into it.

As I waited for Hannah, I let my mind return to a boy who had waited for me outside my dojo, one difficult evening months ago. He had been unsure of himself and was more than a little frightened. Pavel had made my dojo his home, planting himself on my office couch, content to remain there watching a movie. I remembered him that next morning, broom in hand, diligently sweeping the dojo floor. It was the last image I had of Pavel alive.

The light on the second floor went out and I cleared my mind. In another minute, the front door opened. Hannah Cole was wearing a lightweight long dark coat and was carrying a small briefcase. The contents of the case did not interest me. She locked the door, then came down the steps in front of me, looking neither to her right or left. I took the gun from my belt, flipped off the safety, and stepped out of the shadows.

Acknowledgments

In the Name of God is a work of fiction. However, as there is no better example than true life, some characters' traits may have been based on real people. These behaviors and qualities have been used purely to flesh out fictitious personalities. Similarly, while some locations are real, others are also the result of my imagination. The real life locations have been used fictitiously as well or have been altered to work within the context of the story.

What is not a product of my imagination is the tremendous assistance I have had through the writing process. Thank you to Sima Abarbanel, Cheri Crow, David Gordon, Julian Gordon, Jesse Mashbaum, and Martha Nathanson for your keen eyes, encouragement, and input. A special thanks to Howard and Aileen for allowing me to use the "Howard & Aileen Show." To Dr. Chuck Leve and Warren Alpertstein, please accept my sincere appreciation for your anesthesiology and legal suggestions to keep the applicable events accurate; to Sam for your consults;

Professor H.I. Sober for *ha-derech*; to Elliott King for the match-making; Kevin Atticks and Andrew Zaleski for your advice, hard work, and diligence. A singular thanks must also go to AJ and Jeff. You've been a great source of enthusiasm, advice, and comfort for this project and beyond.

Finally, to Becky: this book would not be as polished or as professional if not for your input. While you say you dislike writing, you do it magnificently. Thank you for your help and support...always.

If I have left anyone out in these acknowledgments, it is only because — as I have frequently said — I have no memory left. Please forgive the oversight.

The future of publishing...today!

Apprentice House is the country's only campus-based, student-staffed book publishing company. Directed by professors and industry professionals, it is a nonprofit activity of the Communication Department at Loyola University Maryland.

Using state-of-the-art technology and an experiential learning model of education, Apprentice House publishes books in untraditional ways. This dual responsibility as publishers and educators creates an unprecedented collaborative environment among faculty and students, while teaching tomorrow's editors, designers, and marketers.

Outside of class, progress on book projects is carried forth by the AH Book Publishing Club, a co-curricular campus organization supported by Loyola University Maryland's Office of Student Activities.

Student Project Team for *In the Name of God*:
Andrew Zaleski, '11

To learn more about Apprentice House books or to obtain submission guidelines, please visit www.ApprenticeHouse.com.

Apprentice House
Communication Department
Loyola University Maryland
4501 N. Charles Street
Baltimore, MD 21210
Ph: 410-617-5265 • Fax: 410-617-2198
info@apprenticehouse.com

CPSIA information can be obtained at www.ICGtesting.com

225158LV00001BA/223/P